# THE RIVER IS DARK

## — A THRILLER —

# JOE HART

**THOMAS & MERCER**

Published by Thomas & Mercer, Seattle

www.apub.com

Amazon, the Amazon logo, and Thomas & Mercer are trademarks of Amazon.com, Inc., or its affiliates.

ISBN-13: 9781477825778
ISBN-10: 1477825770

Cover design by Elderlemon Design, www.elderlemondesign.com

Library of Congress Control Number: 2014939861

Printed in the United States of America

# ALSO BY JOE HART

Novels

*Lineage*
*Singularity*
*EverFall*

Short story collections

*Midnight Paths: A Collection of Dark Horror*

Short stories

"The Line Unseen"
"The Edge of Life"
"Outpost"

*For my kindred spirits who can't get enough of being afraid—this one's for you.*

# PROLOGUE

His mother screamed again.

She screamed, sounding like her lungs were going to come out. Eric ran. He flew up the stairs two at a time, something he did only when racing Champ or his dad, trying to beat either of them to his room on the second floor. He couldn't hear his dad anymore, and that scared him even worse than his mother's screams. He knew Champ was dead, the faithful golden retriever's body in the garage entry, a blood-sodden and twisted mess that didn't resemble his closest friend of five years. Now, instead of a lighthearted race, terror propelled him up the stairs with an unseen hand that both quickened and slowed his movement. He heard the thing roar something that resembled words in the kitchen, and his mother's screams took on a new pitch, making him want to fall to the floor and clap his hands to his ears. He wanted never to hear anything like it again. But he couldn't disobey her, not now, not after how her eyes looked. They said, *Run away and don't look back*. So he did.

His toe caught on a runner, and he cried out as he sprawled onto the landing just before the upstairs hall. His knees burned on the carpet, and his shoulder popped as he thrust his hands out to stop his face from connecting with the floor. Eric leapt to his feet as he heard his mother shriek again, like the sound of air escaping from a pinched balloon, and then abruptly fall silent. The quiet of the house was so horrible that he nearly fell a second time, the strength gone from his legs. He knew what the silence meant. His parents and dog were dead, and he was alone with *it*.

His parents' bedroom loomed closer as he ran down the hall toward its darkened doorway. His own room flashed by to his right, but he knew there was no help there. The only phone upstairs was in his parents' room; they had promised him that when he turned twelve he could have one put in next to his bed. That promise felt alien now, something unreachable and strange, like a dream fading fast in morning light. Eric wished that he would wake up now, the blood and the screams just a cloudy nightmare that would drain away to nothing, and Champ would saunter into his room any moment, the ever-present guilty look plastered across the dog's face.

Eric heard a wet thump in the kitchen, like the time his dad dropped a whole pizza on the floor just after taking it out of the oven. Footsteps, heavy and slow, moved below him, and he bit back a scream when he saw a shadow darken the foot of the stairs. As quietly as he could, he shut his parents' door behind him and locked it. The room was dark, but he made his way directly to his father's side of the bed and grasped the cordless phone from the charger. The buttons lit up the space around him and made his finger glow green as he punched the three numbers and slid down to the floor. There was a moment's hesitation, and then a clicking in the receiver. A woman's voice came on the line, the sound of her words too calm and collected for the insanity that surrounded him.

"Nine-one-one, what is your emergency?"

Eric stuttered the first thing that came to his mind in a frantic whisper, and lay on his belly when the sounds of the stairs creaking under a heavy weight met his ears. The stairs had never sounded like that before, not even when his dad treaded on them in his thick winter clothes and boots.

"Are you okay?" The lady sounded more anxious now, and somehow it made him glad. Someone knew he was scared and she wanted to help.

"I'm hiding under my parents' bed," Eric whispered as he slid beneath the wooden frame. "It's coming down the hall. Please send help. My mom and dad are dead, and so's Champ."

"Help is on its way, honey. You just stay on the line with me and everything will be all right."

A bang echoed in the hallway, and he knew what it was: his door rebounding off the wall inside of his room. *It's in my room.*

"Are you there, honey?"

"Yes," Eric whispered, but quieter now. It was close and it would hear him. It would pull him out from under the bed and do to him what it had done to Champ and his parents. Hot tears squeezed out of his eyes as the door to his parents' room rattled in its frame.

"Are you okay?"

"It'll hear you," Eric breathed, his voice no longer anything he recognized.

The door burst open with a cracking sound, and pale light spread onto the floor, along with splinters from the shattered jamb. Eric registered the woman's question one more time before he pushed the off button and silenced her voice. He tried not to breathe, although his lungs wanted nothing more than to heave in huge amounts of air. Stinging tears slid off his cheeks and fell to the carpet inches below his face, and he was sure it heard them land, because it moved closer. He could smell it, a rank and powerful scent that reminded him of spoiled milk. *Please let it go away, please make it leave.*

It was closer now, and he could hear it breathing, sniffing him out. A high whining sound began to fill the air, slight at first but gradually getting louder, and in the moment before the bed flew up and away from him, Eric's hope flared and died with the keen of sirens and his own scream in his ears.

3

# CHAPTER 1

His eyes came open with the grating wail of the alarm clock on the bedside table.

Liam blinked at the ceiling and wondered for the hundredth time why he even set the damn thing each night. Routine, that's why. The doctor said routine was good for sleep. Routine. With a grunt he rolled over and slapped at the button, eventually silencing the screeching clock. He listened. The popping sound of the late-summer sun warming the floorboards of the old farmhouse kitchen, the jangle of the wind chimes on the front porch, a breeze pressing its breath against the old windows in the bedroom, a car passing on the highway and then gone. He sighed and lay back, thinking about the gun in his closet, tucked out of sight on the high shelf, always there in the morning, in his mind, asking its question.

As he showered, he rubbed his jaw, feeling the growth there. He should shave, otherwise the whiskers would become like steel wool and his fair complexion would suffer a "red tide," as his dad used to call it. He hissed a laugh and shut off the water.

The shave felt good, but not as good as when his father used to do it with the straight razor. The feeling after his father's shaves was unequaled, something he couldn't put his finger on. He thought of the barbershop: the tangy smell of leather that covered the heavy rotating chair; the musk of the shaving cream on his face; the feel of the blade, so sharp against his skin, yet held with a sure hand that relaxed him when his father shaved him. He paused, shaking the disposable razor out under the hot water, and watched the black stubble flow away down the drain. Without looking in the mirror above the sink, he grabbed the pearl-handled round mirror from the drawer to his left. As he did each time he picked it up, he remembered his dad holding it out in front of him when he was ten, after his hair had been particularly long. He could still see his father's smiling face above the mirror, a face that his own would resemble more and more as the years went by, minus the ever-present cigarette in the corner of his dad's mouth. He recalled the thought that went through his young mind, so happy in the moment that the black realization hit him like a thunderclap and nearly sent him out of the barber chair: someday, he would look into that mirror and his dad would be gone, and there was nothing he could do about it. The memory never failed to assault him when he picked the mirror up.

He gazed at his reflection, noticing the patch of whiskers he always missed on the right side of his chin, as well as the lines around his eyes that seemed to deepen with each restless day and every night of shallow sleep. The thought of more sleep sent a tremble of yearning through his body. Instead, he toweled off his face, laid the mirror back in its resting place within the drawer, and went to make coffee.

The day was as bright as he expected, and he ate a protein bar with his coffee on the front porch, soaking in the morning sun as well as the thick caffeine in the large cup. His mind went over the plans for the day without conscious thought. He was low on bread and deli meat and he needed toilet paper. Town it was then. And maybe he'd stop today on his way home. It wasn't far off the highway. He could pull onto the exit and follow the road down to the stoplight, turn right, and go through the outskirts of the little

5

suburb. His body would take him down the correct streets, turning and braking like an automaton, and he would park his car outside the apartment building like he had so many times before. He would walk up to the entrance and see the paint peeling off the siding, not enough to look trashy but still noticeable. He'd touch the rough brick beside the intercom, feel the grit bite into the skin of his knuckles as he tried to get his finger to push the button beside the name he knew so well. He wouldn't leave until he did. Not like the last time, when he'd stood there for over ten minutes, until his knuckles bled from where he rubbed them raw against the brick.

The phone rang inside the house, pulling him back to himself so fast, he jerked coffee over the rim of the cup and onto his pants.

"Shit," he said, and rubbed the scalding spot on his thigh. The phone belted out another demand to be answered, and he moved through the kitchen to where it hung beside the fridge.

"Hello?"

"Is this Detective Liam Dempsey?"

"No—I mean, yes, this is. Who is this?"

"Mr. Dempsey, this is Senior Special Agent Todd Phelps with the Bureau of Criminal Apprehension."

Liam's mind sped forward a hundred times faster than he could think, but he came up with no connection to him or to what had transpired ten months before. "Yes?" he answered.

There was a pause, a familiar one. Familiar since he'd paused the same way dozens of times in the last eight years.

"I'm very sorry to have to tell you this, but your brother, Allen, and his wife were the victims of a home invasion last night. They did not survive."

The icy tip of anticipation plunged into his chest fully, and he leaned back on the counter behind him. He let the words roll over him, let them sink in like water on dry soil. His brother was dead, and so was Suzie. He squeezed his eyes shut, a third shoe dropping, one he didn't know existed until then.

"Mr. Dempsey? Are you there?"

Liam gritted his teeth and nodded. "Yeah, I'm sorry. What happened?"

"Details aren't entirely solid at this point, but from what we know, an individual or individuals entered your brother's home last night and murdered both your brother and his wife. We have several leads already, and I assure you that we will find those responsible for your loss. I'm very sorry."

Liam heard concern in the man's voice, but something else also: impatience. The agent on the other end of the line wanted, *needed*, to get off the phone. This wasn't his specialty, and he wanted to be done with it. So did Liam.

"Thank you. I'll need a few hours to get some things in order, and then I can be down there."

"That's perfectly fine, sir. If you need to get in touch with me before then, please don't hesitate to call." Phelps rattled off a number that Liam tried to hold on to and then let slide away beneath the crushing feeling on the top of his head. He was in the jaws of a massive vise, the handle turning slowly but surely, the steel around him unforgiving as it closed in.

The agent said something else, but Liam didn't catch it. "I'm sorry, what?"

"I just said that you can take as much time as you need."

"Thank you," Liam said, and stretched his arm out to hang up the phone. The cradle didn't grab the earpiece when he let go, and it fell to the floor and exploded into three separate pieces. He stared at the rechargeable battery, with its electrical tail sprouting from its casing, and without thinking about it, he picked it up and hurled it as hard as he could into the living room. It hit something that fell over with a crash, but he didn't notice as he slid to the floor and closed his eyes to the sunshine of the young day.

———  ———

The Chevy's tires growled as Liam turned left and headed southeast, away from the open country he was used to. The cab was quiet, with only the hiss of air traveling around the vehicle and his measured breaths. He glanced at the stereo and studied it for a moment, like it was an artifact from another planet. He considered turning it on just to drown out the quiet and his thoughts, but dismissed it. Music wouldn't hold back the churnings of his mind. Songs didn't mean anything to him anymore. What was the last song he'd heard? He knew the question was of no importance, but for some reason it felt criminal not to remember. Another question, the important one, finally shouldered its way to the front of his thoughts, and he clenched his jaw. When was the last time he'd seen Allen?

His stomach surged upward for the umpteenth time, and he swallowed the taste of bile on the back of his tongue. The song his father used to sing began to play on a loop inside his head, the words rounded off into slurred vowels and consonants, but the melody so sad and clear it made the corners of his eyes sting. He shrugged his shoulders and brought the travel mug to his lips, letting the cooling coffee trace a path down his throat.

The truck went over a bump in the road, and he heard his bag shift behind him. He hadn't really contemplated the things that were in the duffel bag; the time after the phone call was indistinct, hazy with hurried motions and punctuated by several pauses when he merely stared at the wall for minutes on end. He knew there were some clothes, his toothbrush, and his iPad in there.

And the gun.

He fidgeted with a frayed piece of the steering wheel cover and tried to discern what made him reach onto the top shelf and feel with a hand until his fingers met the cold, dusty steel. He hadn't shot the Sig in well over a year, but without thinking, he'd snapped the magazine free, checked the rounds therein, slammed it home, and placed the SP2022 at the bottom of the bag, beneath a pair of worn jeans.

The miles became meaningless as he drove, landscape shifting without recognition outside the windows. The flat plains and fields filled with farmers' crops became lined with encroaching trees, their arms flush with flags of green leaves. The land began to roll up and down, cresting on hills that overlooked the occasional stream or river winding through the earth like the track of some great serpent long extinct. The ground became rockier, the faces of stones peeking from beneath shaggy overgrowths of reeds and grass on the edges of the road.

Liam noted none of it. He drove, his senses closed to all but piloting the truck.

It was shortly before noon when Tallston came into view. When the Chevy crested the last hill before the town, he wasn't prepared; even with the sickening pulse of grief in his stomach, the sight still moved something inside him.

The city sat at the bottom of a depression, its left side hugged tight by a line of bluffs that soared a hundred feet above the town in some places. The muddy twist of the Mississippi flowed opposite the bluffs, hemming in the town with its curves. The city sprawled in a general crescent shape, its design embedded in the natural surroundings. It was as if the first settlers had wanted the city to blend with nature instead of declaring its blaring progressive presence, which was common in other towns of its size. The city's name itself came from the sentinel bluffs. *Tall Stone* became shortened, robbed of its phonetic history by hurried tongues. At least that's what Allen had told Liam when he'd opened his practice here twenty years ago.

Liam sighed as the truck coasted down the steep hill and into the outskirts of town, past a sign that declared, *Welcome to Tallston, the jewel of Minnesota*. A few yards after the greeting, another sign stood in the high grass beside the road, this one smaller yet still imposing with slanted letters that blazed against a black background: *Future home of Colton Inc. Where industry meets nature.* LIES was spray-painted in dripping white letters across the lower half of the company's message.

The road wound around two corners and fell away once more, and Liam stretched his jaw, surprised at the feeling of his ears popping from the descent. A few homes dotted the sides of the road, their fronts obscured by thick growths of trees and hedges. Soon the highway became Main Street, a long, curving swath that cut the town into halves, which were divided in cross sections by multiple side roads shooting off left and right in between the businesses that studded the blocks.

Liam slowed the truck to a crawl as he entered the street—"the drag," his brother had called it once. Tallston knew its place as a tourist locale, and kept its buildings in check, not allowing much room for trend. Instead, the colors and architecture reminded Liam of a golden era long since passed, when tail-finned Studebakers might have cruised on a warm Saturday night, numerous elbows cocked from the windows, with the occasional catcall issuing from within whenever a pretty girl in a poodle skirt passed by. On the left side, the glass windows of a bakery displayed cakes and brightly colored cookies. Beside it was a nail salon, a hardware store named Brenton's, and what looked to be a conglomeration of businesses boxed together into one storefront with a sign proclaiming *The Square*. On the right was a drugstore, a long textile mill, a dentist's office, and a small café nestled next to an overbearing two-story stone building with no lettering on its front.

Liam pulled into a parking space in front of the café and shut the truck off. Despite the roiling in his stomach, he knew he should eat and his coffee was long gone. He let his hands fall to his lap and rest there while he studied the people making their way along the sidewalk beside the storefronts. Their garish clothing screamed *tourist*, just as the town around them echoed the same.

Liam climbed out of the Chevy and pocketed the keys after locking the truck. When he pulled open the door to the café, the smells of cooking food and aged wood surrounded him. The eatery was narrow and long, with several booths lining its right side. A row of tables sat to the left, and at the far end a bar ran parallel to the back wall, the red upholstered stools before it showing their age with wisps of cushion poking through in various places. One booth held a couple drinking coffee, and a lone man in a long threadbare coat sat at the bar. Liam made his way between the tables and booths until he reached the counter, and took a seat several spots down from the man in the coat. A waitress in black dress pants and a black polo looked up from reading a newspaper and smiled.

"Good morning . . . or afternoon?"

Liam nodded and tried to return the smile. "Afternoon now, I think."

She grabbed a menu from beneath the counter and slid it before him. "Well, we serve breakfast all day if you haven't had any yet, and our special is roast beef covered in gravy with mashed potatoes and a fresh garden salad. Would you like anything to drink?"

"Coffee, please," Liam said, and looked down at the menu. The descriptions and pictures of the food designed to entice only made his stomach seesaw. When the waitress placed the cup of dark, steaming liquid before him, he slid the menu back to her. "I'll just have the club sandwich." With a nod, she retreated to the kitchen doors and disappeared from view.

"The club's shit, just so you know."

Liam turned to the man at the counter, who gazed at him from under a tangle of dark hair streaked with gray. His face was long and narrow, with sallow cheeks that fell in like slack sails. He was unshaven, and when Liam looked at the man's hands wrapped around a similar mug of coffee, he saw long yellow fingernails with dirt caked beneath them.

"That so?" Liam said, not wanting to talk and saying as much with the dead tone in his voice.

The unkempt man nodded. "I don't know where the hell they get their bacon, but it doesn't taste like any pig that I've had before." The man waved a hand in disgust, and Liam caught a waft of body odor from his direction.

Liam sipped from his cup and was surprised at how good the coffee was. He could almost feel the caffeine bolstering him, straightening his insides, which felt folded and broken.

"Good coffee, though," the man said, as if reading his mind. Liam adopted silence to get his new friend to stop addressing him, and merely nodded. "You're from out of town," the man continued. It wasn't a question.

Liam glanced in his direction. "Yeah."

"Lots around these days. You don't look like a reporter, though."

Liam stiffened. He hadn't been in town for more than fifteen minutes and already the confrontation he'd been dreading was upon him. "I'm not."

The man sipped his coffee and looked past Liam to study something on the wall. "Yeah, killing always brings the vultures. I knew they'd come after the first ones, but now it's bound to be twice as bad."

Liam paused, his cup hanging a few inches below his mouth. "What do you mean, 'the first ones'?"

The man's bloodshot eyes flicked back to Liam's face, and he squinted. "Wasn't two weeks ago Jerry and Karen Shevlin were found the same way as the ones last night. Their boy was luckier, but not by much. Lost an arm from the elbow down and hasn't woke up yet. Poor little bugger, he can't be more'n ten or eleven."

Liam set his cup down and turned to fully face the man. "You're telling me there was a double murder here last week?"

The man nodded, his clumpy hair bobbing with the motion. "Yeah, local authorities tried to keep it quiet right away, but it got out after only a day or so. Now this new one last night." The man shook his head. "And the doctor along with his wife at that. Sad, sad business."

The door to the kitchen banged open, and the waitress came out holding a plate with a soggy-looking sandwich and a pile of wilting French fries. Her eyes flitted to the man down the bar, and her mouth dipped at the corners.

"Nut, I told you not to bother people, or Dale will boot you out again."

Before the man could respond, Liam spoke. "He's fine, not bothering me at all."

The waitress gave Nut another stabbing look, and then smiled at Liam. "Anything else I can get you, hon?"

"I'm fine, thanks," Liam said.

The waitress moved off to check on the couple in the booth, and the man at the bar leaned forward conspiratorially. "My real name's not Nut, but everyone calls me that. Nice to make your acquaintance," he said, holding out a dirty hand.

"Liam Dempsey," Liam said, and shook hands with the man, taking in the surprise and calculation in Nut's eyes.

"You wouldn't be—" Nut began, but Liam stood, already reaching for his wallet. With a flick of his hand he laid a twenty on the counter, and moved past the waitress and out the door without looking back.

# CHAPTER 2

He tried to call the number Agent Phelps had told him earlier that morning but each time he dialed, the digits slipped away from his memory like sand through fingers.

Liam punched the end button and stared through the truck's windshield, his heart thudding faster with a feeling he hadn't experienced in almost a year. He willed his pulse to slow before bringing up the browser on his phone. In less than a minute, he found directions to the sheriff's office and threw the truck into reverse.

The Tallston sheriff's department sat four streets south of the café, built beside an imposing three-story brownstone that served as the town hall. Liam strode up the concrete entrance ramp and pulled open the glass door emblazoned with a gold shield, the words *Tallston Sheriff's Department* curved around its upper half. A cool wave of air-conditioning washed over him as he stepped through the door, effectively cutting off the day's burgeoning heat. The lobby of the office was simple, with a reinforced steel door set in the left wall and a Plexiglas partition directly ahead. A round hole the size of a grapefruit was cut in the center of the glass, and a plump woman in a brown uniform rested behind the desk, a black headset tipped up so that it touched the taut strands of her ponytailed blond hair.

"Is the sheriff in?" Liam asked as he stepped up to the window, leaning forward so his voice would carry through the porthole.

The woman raised her eyebrows and seemed to take him in for a moment before shaking her head. "No, he's not at the moment. Can I help you with something?"

"Is he at the Dempsey house?"

Her eyes narrowed. "Who are you, sir?"

"I'm Allen Dempsey's brother. I need to speak with the sheriff or the BCA agents assigned to the case."

The deputy's face softened. "I'm very sorry for your loss. They should be back from the crime scene sometime later this afternoon, if you'd like to leave them a message."

"Thanks, but I'll try to catch up with them there," Liam said, turning away.

"Sir, you won't be allowed at the—"

Her words were lost to him as he pushed through the door, into the heat of the afternoon.

His brother's house sat atop one of the highest bluffs overlooking the town. Liam almost didn't remember how to get there; over ten years had passed since his last visit, and the hurried drive away from the house was a blur that he couldn't fully recall. He followed the faint memory up a fork in the main street at the very end of town, the smooth pavement turning to even smoother concrete as his pickup climbed up and away from the city below. He made a left turn at a T at the top of the hill and followed a wooded road until he spotted the ornate mailbox adorned with his brother's name. He shook his head, out of habit, at the *Dr.* before *Dempsey* emblazoned in silver on the mailbox's side, and turned down the private drive. After two curves, he saw the rear end of a sheriff's cruiser and a flapping strand of yellow *Do Not Cross* tape, its message vanishing and reappearing with the touch of a light breeze. Liam parked behind the cruiser and got out, his stomach feeling lighter than the rest of his body, the sunshine too bright even through his sunglasses. A young deputy leaned on the hood of the cruiser, and when Liam shut the truck's door, the man turned toward him and stood, the twin reflective lenses of his shades following Liam's approach.

"What can I do for you?" the deputy said when Liam was still five steps away.

"I need to speak with the sheriff and agents in charge of the investigation."

The deputy put up a hand in a halting motion, even though Liam had already stopped. "This is a crime scene, sir. I need you to get back in your vehicle and make an appointment at the department in town."

"I'm the doctor's brother," Liam said.

The deputy dropped his hand, but his posture didn't change as he continued to study Liam. "I'm very sorry, but this is a secured scene and I can't let—"

"Could you please let the sheriff know that I'm here and I'd like to speak with him?"

"Sir, I understand you're upset, but you need to get back—"

"Listen, I'm not going anywhere until you go get your superior officer or the BCA agent I spoke with this morning." Liam pulled off his sunglasses so that he could stare at the deputy without obstruction. Something in his gaze must have spoken to the younger man, because without another word, the deputy spun, ducked under the string of tape, and walked to the house looming over the other cars in the driveway.

Liam crossed his arms and stared at the sprawling one-level home. Two hand-carved pillars propped up a wide overhang that shaded the front entry from the sun. Several sets of floor-to-ceiling windows glared back at him like corpse eyes, darkly accusing in the bright day. A stall of the attached garage gaped open, revealing what must've been his brother's latest vehicle: a shining black Cadillac Escalade. Or maybe it was Suzie's. Liam felt his teeth grit together, and he turned to face the dense woods on the left side of the drive-way, until he heard the sound of footsteps.

Two men walked toward him, trailed by the deputy. The first was tall and clean-cut, wearing a dark suit with a maroon tie. His face was smooth, with dark hair parted in a precise line on the left side of his head. The other man was shorter and powerfully built; a round belly that carried an extra thirty pounds Liam was sure hadn't been there in his younger days hung over a duty belt laden with all the tools of law enforcement. The sheriff had nearly white hair and a neatly trimmed mustache of the same color.

The taller man reached Liam first, holding his hand out. "Mr. Dempsey, I'm Senior Special Agent Todd Phelps, this is Sheriff Barnes." Liam shook hands with both men, the agent's grip overly strong while the sheriff's was firm but polite. "I apologize for not answering earlier. We are in the middle of the investigation and I couldn't—"

"I'd like to know why you didn't tell me my brother and his wife were the second of two double murders in the same town within the last week," Liam said.

The agent's eyes narrowed somewhat, but his voice remained even. "At this point in the investigation I wasn't at liberty to reveal all the details surrounding your brother's murder. We're not even sure the events last week are related in any way."

Liam shifted his eyes from Phelps to the sheriff's round face. "You're telling me that a double murder in the same small town a week before isn't connected?"

"At this time we're not sure, but believe me, we're doing every-thing possible to follow up on the leads we have."

"Was there anything stolen from either scene?" Liam asked, glancing over the agent's shoulder at the house.

He felt Phelps's eyes running over his face like the touch of crawling insects. "Mr. Dempsey, where are you a detective out of?"

There was only a beat before Liam responded and met the agent's gaze. "Minneapolis Homicide, and I'm not a detective anymore."

Phelps pushed his tongue against the back of his lower teeth. "Well, we can't release any information at this point. Now, if you'd like to meet with either the sheriff or myself later this evening, we'd be happy to do so."

A tremble of anger flowed through his body at the brush-off, but he mentally restrained himself. "Yes, please call me at the earliest convenience. I'll leave my number at the sheriff's office."

Without another word or look, Liam spun on his heel and walked to his truck. He threw the Chevy into reverse and backed out of the drive until he was able to turn around on the wider road at its mouth. He cursed under his breath as he urged the truck away from the crime scene and back into the waiting town below.

He found a quaint hotel at the south end of Tallston and checked in, telling the woman at the front desk that he'd be staying through at least the weekend. His room was on the third floor, one of a dozen. The accommodations were both comfortable and cramped, with a bed tucked so close to the bathroom that he was sure if he needed to piss in the middle of the night he would only have to roll over and let fly. A bank of windows graced the far side of the room, and when he walked to them to look out, he saw that the hotel was closer to the Mississippi than he originally estimated. The dark-brown river ran in a wide arc only a stone's throw from the rear parking lot, and he could see the untouched canopy of leaves in the wilderness across the water. It looked like the forest ran on forever in unbroken wilds that rolled in waves of emerald as the wind made itself known again. After calling the sheriff's office to leave his name and number, he headed back downstairs.

The hotel had a small bar tucked in the back of the building, almost as an afterthought, and Liam noted the sensation of claustrophobia as he entered the space, the low ceiling only a foot above his head. The bar itself was a mahogany log, halved and angled into three pieces that created a half circle. A scattering of tables sat against the opposite wall, and two doors, one at each end of the room, were marked accordingly for men and women. A petite, blond woman with close-cropped hair sat at the far end of the bar nursing a water; her eyes registered him as he entered, and then moved away. A balding bartender, the hair growing off the back of his shining pate so long he could have sat on it, leaned on the polished wood as Liam took a seat on a barstool that let out a squeak of protest.

"Getcha?" the bartender said, tossing a napkin Liam's direction.

"Bud Light and a shot of Crown." While the bartender busied himself with the drinks, Liam glanced around the room once more and noticed the woman staring at him again. He met her eyes and held them until she looked away, his expression as uncaring as he felt.

The bartender set the beer and shot glass before him. "Seven fifty."

"I got it," the blond woman said, rounding the bar as Liam dug for his wallet. He looked up at her as she nodded to the bartender, who shrugged and wrote something on a notepad before busying himself with a glass that was already clean. The woman set her water down a few inches from Liam's beer and motioned at a barstool to his right. "Mind?"

Liam sighed and looked down at the bar. "Go ahead."

He heard her laugh lightly as she took the seat beside him. "You're not very appreciative of a girl who just bought you a drink."

He glanced at her before taking a sip of the flat beer. "Sorry."

She tossed her head to the side. "It's okay. You just look like someone who could use a little kindness."

"Thanks, I'm just preoccupied," Liam said, picking up the smudged shot glass.

"Troubles for each and every one, my dad used to say."

Liam threw the shot back and let the whiskey burn all the way to the base of his stomach and back before looking at his beer and wondering how fast he could finish it.

"You just passing through?" the woman asked.

"Kind of."

"Me too. Interesting town, though. I heard there was a double murder here last night. Did you hear anything about that?" Liam tried to hide any reaction, and shook his head before downing half his beer. "I mean, how horrible. It sounds like it was pretty brutal. A doctor and his wife, if I'm not mistaken."

Liam turned his head just enough to look at the woman and saw that she was staring at him intently, the look of a child waiting for a firework to go off.

Liam tipped his head back to study the low ceiling. "What station you from?"

"What?"

"I said, what fucking news station are you from?" He focused his gaze on her and felt a spark of satisfaction at the surprise on her features. She opened her mouth once for rebuttal, then closed it before deflating a few inches in her seat.

"KQSL Channel 9, out of Saint Paul. I'm Shirley Strafford," she said, holding out a manicured hand.

Liam tipped the rest of his beer back and stood in one motion. "Thanks for the drink," he said as he walked toward the outline of the entryway.

"Mr. Dempsey, if I could just have a minute."

Liam heard the bartender grumble something and Shirley's reply—"I can talk to anyone I want, thanks"—before he walked out the front door of the hotel and toward his waiting truck.

Liam spent the next two hours driving around the small town, getting his bearings as he paused at each intersecting street. He coasted past businesses, homes, several two-story apartment buildings, and a park set on the banks of the river. He stopped at the park and took in the large menagerie of playground equipment, the swaying swings, and the creeping merry-go-round turning clockwise with the breeze. It was eerie to see a place made for laughter and people so empty. He knew why there was no one here; if he had children, he wouldn't let them play alone in this town either.

Liam got out of his truck and walked across the well-trimmed lawn and the sand of the playground, onto a wide wooden boardwalk that ran parallel with the park. The boardwalk threaded through a dense copse of hardwoods and then emptied out to a panoramic view of the river. Jagged chunks of rock stretched away from the boardwalk until the ground dropped into the swift water beyond. Across the river, Liam spotted the corner of a building, its general outline barely visible behind the thick growth of trees and brush that encumbered the opposite shore. The structure looked to be at least two stories high, and the last vestiges of a pier poked above the water like an ancient sea creature waiting for a meal. A sign with the same message as the one on the way into town from Colton Inc. grew out of the long grass next to the sunken pier.

Liam stood there for a long time, watching the sun gather on the brown water and turn it into a reflection of the reddening sky so that it looked like a flowage of blood. His hand stole to the pocket of his jeans, and he traced the edges of the straight razor that lay against his thigh. It was a custom blade made by a friend of his father, for the barber. Instead of the customary pinion mounting that most razors had within the handle, his father's locked when opened, and the handle was flat black, the once-polished ebony stone scuffed and abraded by years and years of use. Liam remembered when he asked his father why he always used the same razor day in and day out. The older man had merely smiled, the cigarette tilting up in the corner of his mouth, and said if a man does something well, his tools should be precious to him. The blade had shaved more faces than Liam could count and was still sharp enough to split hairs. He'd taken to carrying it wherever he went after his father passed away, the feeling of it in his pocket never failing to help calm him.

His phone vibrated in his other pocket, letting out a chime that startled him from his reverie. When he looked at the glass display, the number calling only said *Blocked*.

"Hello?"

"Is this Mr. Dempsey?"

"Yes."

"This is Sheriff Barnes. Would you still like to stop by for a bit?"

Liam turned from the river and began walking toward his pickup. "Yes. Are you at your office?"

"Yep, you can park around back of the building. I'll let you in the door on the east side."

"Sounds good, thank you."

There was a pause, and then a grunt from the other end of the phone. "I'll see you in a few."

The connection broke, and Liam stared at the blank screen for a moment before hurrying to his truck.

Liam was about to knock on the rear door of the law-enforcement building when it cracked open, with the sheriff's round face, slightly redder than it had been at his brother's house, visible in the gap. Barnes motioned him inside and led him down a corridor with several doors mounted in the left wall and three vacant cells on the right, their doors open as if each expected to be filled quite soon. The sheriff's office was a small room at the front of the hall, the space within occupied mostly by an elephantine desk piled a few inches thick with papers and manila folders. A framed picture of Barnes knee-deep in a clear stream hung on the wall; his eyes were alight with happiness and his arms held a massive king salmon.

"Have a seat, Liam—may I call you Liam?" Barnes said, motioning to a cushioned chair several years past comfortable use.

"Sure," Liam said, sitting.

Barnes slumped into his own chair, which deflated a few inches beneath his bulk. He rubbed his eyes and then stroked the white hair on his upper lip before glancing at Liam. "I'm sorry about your brother and his wife."

Liam swallowed and stared at a spot over the sheriff's left shoulder. "Sir, no offense, but I've been told how sorry everyone is from the moment I got here and no one's answered any of my questions." When he looked again at Barnes, the older man's eyes were focused on the piles of paperwork covering his desk.

"You're justified in being angry. All I'm saying is, Allen was my doctor—he was most everyone's around here unless they wanted to drive over to Fairview Hospital in Dayton. Suzie was a good woman, helped organize a lot of the community functions. They'll be missed."

"Suzie was wonderful."

"Didn't get along with your brother?"

"Did he ever mention me?" Barnes didn't say anything, only nodded. "Let's just say we weren't on speaking terms. I hadn't seen him since my father died two years ago, and the time before that was five years earlier."

"You two have a row about something?"

Liam settled back in the chair and fixed Barnes coldly, unblinking. "Sheriff, I don't have the time or patience for your insinuations. I came down here to take care of my brother and sister-in-law's affairs, and maybe glean some insight as to why they were killed. What I find is a community with two double homicides in less than a week and belligerent law enforcement that's set on keeping me in the dark. Transparency breeds trust, so if you think I had something to do with my brother's murder, say it now so I know where you stand."

To Barnes's credit, the man didn't move a muscle. After a beat, he pursed his lips, making his mustache rise in a wave, before exhaling. "I don't think you're involved. It's just been a hell of a week and I'm in no mood to have someone else walk on my toes. They're sore as hell already."

"I just want to know what you can tell me, not anything that might jeopardize the case," Liam said.

Barnes sighed again. "It started last Tuesday night. Jerry and Karen Shevlin were the first victims. Someone broke into their home in the evening, sometime around nine. Killed them, along with their dog. Their son, Eric, locked himself in their bedroom and called 911. Officers got there shortly after he hung up, found him on his parents' floor bleeding profusely. It was pure luck there was a unit less than a mile away when the call came in, otherwise things might've been different. He was rushed to your brother's practice, and Allen got the bleeding stopped before the boy was airlifted to Fairview. He's in a coma, hasn't woken or said a word."

Liam absorbed the information, calculations overriding emotions, the feeling like slipping into a comfortable pair of shoes. "And my brother's house? Same forced entry?"

"I can't say."

"Did Allen and Suzie know the Shevlins?"

Barnes licked his lips, considering. "Yes, Allen and Jerry were best friends."

"How were they killed?"

"I can't say."

"Doesn't look like you have any suspects in custody," Liam said, motioning to the hallway and empty cells.

"No, not yet. My deputies and I are support now for the BCA and their forensic team. This is way over our heads. I hesitated for only a heartbeat last week when I saw the Shevlins' place before calling BCA for help."

Liam nodded. He'd worked extensively with several BCA agents during his career, and all had been excellent, trustworthy, and competent. Phelps exuded none of their traits. "How were Allen and Suzie discovered?"

"They took the local paper. The delivery boy stopped by for payment early this morning and saw them through the front window."

"Was my brother questioned after the Shevlin murders?"

"Yes, but he and Suzie were in shock. They didn't know a thing."

Liam chewed the inside of his cheek. This wasn't going anywhere, and he deduced from Barnes's reactions and answers that there wasn't a whole lot more than what he was telling him. They were almost as much in the dark as he was.

"You're quite a bit younger than Allen," Barnes said, appraising Liam again.

"Sixteen years. I was a planned oops, my dad used to say."

Barnes chuckled. "You're young for a detective too."

Liam felt the familiar tightening in his chest and swallowed. "Yeah, guess I was too dumb to be on the beat."

Barnes smiled, and it looked like a lot of effort. "Is there a reason—"

Liam stood and reached across the desk to shake the sheriff's hand. The older man stopped speaking and returned the gesture. "I appreciate all your help, Sheriff. Do you know when the bodies will be released for burial?"

Barnes blinked and nodded. "Tomorrow, I believe. Agent Phelps wanted the autopsy results as soon as possible."

"Could you notify me when they release them? I want to get back home as soon as I can wrap everything up here."

"Sure."

"Thank you," Liam said as he exited the office. His footsteps clicked and echoed back to him from the far walls of the cells, and the crushing feeling in his chest accelerated him out of the door and into the evening air.

# CHAPTER 3

He found a pub on a side street that looked like it served food.

The inside was larger and cleaner than he expected, and when he sat at a table in the back of the room, it was only a few seconds before the locals returned to their drinks. The menu was featureless, and his appetite hadn't returned. He ordered a cheeseburger basket, and nursed a Guinness until it arrived. He was about to make an attempt at actually eating when the door to the bar opened and a woman walked in.

She was tall, maybe five feet nine, and wore a knee-length skirt. Her dark-brown hair was swept away from her brow by a black headband and hung almost to her shoulders. She clutched a purse close to her side, and as her eyes passed over him without lingering, he remembered the dances they'd shared, the feeling of her slender back beneath his hand, how her lips felt against his, even the way her skin smelled.

Liam set his burger in the basket and stood. The woman turned away from him and tried to lean on a barstool as she waited for the bartender to finish with another patron. Liam threaded his way between a row of tables and put a hand on the bar a couple feet from where she stood. He watched her eyes glance at him, traveling up his forearm to his face before sliding away, and then coming back. She pivoted, her mouth open, the beginning of a question on her tongue.

"Hi, Dani," Liam said.

She tried to say something—he could see a word forming in her mouth—but then she simply stepped around the barstool that separated them and hugged him, tears already spilling from her eyes.

He led her back to his table after she put in an order for a vodka tonic. After the waitress dropped off the drink, she sipped it and stared at him over the rim of the glass. He crossed his legs and sat back in his chair, looking at the spots where her tears dried in ghostly, crooked lines on her cheeks.

"I can't believe you recognized me," she said after a few minutes of them trading gazes.

"Ditto," he said, cradling his beer in one hand. "But in all fairness, you haven't changed that much."

Dani huffed laughter as she wiped again at the trails of tears. "In ten years? Yeah, right."

"No, really," Liam said. "I knew it was you right away."

She brushed her cheek one more time and then looked at him, her green eyes unwavering in the low light of the bar. "You look different."

He tried to smile, but it crumpled and refused to take hold. "It's been a long time."

"Yes, it has."

Liam searched her face and found himself studying the angles of her nose, the sharp lines of her eyebrows, the red of her lips, just as he had when they'd danced so many years before. He took a long drink of his beer, then set it down on the table.

"It's horrible," she said after a moment. "I can't even bring myself to accept it yet."

"I know what you mean. It's a shock."

"I just can't—" Dani's eyes filled with tears again, and she shook her head. "Sorry. I'm still trying to wrap my mind around it. Suzie and I were pretty close, even for cousins."

"She wouldn't have had just anyone as her maid of honor, I'm sure."

Dani jerked her head, the tears she fought to hold back streaming down her face again. She rubbed a shaking hand across her forehead and took a long pull from the glass before her. "You never think you'll have to deal with this sort of thing, you know? You do your regular routine every day, and it's easy to forget this type of stuff happens all the time." Liam didn't move; instead, he fought the bindings of panic beginning to tighten in the center of his chest. "You just don't think it will ever happen to you. It's terrible of me, but I didn't want to come. I wouldn't have, but there's no one else on Suzie's side of the family besides my parents, and they're on a cruise vacation." Dani wiped her eyes again.

Liam struggled for words of comfort. Words he'd spoken before to families he didn't know, wives, husbands, children, mothers, fathers. But now, he found nothing in the reservoir deep within him. It was hollow and empty, a tomb of dried emotions that lay silent in a dark place he couldn't reach anymore.

"I'm sorry," Dani said after a moment.

"For what?" Liam asked, rising from the depths inside him.

"Here I am sobbing and carrying on, and it was your brother. Suzie and I were close, but I'm sure not as much as you and Allen were."

Liam curled his mouth at one corner and reached for his mostly empty beer. "Allen and I weren't on the best of terms as of late."

"Oh, I'm sorry."

Liam shrugged. "We . . ." He shifted in his seat. "We just didn't keep in touch anymore. He had his life here, his practice, Suzie. I was always busy. It just wasn't conducive for us."

Dani looked at her lap. "I hadn't seen Suzie for quite a while either. I think the last time was at Christmas two years ago. My mom

29

and dad and I all came here for a weekend. We stayed with Allen and Suzie. It was nice." Dani's face contorted with grief again, and Liam reached out to grasp one of her hands in his own. Her fingers wrapped around his, and she squeezed as a sob hitched through her chest. "I'm sorry, I just can't believe they're gone," she whispered.

She took another drink of her vodka and glanced at him before staring at the table. Her hand remained in his, and neither made any move to release the hold. "Do they have any leads?" she finally asked.

"Not that I can tell. They're being pretty close-lipped about the whole thing. I met with the sheriff tonight. I got the feeling he doesn't know much more than I do."

"It makes me so angry," Dani said. "What did Allen and Suzie ever do to deserve this?"

Liam said nothing. The door to the pub opened, and Liam watched the shaggy head of Nut appear and slouch to the bar, where he began to talk to the bartender.

"Dani, I have to speak to someone," Liam said, his eyes never leaving the vagrant's back. "Can you give me your number so I can get ahold of you tomorrow? Maybe we can help each other make arrangements?"

Dani glanced over her shoulder and then back at Liam. "Sure," she said, and reached into her purse, pulled out a business card, and handed it to him.

He saw the confused look on her face and squeezed her hand once more. "Are you going to be okay?"

Dani finished her drink and made an effort to smile. "Yes, I'll be fine."

"I'll call you tomorrow."

Liam stood and left his beer and food on the table. He moved in a straight line across the pub toward Nut, who had an overfull glass of beer clutched close to his chest. The older man spotted Liam when he was two steps away; his eyes widened and a bit of beer slopped from his glass onto the floor. Liam saw the indecision on the bum's face and wondered if he would have to pursue him out of the pub.

"I need to talk to you," Liam said when he was within arm's reach of the man.

"Uh," Nut said.

Liam jerked his head toward a corner table in the back of the pub and saw the bum's shoulders slump. Liam let him go first, and as they made their way to the back of the bar, he saw Dani rise from her seat and walk toward the door. He felt her eyes on the side of his head, but he locked his gaze on the back of Nut's dirty coat. Nut set his beer on a wobbly table and sat in the chair closest to the wall, while Liam took a seat beside him, effectively blocking the vagrant's only escape route.

"Listen, I don't know what this is about, but—"

"How much did you get from the reporter for giving her my name and what I looked like?" Liam asked.

Nut opened his mouth to protest, but Liam reached over and pulled the glass of beer out of the other man's hand. Nut watched Liam drag the glass away and frowned.

"Fifty bucks," Nut said. Liam pinned him to the wall with a glare until Nut squirmed. "I'm sorry, okay? You make do with what you have, and I was short this morning."

"Short on beer funds."

"Yeah, well. How the hell did you know anyway?" Nut asked.

"You're the only person outside of the investigation that knew I was in town."

Nut nodded, dropping his head so that he looked at the pitted tabletop. Liam slid the beer back in front of him, and Nut raised his eyes again.

"I want to ask you a few things," Liam said.

A smile broke out on the man's stubbled face, and he grasped the beer. "Sure, whatever you want to know, buddy."

Liam glanced around the room to see if their table was being observed. The rest of the diners and drinkers seemed to be immersed in their own conversations; he caught no one eavesdropping or even looking in their direction.

"Tell me about the Shevlins."

Nut tipped the glass to his lips and sucked down almost half its contents in a few swallows before wiping his mouth on a stained sleeve. "Rich as rich could be," Nut said, lowering his voice. "Kind of the flagship couple for Tallston—old money and good looks combined. Jerry was born with two silver spoons, one in his mouth and one up his ass. His daddy was a land baron of sorts, owned thousands of acres across the river. From what I understand, he leased it to crop farmers, mostly wheat if I remember right." Nut paused to slurp more beer. After stifling a belch, he continued. "His daddy sold most of the land about twenty years ago, and Jerry became a businessman before he was twenty-five."

"What did he do for a living?" Liam asked.

"One of them day traders or some shit," Nut said. "Invested in God knows what."

"How about his wife, what was she like?"

"Easy on the eyes, Karen was. Don't remember quite when she moved here. Don't recall seeing her around much before she became Jerry's girl in high school. They were homecoming king and queen, got married right out of school. Only thing that marred their perfect life was the death of their first child."

"What happened?" Liam asked.

Nut finished the last of his beer and set the glass down on the table next to Liam's elbow, staring at it until Liam motioned to the waitress to bring another. When the empty glass was gone, Nut took a long pull from the fresh brew and sat back in his chair.

"Where was I?"

"They lost their first child."

"Oh yeah. Rumor was that their first boy died of complications at birth. There's a little tombstone in their backyard where they buried him. That sobered them up a little, and it must have been too traumatic for them to go through it again, since they adopted Eric years later."

Liam's mind hummed with flickering thoughts. Connections like strings began to attach themselves to a bleary map in his head. "Did Jerry or Karen have any enemies in town? Did he have any business deals that went wrong?"

Nut drained more of his beer and appeared to search his mind, his dark eyes rolling almost straight up at the ceiling. "Not that I know of. The deal with Colton must have gone through fine, since the project across the river is still scheduled to start soon."

"Colton Incorporated? Is that what the signs are for all over town?"

"Yep. Colton is out of Sweden somewhere, I believe. Huge paper company with depots all over the US. They purchased the land across the river from the Shevlins over a year ago. Talk around town is they're gonna tear down the old foundry and build a processing plant for pulp and whatnot. I suppose they'll use the river for transport— that's why they chose the spot."

"How does everyone feel about the plant going up in a small town like this?" Liam asked, something catching on a burr in his mind.

Nut shrugged and nearly finished the second beer. "Mostly good. Be more jobs created. There's a small activist group that's trying to stop it from going through. They say that by cutting down the trees on the other side of the river it'll damage the ecosystem or some bullshit. Buncha hippies, if you ask me. I'm sure that big shot from Colton is fit to be tied about these murders, though. Something like this might put a hold on the city's vote that's coming up."

"Who's the big shot?"

Nut finished his beer, and without prompting, Liam had another brought to their table. "Name's Donald something or other. He's rentin' a big place on the south side of town, right smack on the river. He and his team of suits have been here for a few weeks, buttering up the local government, I assume. The mayor's got his head up his ass, so he'll believe anyone with a little money to wave around under his nose." Nut sipped his beer, and Liam saw the other man's pupils tightened to pinpoints under the influence of the alcohol. "You know that shithead wanted to cut the local soup kitchen out completely? I mean, there's not a lot of us around town without places to go, but you can't take that away from us. Some of my friends aren't as industrious as I am, and they count on at least one meal from that place every day."

"You mean they're not as good at selling information?" Liam asked.

Nut licked his lips and blinked. "I'm taking that as an insult."

"Good." Liam opened his wallet and pulled out a fifty-dollar bill. He watched Nut's eyes follow it as he placed it on the table between them. "You're with me now, okay? If you hear or see anything else that you think might be important, I want you to call this number." He pulled a piece of scratch paper out, grabbed an errant pen from a nearby table, and jotted his cell number down. "Anything, do you understand?"

Nut nodded, still staring at the fifty within his reach. "You some kind of cop?"

"Not anymore." Liam stood and turned to the bar to settle up the bill.

"I'm sorry I told those vultures your name."

Liam stopped and studied the homeless man's drunken eyes, and nodded. "You do what I asked and we'll call it even." Nut smiled and raised the dregs of beer to him in a toast.

Liam paid the tab and made his way outside into the deepening dark of the night, wondering what the hell he was getting himself into.

⌣

Sleep wouldn't come. It never came like before. He remembered the sensation of drifting off, the steady pull of exhaustion dragging him down into a soft slumber. He would awake sometimes in the early-morning hours in slight surprise at having fallen asleep without realizing it.

But those nights were gone.

What he had now was waiting. The slipstream of time slowing to a crawl, the minutes stretching into hours, his mind and body helpless with the compulsion to check the clock constantly.

He stared up at the hotel ceiling, longing for a drink. Something powerful. Several pulls of whiskey would do the trick. But he didn't want to get drunk, and passing out wasn't the same as sleeping; it was similar, but without the rest. He tried the breathing exercises the doctor had taught him. Inhale, hold, exhale slowly and count to ten, until all the air was out. Repeat. Think of the states and their capitals. Retrace the roads he had driven on that day, see the landscape in reverse, strive to make it all the way back to where he had left from.

Liam sighed and rolled over, trying to keep his eyelids closed. He pictured Dani standing at the bar. She was still beautiful, just as he remembered. God, he hadn't thought of her in years. He wondered if she was married. He couldn't see how she would be single, but if there was a man in the picture, wouldn't he be here with her for support? He could still feel the warmth of her hand in his own. It was a sensation he hadn't felt for some time, the touch of another. Liam closed his fist lightly, allowing the illusion to continue. He slipped toward the edge of sleep . . . and saw the black eye of the gun barrel.

His eyelids flew open and he sucked in a breath, his heart speeding up from a plodding walk to a sprint in less than a second. His brow furrowed, breath shuddering within his chest, the air hot as sweat broke out over his body. He clenched his eyes shut and forced away the sound of the gunshot ringing in his ears.

# CHAPTER 4

The sound of thunder woke him.

Liam opened his eyes to the surrounding hotel room, battled the immediate confusion of where he was, and let the memory of the day before settle over him. He turned his head to look at the clock: *6:15*. The last time he saw the clock it was 3:10. Three hours of sleep. He inhaled and then breathed out. It would have to do.

He drank two cups of coffee in the little kitchenette off the hotel lobby and gradually began to feel like he was awake. His stomach was an aching, flaccid sac that cried out for food. He managed to choke down three hard-boiled eggs and a slice of toast, promising himself that he would make more of an effort to eat regularly. If he couldn't sleep, he'd at least give himself fuel to keep moving.

The morning was cooler than the previous day. The sky was bruised in the east above the hulking bluffs, a few lacerations of sunlight leaking through mottled clouds as they attempted to close the wounds fully, with the occasional sound of thunder.

As he snapped the door of his truck shut, intent on taking care of his brother's final arrangements, Liam realized he had no idea where Allen and Suzie banked, invested, or lawyered. He sat still behind the steering wheel before drawing out his phone and searching the online

Tallston directory for lawyers. There were three in town. Luckily, he picked the correct one on the first try. The secretary who answered said that without ID she couldn't say whether or not his brother and sister-in-law did business with them, but if he'd stop by, the owner would be happy to speak with him.

Liam hung up and drove to the north end of town, turning down two wrong streets before he saw the squat brick building with *Fenton Law Office* on its front. The reception area was small but comfortable, the walls a cool green. A stern-faced woman in a business suit sat behind a counter and studied Liam as she punched an intercom button on her phone and murmured something into the headset she wore. A few minutes later a middle-aged man in a tweed suit appeared from behind an oak door at the far end of the room. His hair was dark and flecked with gray at the temples, and his blue eyes sat amidst delicate lines of crow's-feet that spoke of a good nature.

"Mr. Dempsey, I'm Chris Fenton. So sorry for your loss," Fenton said, shaking Liam's hand.

"Thank you," Liam said.

"Please come in."

Liam followed the lawyer into a spacious office lined with dark wood baseboards and rows of modern bookcases filled with leather-backed tomes. Fenton slid into a seat behind a massive desk, and Liam sat in a plush chair across from him. The lawyer moved several sets of folders and then interlaced his hands before him on the desk, his eyes morose.

"Terrible, terrible thing. Allen and I were friends. We golfed together once a week. It's quite a shock. I'm so very sorry."

"Thank you." Liam struggled for something else to say, but he had nothing to offer, his brother an angry enigma that he had kept in the back of his mind until yesterday.

"I'm sure you'd like to get things in order as quickly as possible, which I should be able to do for you. Not that the family resemblance between you and Allen isn't apparent, but I will need to see some ID, just a formality." Liam brought out his wallet, and after only a few seconds of examining his driver's license, Fenton handed it back to him. "I managed to gather all of Allen and Suzie's paperwork here. There's only a few things you need to sign, actually. Their finances and wills were in excellent shape." The lawyer paused as he shifted documents and looked across the desk at Liam. "You are the last living relative, correct?"

"Yes," Liam said. "My mother's been gone a long time, and my father died two years ago. There's no one else close except for Suzie's side of the family."

"Yes, well, I'm not sure how to say this, so I'll just say it," Fenton said. "Your brother didn't name you in his will or on any of the insurance policies. It looks like their liquid assets will be distributed between four different charities, one local and the others international. The house is to be sold and the revenue is to be divided in the same way."

"I'm not surprised," Liam said, feeling a small rise of anger at his brother before it became absorbed into the bitter miasma surrounding Allen's memory. "I'm happy to sign whatever you need to get things under way."

"Okay, but there is one other matter." The lawyer studied him. "Suzie took out a policy several years back, and the sole benefactor is you."

There was a beat of silence. "What?"

Fenton leaned forward and turned a binder of papers toward Liam so that he could read them. "She created this insurance policy unbeknownst to Allen, or it appears that way. You're listed as the recipient of the policy amount."

Liam's head swam with confusion and a new wave of sorrow. Suzie, always kind, always thinking of him. "I didn't know anything about this. I haven't seen either one of them for over two years."

"Yes, I understand. This was created on June 11, 2011."

Liam closed his eyes, remembering the date. *The day after Dad's funeral.*

"I'll just need your signature on the bottom of these, as well as your bank account information for the deposit."

"How much did she set the policy for?"

Fenton glanced up at him. "Five hundred thousand."

Liam cringed internally. Half a million dollars. More than enough motive to kill.

"I don't want it."

Fenton stopped scribbling something and looked up at him, his eyes slits. "What?"

"I don't want it. I'm refusing the policy."

"Well, Mr. Dempsey, you can't really refuse it, you'll—"

"Then I'll donate it. Give me a few days to think about where I want it to go, and then we'll do the paperwork."

Fenton sat back in his chair, appraising him. "Sure, we can do that."

"Can I take the rest of the paperwork to look over in the meantime?" Liam asked, motioning to the folders on the desk.

"Yes, by all means. I've got all the places that you need to sign marked. Like I said, the execution of the will doesn't really require anything, so yes, go ahead."

The attorney closed the documents and handed them to Liam, whose heart picked up its already hurried pace.

"Thanks very much for your help. I'll be in touch soon," Liam said.

The two men shook hands as they stood, and without waiting for the lawyer to say anything more, Liam opened the office door and moved as quickly as he could outside, leaving Fenton to stare after him.

Liam flipped through the pages of his brother's life. He searched the numbers and words of Allen's last testament, trying to build a picture out of the symbols or patterns in the paperwork. Nothing stood out to him. He looked for monetary connections to the Shevlins, and other than Allen and Suzie being named Eric Shevlin's godparents, there seemed to be no indications of debt or loans between the two families. The will was straightforward. His anger at Allen for not being named in the will dulled with each passing second, and soon it was just another facet of his brother's familiar rancor.

Liam sat back and rubbed his eyes. They felt swollen, coated in lead. He glanced at the separate packet of papers that lay to the left of everything else on the small table. Suzie's policy. He stared at the number on the paper. He knew why she'd done it, but her kindness was now a curse. Phelps would gain access to their records, if he hadn't already. He would see the policy, and it would be a klaxon going off, a neon arrow pointing to Liam as a suspect. The rumblings of anxiety constricted his chest, but there was something else there too. A warm flame of pride, soured only by grief at the thought of Suzie going behind Allen's back to make sure he would be taken care of if anything happened to them.

"She was too good for you, asshole," Liam said to the empty hotel room.

The sudden chime of his phone made him jerk, and when he looked at the screen, he saw that the number was unavailable again.

"Hello?"

"Liam, this is Sheriff Barnes. Could you come by the station sometime today?"

"Of course. Has there been a development?"

Barnes hesitated. "Nothing groundbreaking, just something I thought you'd like to see."

"Okay, I can be there in ten minutes."

"Good. Hit the buzzer near the back entrance and I'll let you in." The sheriff hung up.

Liam stood, ready to head out of the room, but he paused. After a few seconds of thought, he reached into the bottom of his bag and found the hard angles of the Sig, softened by the holster hugging it. He undid his belt and threaded it through the concealment holster. The holster molded to his lower back on the inside of his jeans and when he tightened his belt, he could barely feel the weight of the gun there.

With a flip of his T-shirt and a quick check to make sure the handgun wasn't visible, Liam turned off the lights and left the room.

Liam approached the rear door of the station, the clouds overhead expanding with bloated bellies that spoke of a deluge. There were two squad cars parked in the rear lot, along with a late-model Land Cruiser. Liam eyed the shiny vehicle as he passed it, noting the severely tinted windows and the chrome spokes within the rims. He was just about to push the round button mounted beside the door when it opened from within and the sheriff's deputy he'd seen at his brother's home the day before stepped outside.

The young law officer recoiled and rolled his eyes as he exhaled. "Wow, you scared the hell out of me."

Liam smiled. "Sorry, the sheriff told me to ring the button."

The deputy nodded, holding the door open for him. "No problem, go ahead. He's in a meeting, might have to wait a minute."

"Thanks," Liam said, slipping past him, out of the dingy light of the day and into the stark fluorescent glow of the jail. As soon as the door shut behind him, he heard a raised voice down the hall. It didn't sound like Barnes, and Liam walked as quietly as he could toward the closed door of the sheriff's office. Gradually, the words became less garbled and more distinct.

"You do realize the importance of this project, Sheriff?"

"Yes, of course I do, and I'll do my best to impress it upon the agents handling the cases, but with all due respect, Mr. Haines, there has been loss of life. A construction project doesn't really come into play during a murder investigation."

Liam leaned against the wall to one side of the sheriff's office and tilted his head to hear the conversation better.

"I can say, on behalf of Colton Incorporated, that we are very sorry for the town's losses, but the amount of financial backing that is riding on the town's vote next week is quite substantial."

"I don't know what else to tell you, Mr. Haines. There's been concern raised and people are scared. It will be up to the city council whether there will be a postponement of the vote," Barnes said. The old man's voice was gruff and bland, without emotion or energy. "We're doing all we can."

There was a long pause, and Liam stepped away from the door as he saw the handle begin to turn.

"Just see that you keep us updated."

The door opened completely, and Liam was ready for it. He took a step forward as though he were only just now walking down the hallway, and nearly bumped into a man in a black button-up shirt and gray slacks.

"Oh, I'm sorry," Liam said, and stepped out of the man's way.

Haines had wide shoulders, which he held back in a stiff posture, his chest thrown out. He looked to be a few years older than Liam and was clean-shaven, his features angular, with a knitted black brow that almost formed a line over his squinting eyes.

Haines sized up Liam for a split second, and then pushed past him without a word. Liam stepped into the sheriff's doorway and watched the other man until he disappeared through the rear entry.

"Top of the morning to you," Barnes said in a deadened tone, his voice unchanged from the conversation with Haines.

"Not that I heard, but it sounded like things are looking up for you," Liam said, walking into the office and raising his eyebrows.

Barnes stared at him for a moment, then snorted a short laugh. "Shut the door and come sit down."

Liam did as he asked and waited expectantly. Barnes exhaled a drawn-out sigh and rubbed his mustache.

"I looked into your record," Barnes said at last.

Liam's heart stutter-stepped, then began to slam in his chest. "I see. And how did you—"

"Just because I'm a small-town sheriff doesn't mean I don't know people."

Liam's temper flared with his rising panic. "So what the hell does my record have to do with what's going on now?"

"Everything," Barnes said, leaning back in his chair.

"Listen, I don't know what Phelps told you, but I haven't been to this town in years. I haven't spoken a word to my brother or his wife since the day I buried my father. I did not kill them."

"I know, Liam. You misunderstand. I read about what happened to you ten months ago, but that's not what interested me. What interested me was your arrest record and case-closure percentage. They were off the charts. There's a dozen entries in your file by your superiors noting your ability to read a suspect just by speaking with him. Not to mention the commendations. You were a damn fine detective."

Liam sat with a retort stuck in his mouth, the angry words dissolving like an ill-tasting pill. "I guess I'm not following," he finally said.

Barnes interlaced his fingers over his formidable belly and closed his eyes. "Son, I'm about a year away from retirement. My wife's father just passed away, God rest his wretched soul, and he happened to leave us enough money to buy the cabin on the Sheldon River in Colorado that I've had my eye on for the last ten years. I love to fly-fish, Liam.

I love the solitude of it, always have. The feeling of the river parting around your waders, the zip of the line overhead, the hit as a nice trout takes the bait." Barnes opened his eyes and looked at Liam. "There's really nothing like it."

"Sounds nice."

"You can't even imagine," Barnes said, the barest of smiles on his face. "What I'm getting at is, no matter where I go after I retire, this is where I grew up. I know the people of this town, I knew their parents, and I know their kids. I've gone to the same diner to eat lunch and bought my shoes at the same shoe store for the last fifty years. I love this place, and what's going on here just isn't fair."

"This have something to do with the polite man I met in the hall?" Liam asked.

"Dumbfuck," Barnes muttered. "Donald Haines. He's the head manager on the latest Colton acquirement. The old foundry and the land it sits on across the river."

Liam nodded. "I was filled in on the project by someone already."

Barnes scowled. "By whom?"

Liam considered it for a few seconds and saw no harm in being honest. "Nut."

Barnes's scowl deepened. "Damn gossiping drunk." The sheriff pointed a stubby finger across the desk at Liam. "He's a nosy bastard, been hanging around bars and cafés too long in this town." Liam held his tongue, and Barnes regained his composure and continued. "That shithead Haines sees the murders as an inconvenience to the project across the river. He's heard rumblings that if the killer isn't caught, the city council might not convene and vote on whether construction can begin. Prick."

"What does this have to do with me?"

Barnes put both of his meaty hands palm down on his desk and looked Liam in the eyes. "Allen and the Shevlins weren't just murdered, son. They were cut to pieces." Liam swallowed and waited, not looking away from the sheriff's unwavering stare. "I've never seen anything like it in my life. It was . . . inhuman." Barnes pointed a finger at Liam's chest. "Phelps isn't handling this the way he should—he's rushing. I've seen hurried law work before and it always ends up badly. Do you agree?"

"Definitely."

"Good. So from what I've read about you and from what I've seen of Phelps, you're the better cop. You have the experience to help find this guy, whoever he is. Now, my question to you is can you handle working on something this close to home? Can you put aside any feelings that might muddle the investigation?"

"Yes."

"Are you sure? Because I'm not solely concerned with the town's well-being here. If I'm to go out on a limb, I want to be sure you're not going to shake it so much that I fall off and break my ass."

Liam nodded once.

"On the other hand, I will not let my town be terrorized and become the hunting ground of some psycho when there's an answer sitting right in front of me." Barnes blinked a few times, and Liam saw the emotion written in his features. "Even if you and your brother didn't see eye to eye, Suzie was still a special woman and she didn't deserve to die like she did." Barnes nodded once, affirming his own words. "You got a gun?"

"Yes," Liam said, feeling the floating sensation of being in a dream.

"Registered to carry it?"

"Yes."

"Got it on you now?"

Liam said nothing.

"Good."

The older man stood and turned toward the door, placing his hand upon a manila folder on the corner of his desk. "I just got the autopsy reports back on Allen and Suzie. They're in here, along with the Shevlins', as well as some crime-scene photos and notes." Barnes reached into his pocket and drew out a small set of keys, laying them on top of the file folder. "Keys to your brother's place. You're allowed to go back in there—forensics is done with everything. There's also a business card in the folder for a cleaning company out of Dayton that can handle the mess in the house." Barnes turned his head and fixed Liam with a penetrating look, tapping the folder once. "Think I'll go up front and get myself a cup of coffee."

The sheriff moved around his desk and swung the door open as if Liam wasn't there anymore. Liam listened to his footsteps echo in the hall and fade as they neared the front offices. After a moment, a door slammed and all was quiet again.

Liam stood and put the house keys into his pocket, then grabbed the file folder from the desk. He scanned the area behind the sheriff's desk until he spotted the small copier in the corner of the room. He slipped the stack of paper out of the folder and placed it into the feeder tray at the top of the copier. With a punch of the green button on the machine's face, it hummed to life, sucking greedily at the pile of papers in its tray.

# CHAPTER 5

Liam laid the sheaf of papers on the passenger seat and started the truck.

Reaching into his pocket, he found Dani's business card and pulled it out, really seeing it for the first time: *Dani Powell—Web Design—Freelance Artist*. So she'd gone ahead with the musings she'd spoken of the night of Allen and Suzie's wedding. He remembered the feeling of her breath on his ear as they danced. She'd told him about how much she'd like to draw and create art for a living, and he had listened, feeling privileged at how close she stood to him.

He punched the cell number into his phone and waited. On the third ring, Dani answered.

"Hello?"

"Dani, it's Liam."

"Hi, how are you?"

"Fine. Look, I don't know how to ask you this, and you can tell me I'm crazy if you want, but I was able to come by some information concerning Allen's and Suzie's deaths. Would you be interested in looking over it with me?" Silence hung thick on the other end of the line, and he mentally cursed himself for calling her. Of course she didn't want to go over the details of her cousin's death. And why was he asking her? Out of respect, believing that she would want to be involved—or were his motives completely selfish? "I'm sorry, I didn't—"

"I'd love to help," she said.

"Really? Because what I have isn't pleasant in the least."

"No, I want to. I owe it to Suzie if I can help in some way. Thank you for offering. Should I meet you at your hotel?"

"Yeah, that'd be great," Liam said, putting the Chevy into drive. "It's the Riverside Inn on the south end of town. You can't miss it."

"Okay, see you soon."

"Okay, bye." He hung up and stared at the phone in his hand. A fluttery feeling began to course through the base of his stomach, and he squelched it with a glance at the papers in the passenger seat. This wasn't a teen study session with a pretty girl; it was a murder investigation that he wasn't even supposed to be involved in. And now he'd implicated a woman who in no way deserved to be a part of this mess. Annoyed, he tapped a finger against his temple as he drove toward the south end of town. The clouds above the bluffs were even lower than before his meeting with Barnes, and he expected heavy raindrops to start falling any minute.

The inner turmoil hadn't abated by the time he pulled into his hotel parking lot, and he decided that, after sharing his thoughts and the information with Dani, he would leave her out of any further action he might take. And what was he going to do? Go after the killer alone? A familiar stirring of energy rose in his chest at the thought of finding the person responsible for the murders, and even with only three hours of sleep, a focused calm fell over him, with just a suggestion of weariness at the wings of his senses.

He parked in a spot at the corner of the lot and retrieved the papers, and had taken three steps from the vehicle when Shirley Strafford and a man holding a camera and tripod over his shoulder came around the far side of the building and obstructed his path to the hotel doors. The reporter's small, perky face held a sickly sweet smile, and her eyes flashed a challenge to him as he slowed his walk, his jaw tightening.

"Mr. Dempsey, a quick word with you?"

"No, thanks," Liam said, and tried to sidestep the woman. She moved to block his way, a wireless microphone clutched in one hand.

"It will just take a second," she said, pushing the mic into his face. "Have there been any new developments in the case of your brother's and sister-in-law's murders?"

Liam tried to move to the woman's other side, but she blocked him again.

"Could you tell us how you feel about the brutal nature of the crimes committed here in the last week?"

"Please move," Liam said, stepping back a few feet from the reporter's reach.

"If you would give us a little of your time, we'd be happy to let you get on with your day," Shirley said, and gave him another smile.

Liam brushed past her before she could step in his way. He felt her microphone graze his cheek as he reached for the door handle, but the cameraman put a foot in front of the door and lowered the camera away from his face.

"Look, bud, give us a couple minutes and we'll leave you be."

Liam let go of the door handle and dropped his head. "Okay," he said as he folded the papers he held in his hand and tucked them into his back pocket.

"That's a trouper," the cameraman said, and began to raise the viewing lens back to his eye.

With a fluid motion, Liam stepped forward and pressed the red power button on the back edge of the camera. "What—" the man began, but Liam released the camera and grabbed his face. He slammed the man's head into the brick wall of the entry and heard a muffled cry of pain as the cameraman's eyes fluttered.

"Listen to me," Liam hissed, and turned his head and fixed Shirley with an icy glare. "My fucking brother and sister-in-law were just murdered. Believe it or not, I'm not in a mood to discuss it. Do we have an understanding?"

The cameraman nodded as far as Liam's grip would allow him, but Shirley merely grimaced at him, her false smile replaced with a look of disgust. Liam pressed a little harder on the man's face and he whimpered. Finally, the reporter's shoulders drooped.

"Okay, fucking let him go!" Shirley yelled.

Liam released the cameraman and readied himself for an attack, but none came. The man merely rubbed his face and shot a hateful look at Liam. Without another pause, Liam swung the door open and walked toward the stairs, giving a smile to the young man who stepped from the room behind the front desk.

"Everything okay, sir?"

"Just fine, thanks," Liam said, and he bounded up the stairs two at a time, leaving the hotel employee to stare at the retreating reporter supporting her staggering cameraman outside.

Fifteen minutes later there was a knock on his door. Liam moved to the front of his small room and stopped, wondering if the sheriff would be in the hall with Shirley and the cameraman, his eyes morose and filled with disappointment.

"Who is it?" he asked.

"It's Dani."

Liam unlocked the door and opened it. Dani wore a pair of hip-hugging jeans and a long-sleeved T-shirt. Her hair poked out from a tight bun in different directions, and her eyes looked clear, as if she'd gotten some sleep. He nearly grimaced at how horrible his appearance surely was.

"Come in," he said, standing back. She stepped by him, and he caught a faint whiff of perfume, something like ripened peaches. "Sorry for the state of things," he said.

"It's fine," Dani said, turning in a small circle as she looked around the room.

Liam picked up her business card from the table beside the bed. "So you're an artist, just like you wanted to be."

She glanced at his hand and laughed. "Well, yes and no."

"What do you mean?"

"I do web design, which is an art form these days, but it's not my passion."

"Not like drawing?" Liam said as he moved past her to the coffeepot that chugged and burbled on the table below the window.

Dani sat in one of the two chairs at the end of the bed. "No, not like drawing. Don't get me wrong, I still get to do it. I set aside an hour every day to sketch and work on some creative aspect, but none of my work has gotten accepted by the galleries I keep submitting to." She looked at him for a long time, her head tilted to one side. "You remembered that I liked to draw."

Liam nodded. "Of course." Dani opened her mouth, then closed it. "What?" he asked.

"I'm sorry I didn't call you after Allen and Suzie's wedding. I know I said I would. It was kind of fast for me. I'd only broken up with my boyfriend a few weeks before and I had classes, but it's no excuse."

Liam waved the words away and handed her a cup of coffee before sitting opposite her. "Do you take cream?" he asked, starting to get up again.

"No, no, it's fine, thank you," she said.

"Are you happy doing the web design?" he asked. He could see she wanted to talk more about the few hours they'd shared on Allen and Suzie's wedding night, but he was afraid the memory might become tainted by words. He wouldn't tell her how long he'd waited,

51

hoping she would call. To her it might've only been a few dances and several lingering kisses, but to him it had meant more.

Her face scrunched up as she half smiled and half frowned. Another of the weightless swells surged in his stomach and he shifted in his seat.

"It supports what I really like to do, so I guess that makes me happy," she said. "Sometimes that's all life is, you know? Doing something different to support what you really want." Her eyes found his as she sipped her coffee, and he suddenly felt very lucky to be sitting so close to this woman. "How about you? Are you still a police officer?"

"Umm, not anymore," he said with as much nonchalance as he could muster.

"Oh, really? Was it not what you wanted to do?"

Liam searched for a way to change the subject and found none. "I'm not sure anymore," he said. Dani studied him, and he felt himself wanting to tell her. Wanting to expose the raw wound that spiked with pain anytime someone mentioned his career. He opened his mouth to say something, to lead into it somehow, but instead he reached out and grasped Suzie's insurance policy form. "Take a look at this," he said as he handed her the paper.

Dani scanned it, and her eyes widened slightly before she looked at him. "Wow. That's a lot of money."

"I know."

"Why did she do this?"

"Because she was kind and my brother wasn't. I suppose she felt sorry for me, even though she was married to Allen. I don't think she ever told him she took out the policy. He would've been furious."

Dani stared at him for what seemed like a full minute before setting the paper down. "Can I ask why Allen and you didn't get along? He was always so outgoing and friendly to me."

Liam sighed and looked down at the floor. "My mother died giving birth to me. Allen never forgave me or my father for it. He once told me I was a mistake that cost more than I would ever be worth."

"That's horrible," Dani said, her eyebrows furrowing.

"Yeah, my dad thought so. He and Allen fought quite a bit before Allen went off to school. Dad raised me alone, and Allen just drifted farther and farther away from us. It hurt my father a lot, but he didn't give up. He always invited Allen and Suzie down for Christmas and Thanksgiving, always sent him a birthday card." Liam paused, the poignancy of the memories surprising him. "The last thing Allen said to me at Dad's funeral was, 'Now that he's in the ground, I can finally forget about both of you.'"

Dani gave a small gasp and her hand slid into his. He looked into her face and realized it wasn't merely the weight of the words he spoke that pulled on the strings of his emotions; it was more the act of telling someone who actually cared.

"I'm so sorry," she said.

"It's okay," Liam said, releasing her hand at the thought of only pity fueling her response. "It was quite a while ago, but now with this . . ." He tapped the policy. "It puts a little different spin on things."

"You mean, it implicates you in their murders."

"Yes."

Dani thought for a moment. "But what motive would there be to kill the Shevlins?"

"That's my only saving grace. No self-respecting cop is going to go down that avenue for too long—there's really nothing to back it up."

"Exactly, and besides, they could say the same of me for what Allen and Suzie put in their will."

"What's that?"

"They gave me their cabin on Long Lake, up north. They knew I loved it there. I don't know how many weekends my parents and I stayed there with them."

Liam nodded. "Yeah, but lake property isn't the same as half a million in cash."

"I suppose you're right," she conceded.

"I'm not too worried about being a suspect—I just don't want to be slowed down by the agent in charge of the case. He could use something like this to run me out of town, and now that I have this, that's the last thing I want," Liam said, picking up the larger stack of papers. He saw Dani look at the documents in his hand and then look away.

"Dani, you don't have to do this. To be perfectly honest I'm not supposed to have this stuff, I just wanted to give you the option to be involved."

She shook her head and set down her coffee cup. "No, I'm fine, just not looking forward to it." She breathed out. "So, where should we begin?"

"With the Shevlins, I think," Liam said, sorting the papers into piles.

A few photos of each crime scene lay amidst the descriptions and autopsy reports. Liam hadn't had the color option on when he copied everything from the folder, and the photos suffered for it. He could only get a general idea of what each picture was with the hazy quality of black and white, not to mention the sheriff's printer may have been the first of its kind ever produced. The scenes in the pictures were monochrome splotches of black blood, pooling lakes of gore, and mangled remains that were entirely unidentifiable. Dani avoided looking at them, and Liam relegated the pictures to a pile near his elbow. After studying them for a few minutes, he concluded that even with the colored originals he may not have been able to distinguish details about the bodies. The sheriff was right: the Shevlins had been hacked to pieces.

Liam picked up a page and sat back in his chair. "Here's some notes that the agent in charge of the case made. 'Crime was committed sometime between nine ten p.m. and nine thirty-two p.m. Assailant entered through the attached garage door, into kitchen. Door was struck with heavy object, possibly murder weapon.'" Liam glanced at Dani, and seeing her face clear and her eyes locked on his, he continued. "'Victims were a male Caucasian, forty-six years old, and a female Caucasian, forty-five years old. Both victims were found in the kitchen area, dismembered and bludgeoned. Wounds indicate a semi-sharp weapon capable of both cutting and blunt trauma. Male's arms were separated from shoulder joints, as well as knees separated below the patella. Female suffered large wound across abdomen, as well as hands and feet being removed at wrist and ankle joints. Both were decapitated.'" Liam paused again, rereading the last line before speaking it out loud. "'All wounds prior to decapitation were inflicted while victims were still alive.'"

"Oh my God," Dani said. "That's horrible."

Liam scanned the rest of the notes before looking up at her. "This means something," he said, turning his head and squinting out the window at the darkening afternoon sky. "This wasn't just a breaking and entering gone wrong, but we already knew that. This was emotional, it meant something to the killer."

He turned and rifled through the other pile containing the information about Allen and Suzie's murders. He read silently for a few minutes, absorbing the information. "It's almost the same MO— entry through the garage door, same murder weapon. But there's one difference: Allen was killed in the same way, but Suzie wasn't."

Dani sat forward, looking over the top of the page at the notes. "What do you mean?"

"It says that Allen was cut to pieces, just like the Shevlins, but Suzie was killed by a blow to the head, that's all. No other wounds whatsoever."

Dani hugged her arms close to her body as if chilled. "What do you think it means?"

Liam set the paper down. "I think the killer didn't mean to murder Suzie at all. I think he did it by accident."

"So you're saying whoever did this definitely knew the Shevlins and Allen and Suzie?"

Liam nodded. "I think so. There's complete correlation as far as how the Shevlins and Allen were killed, but not Suzie." His eyes clouded over, his mind running faster than it had in almost a year. When he came back to himself, he noticed Dani staring at him. "What?"

"How—" She seemed to sort her words. "How do you do this when it's people you know? How do you go over the facts like you're reading out of a textbook?"

Liam studied her face, looking for a hint of disgust but seeing only curiosity and caution. "I don't know."

Dani chewed on the inside of her cheek and then dropped her gaze to the floor. "I wish I was more like that sometimes—able to shut things off when I wanted to."

Liam fought for something to say, but each attempt came up sounding wrong or callous, so he waited. After a few moments, Dani sat back up.

"I'm sorry," he said.

"There's nothing to be sorry about."

Liam wanted to say something more, but instead he reached out and grasped the top paper off the Shevlin pile. It was a transcription of Eric Shevlin's 911 call. Liam scanned it and stopped at the first line. "'A monster's killing my parents.'"

"What?"

Liam looked up from the paper. "That's the first thing Eric Shevlin said to the 911 operator when he called that night. 'A monster's killing my parents.'"

"He was terrified. I mean, could you imagine witnessing something like that? He must've thought whoever was doing it was a monster. Maybe they were wearing a mask."

Liam tapped his forehead with an index finger, an old habit he used to do all the time when on a case. *The tics that come back,* he marveled. "I want to speak to him if he wakes up."

"They won't let you do that, will they? I'm guessing they have a guard stationed at his door and everything, right?"

"Most likely, and if they don't, they should. That kid barely got away with his life. He was going to suffer the same fate his parents did. The killer got interrupted by the police, but there's no guarantee that he won't come back to try to finish him off. I do think that Allen being Eric's godfather and my brother might have some pull." Liam shrugged. "It's all we've got to go on."

Dani finished off the last of her coffee and set the empty cup down. "So what do we do now?"

Liam stood and paced to the door and back again. "I'd like to go to Allen and Suzie's, poke around and try to see if there's anything there. The sheriff gave me the keys back this morning, so we aren't breaking any laws or anything." Liam glanced at Dani. "That's assuming you want to come with. You don't have to, if this is all too much—"

Dani stood and gave him a halfhearted smile. "I've never started a drawing I didn't finish."

Liam grinned for what felt like the first time in years.

# CHAPTER 6

The rain began to fall as they turned into Allen and Suzie's driveway.

Fat droplets splattered against the windshield, and the sky cleared its throat loud enough to be heard over the hum of the Chevy's engine. On the short drive over, Liam filled Dani in on Shirley Strafford and the altercation at the front of the hotel. Dani's reaction surprised and heartened him.

"Good, I can't stand it when she's on."

The mood abruptly changed as they pulled down the long drive and the house came into view. Liam parked a few paces from the closed garage door and shut the truck off. Rain washed down the windshield, obscuring the world outside like an oil painting splattered with turpentine. Lightning cut a jagged gash across the sky, which healed with the sound of repeated thunder.

Liam glanced at Dani and saw that her eyes hadn't left the home since it came into sight. He reached out and placed his hand on hers. "You don't have to come in."

Finally, she tore her gaze away and looked at him. "No, it's fine. It's just strange, you know? I've been here dozens of times and it was always a happy place, fun and warm. It always gave me a good feeling to come here and see them. But now, it's like a place I've never been to before. It's horrible."

Liam squeezed her hand. "I'll be right next to you the whole time, okay?" Dani nodded. "Okay, let's get inside before the storm gets worse."

They left the truck and hurried through the heavy rain to the front door of the house. Liam dug the keys out from his pocket and selected the correct one on the first try. The doorknob turned, and they stepped inside, out of the storm.

The smell met them in the entryway.

It was a raw scent, its edge dulled a little by the hours that had passed between what caused it and now, but Liam still recognized it. Blood. Old or new, the scent was always easy for him to detect. It was like breathing the metallic air of a loose-change jar. Dani put a hand beneath her nose and closed her eyes before sidling up next to him.

The living room stood before them, and Liam noticed that much had changed since his last visit. The entire house looked redecorated, with walls that didn't match the colors of his memory, along with new floor coverings. The hardwood that used to stretch to the kitchen across the room was now a creamy-white carpet. Leather furniture graced the room's edges, and a massive flat screen hung from the far wall. Liam reached out and flicked a switch on his left, which turned on two overhead lights. Dani blanched.

Crusted bloodstains marred the carpet everywhere, with chunks of matted gore thrusting from their centers, like ebony volcanoes oozing rivers of tissue. A wide fan of dried blood lay close to the middle of the room. Pieces of tape marked the outer edges of the stains, no doubt corralling the area for the forensics team to measure and document evidence.

"My God," Dani said.

Liam didn't move his eyes from the scene before him. "Are you going to be okay?"

She swallowed loudly. "Yes, I'll make it."

Liam stepped into the room and knelt before the edge of the nearest blood spatter. He began to map the area in his head, relying on the notes he had read earlier and the taped perimeter. In his mind he saw a mangled body on the floor. His imagination tried to coalesce his brother's face onto the shape, but he shoved it away, effectively making the corpse anonymous. He looked to his left and saw the outline of a severed arm; to his right, entrails spilled like a pile of skinned snakes. Within the largest spray of blood, he saw a severed head pressed on its cheek, the print on the carpet confirming his assumption.

Liam stood and walked to the doorway that led to the hall and bedrooms beyond. A pool of blood no larger than a dinner plate lay in an equally round shape on the floor. He knelt again. This was where Suzie fell, he was sure of it. The scene began to gain motion and life in his mind as he stood and made his way into the kitchen. The dark tile on the kitchen floor looked clean and tidy. After snapping on another light, he saw no footprints, not even a hint of dirt anywhere. Suzie had been meticulous about keeping the house spotless; he remembered that from his short visit before his brother's wedding day.

Liam moved to the door that led to the garage and studied the splintered jamb where the lock had burst through. He opened the door and looked at the jagged tear in the metal exterior near the handle. Leaning nearer to the puncture, he saw that the shining edge looked slightly red. When he placed a finger to the hole, it came back a deep burgundy. Rust.

Liam walked slowly back through the kitchen until he could see Dani again. "The killer must have followed Allen inside the garage when he got home that night, since the report didn't say anything about forced entry through the exterior," Liam said, stopping at the boundary of the living room, his eyes scanning the floor. "He broke the door open with the murder weapon, I'm almost sure of it. There's a hole in the door where he hit it with something hard and heavy." Liam stepped back and drew a line on the floor with a pointing finger. "He came in this way, fast. Allen met him here." Liam motioned to the border between the kitchen and the living room. "He overpowered Allen right away, probably with a blow from the weapon. Then, I'm guessing, Suzie came into the room." Liam moved to the circular bloodstain. "He hit her once, like I said, meaning more to knock her out than to kill her."

Dani took a tentative step into the room but stopped short of the first piece of tape on the carpet. "But why? Why would he do this much damage to Allen and only try to knock out Suzie?"

"Because he had something against Allen that had nothing to do with Suzie."

Dani frowned. "But what would that be? What enemy would Allen share with the Shevlins? And what could Eric have done to someone at eleven years old?"

Liam rubbed the side of his face. "I don't know, but it's obvious someone hated them. Hated them enough to do this." He let his hand fall away, and for a moment the professional detachment he held before him like a shield cracked, and the realization of whose blood coated the floor hit him like a punch.

His throat tightened at the memory of Allen helping him tie his shoes one afternoon when he was five, before they went to see their father at his shop. How he felt a sense of wonder at seeing his brother's fingers, the strong fingers of a man already, looping and twisting the laces without effort. He remembered Allen glancing up at him, and for a split second being caught off-guard by the look of admiration on his younger brother's face. A tenuous string of connection there and then gone, as Allen stood and turned away, telling him to hurry and not make him late.

Liam clenched and unclenched his hands until the moisture at the corners of his eyes receded. He pivoted away from where Suzie had fallen, knowing that if he looked again he would surely cry.

"Do you think they were looking for something? I know the

reports said that nothing seemed to be missing, but maybe it's still here, hidden somewhere?" Dani said.

Liam shrugged. "I don't think so, just because of how fast it appears to have happened. If they were looking for something, there would have been a drawn-out process, torture, that type of thing." Even from across the room, he saw Dani shudder. "But let's check out the other rooms just in case, okay? Look for a safe or a hidden panel in the closet, something like that," Liam said. Dani nodded and walked well around the stains on the floor to meet him near the hallway.

They searched the bedrooms and closets for anything significant but found nothing. He kept his eyes averted from the pictures adorning the walls and bedside tables, and took comfort when he saw that Dani appeared to do the same. A file cabinet in Allen's study looked the most promising, and they spent a half hour flipping through documents that yielded no link to the Shevlins other than a small certificate from the church where Eric had been baptized that held the four adults' signatures at the bottom.

When it appeared that Liam's assumptions were correct, that robbery wasn't on the killer's list of motives, they made their way back to the kitchen. The afternoon looked darker than it had earlier, and rain still fell in silver lines outside the window, veiling the impressive view from atop the bluffs.

"So what now?" Dani asked, leaning on the kitchen counter.

"There's not much else to look at here," Liam said. "I suppose we can go back to town, maybe find something to eat."

"I don't know if I'll ever be hungry again," Dani said, her eyes locked on the black spatters in the living room.

"We'll have to plan a funeral too. Everyone will expect one," Liam said.

Dani nodded. "I'm dreading that, but after this, it should be easy."

"I'm sorry I put you through this."

She turned toward him and shook her head. "You didn't put me through anything. I came here because I wanted to."

"I know, it's just rough, that's all."

"Like I said, Suzie was basically a sister to me. I owe it to her if I can help figure out who did this, and you obviously have the skills to find them, so you're stuck with me."

Liam smiled. "Okay." He caught himself looking into her eyes for a second too long and turned his head. "Let me just grab a pen and paper here. Maybe on the ride back we can call the funeral home and try to schedule something."

Liam pulled open a random kitchen drawer and found stacks of silverware. The drawer next to it held measuring cups and spoons. The drawer on the end was full of odds and ends, and he pulled it out all the way, looking for a scratch pad and pen. As he shifted the contents around, he spotted a stack of Post-Its along with a pen in one corner. Liam grabbed the two items and was about to shut the drawer when something beneath a small calculator caught his eye.

Pulling the set of keys free from the drawer, he straightened and flipped the plastic key fob over so that he could read the label marked by his brother's hand.

"What is it?" Dani asked when she noticed him staring at the keys.

Liam turned the fob toward her so she could read the letters encased in the plastic: *J & K's house.* Dani looked at Liam, who stepped around the counter and began to walk toward the door.

"Wanna take another ride?"

———

They found the Shevlins' house after passing by the narrow driveway twice on the county road a mile outside of town. The storm doubled its effort as they drove, and more than once Liam had to flip the Chevy's wipers onto high just to make out the centerline. Dani studied the driveway as they passed it by, reading off the address number to him.

"Yeah, that's it," he said, and scanned the sides of the road. A hundred yards from the driveway he spotted a narrow turnaround on Dani's side and pulled into it, dousing the headlights that attempted to light up the thick forest lining either side of the road. A stand of pine trees just tall enough to loom over the Chevy appeared on the left, and Liam swung the pickup behind them, effectively blocking the truck from being seen from the road.

"What are you doing?" she asked as he shut off the truck.

"We have to go in on foot from here. I don't want to risk parking in the driveway and having someone see my truck there. That wouldn't bode well for me. Could you open the glove compartment and grab the flashlight that's inside?"

Dani opened the compartment in front of her knees and handed him the black barrel of the LED flashlight before shutting the compartment door.

"Are you sure about this?" she asked, looking out at the swaying trees and the pitchfork lightning that stabbed the sky in intermittent bursts.

"No, but it's the next step. I think there was something binding the Shevlins to my brother that Suzie knew nothing about, and I think that something might be here."

Dani nodded and gazed at her lap so long that Liam was about to offer to drive her back to town. Then she spoke. "Okay, let's do it."

The wind pounded them when they left the safety and warmth of the truck. The rain became more like stinging nettles as they ran near the ditch on the edge of the road, both of them looking forward and back for any sign of headlights coming their way. By the time they made it to the driveway and hurried beneath the overhanging canopy of trees, their clothes were second skins and water squelched from the soles of their shoes. The driveway was longer than Liam expected, and just when he began to regret not parking the truck closer, the house came into view.

It was an impressive two-story chalet-style home with long eaves and cedar siding. A manicured flower garden sat to the left of the driveway, along with an immense steel outbuilding. The paved drive dropped away and wound down to the two-stall attached garage, where a sidewalk shot off from its front, leading to a wide covered porch. Beyond the house a close-cropped lawn stretched a stone's throw away, extending into the river. The dark water flowed by in eerie silence, as lightning danced somewhere behind them, throwing the yard into a shocking negative flash that cut through the gloom.

Liam reached out and grabbed Dani's hand, pulling her with him as he pelted down the slope to the house. Their footsteps resounded in hollow thumps on the decking as they crossed it to the front door. Liam fumbled with the keys in the twilight and finally managed to fit the correct one into the lock. Before turning it, he glanced at Dani.

"If there's an alarm on the door, we run, okay?"

She nodded, and he turned the lock and opened the door.

Only the muffled patter of rain on the roof met them as they entered. They stood in a foyer, with a large sitting room to their left. A bank of stairs rose to their right and turned, opening up on a landing that fronted what looked like several bedrooms. Liam searched the darkness behind the banister above him, not knowing why the sight chilled him. Dani closed the door behind them, and Liam felt the wetness and heat of her shoulder brush his.

"Let's not turn on any lights, including the flashlight, unless we have to, okay?" he asked in a low voice, uncertain why he felt the need to speak quietly.

"Okay."

They moved together past the stairs and turned a corner, where the kitchen extended under a lofted ceiling. A row of stools sat in a neat line behind an island, and multiple windows gave a panoramic view of the yard and river outside. A spacious living room branched off the kitchen, and Liam searched the shadows that consumed its far end.

"God, it's spooky in here," Dani said. "Way worse than Allen and Suzie's."

Liam nodded. There was something different about the place. Perhaps it was the sprawling size of the home and the utter vacancy within it, or maybe it was the storm. He wasn't sure, but now wasn't the time to comb through the emotions to find a source.

"This is where Jerry and Karen were killed," Liam said, turning in a small circle. The floor in the kitchen looked clean even in the low light, and he saw no obvious stains or matter anywhere in the vicinity. "The cleaning company's been here already."

"I can't say I'm disappointed," Dani said.

Liam suppressed a smile. "I want to find Jerry's office if possible, see if anything stands out."

They moved through the kitchen, the sound of their wet shoes squeaking on the floor like shrieks in the silence. Liam and Dani wound their way through the overstuffed recliners and around a leather corner sofa until they stood at the far end of the house. A bathroom sat beside a closed door at the rear of the room. Liam tried the handle of the door, fearing it wouldn't open. It turned easily. Elation bloomed in his chest as the meager light from outside illuminated an oak desk and a computer, and two file cabinets that sat flush with the wall.

"Got it," he said, and stepped into the room. Liam made his way around the desk and rolled the office chair out so that he could sit. "Here, do you want to hold the light?" he asked Dani.

She took the flashlight and, after a moment of fiddling, turned it on. The light, switched to the lowest setting, shone just enough to allow them to see their immediate surroundings. Liam opened a deep drawer in the desk and pulled the lone folder within it out. As soon as he did, Dani aimed the light into the drawer and pointed.

"Look."

A handgun lay at the bottom of the drawer, its steel flesh gleaming. Liam grunted and turned his attention back to the folder. A few pages within revealed several old stock-exchange records and client contacts. Most of the numbers looked like gibberish to him, and he placed the contents back into the folder and returned it to the drawer. The other drawers in the desk were almost as empty, with only two more binders containing quotes on various land projections and an envelope with two one-hundred-dollar bills inside.

Liam put everything back the way he found it and settled into the chair. Dani focused the light on the desktop, and Liam saw something that made him sit forward.

"That's Allen," Dani said, training the light on the framed photo.

Liam picked it up and studied it. The picture was of the front of Allen's practice. A group of a dozen people stood side by side on a sunny day, a drooping red ribbon hanging before the entrance to the building in the background. His brother held an overly large pair of scissors poised to cut the ribbon. A man stood beside him with a hand on Allen's shoulder, his grin broad and full of white teeth.

Liam grabbed another photograph from the desk's surface and brought it close. It was of Jerry, Karen, and Eric sitting on the deck in front of the house, their hands clasped in one another's, each smiling through the years that had passed since the picture was taken. Jerry was the man with a hand on Allen's shoulder in the first picture.

Liam set both frames back on the desk and stood. "Jerry was involved with Allen's business somehow, otherwise he wouldn't be in that photo."

"Well, they were friends, right? Could he have been there just to be there?" Dani asked.

"Maybe, but I don't think so. My dad and I drove down to see the opening ceremony for his clinic. That picture wasn't taken that day. I think that was a grand reopening or something."

"We could ask around about that—there's nothing to hide there, right?"

"Absolutely," Liam said, stepping around Dani as he moved to the file cabinets. "I just want to take a look in here, then we can go." The words had barely left his mouth when he saw movement to his right.

A shadow strode through the storm outside the living room windows.

Liam sunk to the floor, grabbing the flashlight from Dani's hand as he did so. "Get down," he whispered, snapping off the dull glow of the light. "There's someone outside."

"Is it the cops?" she asked, huddling close to him on the floor, both of them kneeling beside the desk. Liam's heart thundered in his chest, matching the weather outside, and he scanned the yard for the figure.

"I don't know. Do you have your phone with you?"

"Yes."

"If you hear me shoot, call 911, okay?"

"Shoot?"

Liam stood and drew the Sig from the holster at his back. Leaning against the doorway, he peered into the living room and through the windows lining the far wall. He saw no flashing lights or other movement except for an arc of lightning in the distance. Liam crouched and moved out of the office, stopping behind an easy chair. The grip of the pistol felt slick in his hand, and he flexed his fingers as his breath shuddered in and out of him like something alive. With slow caution, he eased to the edge of the chair and peeked around the side.

A shape stood in the corner of the yard.

Liam folded himself back behind the chair. He couldn't see if the person faced the house or the dense woods beyond, but with the lights off inside, he would have an advantage to move without being seen. He glanced at the office and saw Dani's pale face looking back at him, her eyes wide. He held up one index finger, and then moved out from behind the chair, his back and knees bent, his body as low as he could get it to the floor. Lightning flashed again, turning the world outside into a blizzard of light. Liam spun and tried to get a glimpse of the figure, but the light dimmed and dusk resumed within a clap of thunder.

Liam moved through the kitchen, throwing a look at the garage door to make sure it was intact. He winced at the sounds of his feet on the floor, but was sure the pounding rain and thunder masked any noises he made. When he reached the foyer, he searched the rain-soaked drive for vehicles. Empty.

His heart picked up its already brisk pace. If there was no car, then that most likely ruled out law enforcement. If it wasn't the law outside, then there was a good chance it was the opposite.

The killer had come back.

Liam glanced at the stairway and realized why he'd had a sense of apprehension earlier. It was the thought of young Eric Shevlin running up the stairs to hide in his parents' room while they were slaughtered below him, in the kitchen. Liam did a quick pan of the area outside the windows and saw nothing. His angle was now wrong to survey the corner of the yard. He would have to leave the safety of the house to see where the form waited.

Without a sound, he turned the knob and opened the door to the storm. Rain fell in sheets beyond the overhang of the deck. Muddy trails of water flowed over the concrete drive and raced to join the Mississippi at the bottom of the property. Liam closed the door and crept to the corner of the house facing the river. His head swiveled back and forth, his eyes scanning the cascading layers of rain for movement. Leaning forward, he pushed his face around the corner of the house and looked toward the spot where he last saw the figure.

The yard was empty. Without hesitation, he moved down the steps, the gun held out before him, his legs bent, eyes twitching, finger tight on the trigger. Puddles splashed around his feet, but he didn't slow until he reached the far corner of the building. Pausing, he swept the woods for any sign of a deeper shadow before pivoting around the corner. Only swaying trees and brush met him, and after a full minute of waiting, he lowered the gun.

He was sure he hadn't made enough noise to alert the trespasser, and he hadn't seen him depart. Liam turned his head toward the river and the spot where he last saw the figure. A small, rounded shadow sat on the ground just before the tree line. He hadn't noticed it, since the figure had blocked it from his earlier vantage point. He moved toward it, all the while keeping his eyes trained on the dark forest. When he was a few feet away from the object, he glanced down, finally seeing it for what it was.

A tombstone grew out of the ground, the outlines of letters carved into its front. He knelt and moved close to the granite until he could read the words etched into the rock. *Peter Shevlin, June 8, 1993—In our hearts and in God's hands.* A small angel with massive wings hovered over the inscription, its head bowed in mourning.

Liam stood, glancing in all directions as he retreated to the house, his mind trying to make sense of what just happened. An uneasy feeling like a ball of infection began to throb in his stomach. He didn't know what bothered him more: the sight of the shadowed form appearing and disappearing within the storm, or that it seemed to have come to visit the grave of the Shevlins' deceased infant.

# CHAPTER 7

Donald Haines stirred the vodka and lime-water together with an angry flick of his wrist.

He shot his cell phone a poisonous look before downing half the drink, the ice cubes in the glass clinking together. The conversation with Ian hadn't gone well. Not well at all. When Donald mentioned that the project might be postponed because of the recent murders, there'd been only silence on the other end of the line. He could imagine Ian's high-rise office in Chicago, his floor the only one in the building illuminated at this time of night. He could see the man seated behind the hideous art-deco desk in the middle of the room; his dark eyes unmoving from the night around the building, the curling, ever-present sneer on his otherwise stoic face.

"Fuck you," Donald growled, and slammed the rest of his drink.

He tossed the glass onto the countertop and went to the freezer to grab the vodka, wanting—no, *needing*—another drink after the encounter with Ian. The vice president's conditions were clear: get the project under way within the next week, or Colton would find someone else to do it. Donald huffed at the sound of Ian's voice in his ear, so cold and calm, assuring him that they would have no trouble finding a replacement at all.

"Asshole," Donald said to the empty house. Couldn't Ian see that he was doing as much as he could? The cops were out searching for the lunatic right now, and there wasn't any confirmation that the city council *would* postpone because of the recent crimes. He'd also given the mayor an extra thousand dollars. Although the bumpkin took the money, he said there weren't any guarantees, but he'd do his best to push it forward.

Donald sloshed vodka into the glass and didn't even bother with the lime-water before snapping the drink back. God, he couldn't wait to get out of this little shithole. There was nothing here he wanted. No friends, no nightlife, no women to fuck. He walked across the kitchen and gazed out the windows at the storm. The wind hadn't abated since early evening, and the rain fell as if there was a hole in the sky. Turning away from the window, he stalked to the counter where his phone lay, his steps heavier with the influence of the vodka. He checked the time on his phone; it was getting late. He needed to get to bed if he was going to make his tee time in the morning.

Shooting the vodka another longing look, he walked his glass to the sink and set it down. He turned off the single light in the kitchen and was about to grab his phone when a noise made him stop in his tracks.

*Thump, thump, thump.*

Turning his head and listening, Donald tried to discern where it had come from. After a few seconds, it repeated, this time louder, from the far end of the house, near the guest bedroom.

Donald looked out the windows to his left at the swirling trees and spitting rain. *Must be a tree branch rubbing against the house.* He shrugged and moved through the dining room to the door that led into the spacious guest bedroom. As he reached to flip on the light, he had the sudden fear that a hand would stretch out from the darkness to grasp his wrist. The image was so strong he nearly shrank back and shut the door, but instead, he fumbled against the wall until his fingers met the switch.

Light flooded the room and instantly turned the windows into opaque rectangles. Donald moved to the glass and cupped his hands around his face, wary of the storm tossing something hard at the window at that moment. He looked into the night, trying to spy a reaching branch or some other debris that might have caused the thumping, but saw nothing save waving leaves and a pulsing line of lightning that illuminated the dark river at the far end of the yard.

Donald stood back, chewing on his lip, and shook his head. Nerves, frazzled from the call with Ian, was all it was. He needed sleep and a nice round of golf in the morning. Along with a few drinks. Feeling better, he moved out of the room, snapping off the light as he went. He had taken two steps toward the kitchen when the screen door flew open and banged against the side of the house. Donald's heart leapt in his chest and did a drum solo against his ribs. Immediately the fear became anger, as he resumed his course through the house.

"Fucking storm," he said under his breath as he walked to the entry and flipped on the outside light, which illuminated a half circle of the yard and driveway in front of the house. He unlocked the door and pulled it open, immediately catching a face full of wind and rain. Donald squinted against the stinging drops hurled at him by the wind and stepped onto the porch to grab the screen door from where it banged insistently against the siding. With a grunt, he pulled the door shut and stepped inside. When he tried to latch the outer door, it wouldn't stay shut.

"What the shit?" he said, leaning closer to the catch. After a few seconds of inspection, he saw that the tongue of the lock was missing, sheared off and gone. Rage vented like steam from his pores, and he yanked on the screen door as hard as he could, trying to wedge it shut with pure force. The rest of the handle broke off in his hand, and the door sailed open with a bang.

"Fuck you!" Donald yelled, and slammed the inner door shut. He trembled from the anger coursing through his veins and wished

73

he had some outlet to release it. If Ian were here now . . . oh, it would not be good. The thought of pummeling the smug vice president's face into a mass of jelly made him feel better, and he flexed the muscles in his arms, relishing the image of his fist smashing over and over into Ian's teeth.

*BANG.*

Donald flinched in spite of his fury and peered through the darkness of the house toward the guest bedroom.

*BANG.*

The sound was louder this time. Was a fucking tree falling on the house? He moved through the kitchen and dining room until he stood just outside the door to the guest bedroom. He listened, his ear almost pressed against the wood, trying to hear anything inside that would indicate the window was broken. He didn't want to step onto glass with just socks on his feet. Slowly he opened the door, and found the switch before his mind could come up with anything else to scare him.

The window was intact, and nothing else was out of place. He turned in a small circle, looking for anything that could have fallen. The room was spartan to begin with, and there were really no adornments that could have toppled to cause the noise he heard.

"Pussy," he said. "And now you're talking to yourself."

He shook his head and exited the room for a second time, promising himself he wouldn't entertain his imagination again if he heard another sound. Half smiling at his foolishness, he walked toward the kitchen to grab his phone and saw movement in front of him, near the entry. Donald stopped in mid-stride, every muscle in his body going rigid, his skin tightening into a million points of gooseflesh.

The inside door swung open and bumped against the wall.

It rebounded off the coatrack that hung just inside the doorway and slowed, before moving back again with the wind's insistence. One thought flashed over and over in his mind as he watched the door travel its slow arc: *I didn't lock the door, I didn't lock the door, I didn't lock the door.* Now the sounds from before became something different, not random effects of the storm but purposeful and calculated movements. *They were herding me,* he thought, and another shiver of fear swam through his spine.

His eyes searched the dim outlines of the kitchen counter until he located his phone. The shadows of the house, benign before, were now roiling, malevolent shapes that seemed to move on their own. Donald took a shaking step forward and stopped when he heard something else just below the sound of the storm outside. Whispering. The hiss of words from a mouth that didn't want him to hear. Donald's bowels turned to soup, and he forced back the urge to fall screaming to the floor. He needed to get his phone and barricade himself in the bedroom upstairs. He'd call for help, and would crawl out a window if he had to.

He shot a look through the archway to his left, into the living room. The back door was through there, but an even darker layer of shadows hung in the room, and he couldn't get himself to move in that direction. Just a few more steps and he could grab his phone, grab his phone and run. If it was just the storm making sounds and opening doors, he would feel foolish but safe.

His stomach clenched as he heard another susurration somewhere in the dark. He moved forward despite the animalistic feeling in his chest that screamed at him to run. Donald focused on his phone and readied himself to lunge for it. In a second, he'd have it and he could give in to the primal pleadings to flee.

With a little cry that surprised him as it slipped free of his mouth, he sprung forward and thrust his hand at the phone. He felt the rough edges of its case against his fingertips and the relief of knowing he could call for help.

A heavy piece of steel fell out of the darkness and cut through his wrist.

Donald watched it as if from somewhere outside his own body, saw the rusty serrated edges of the blade slice through flesh and bone and shatter the tile countertop beneath. His hand shot forward, free of his arm, and landed on the counter, looking like a fish on a cleaning table. The stump gouted a dark shadow that spread out in an even pool on the counter. Only after a split second of pain did he realize the shadow was his blood as it spattered the kitchen floor.

Donald stumbled back, clutching his ruined arm against his chest like a newborn, the hot wetness beginning to soak through his T-shirt. A hulking shadow moved through the kitchen toward him, ungainly and hunched as it lifted the massive steel blade over its head. He reached out with his good hand and tried to spit out pleas of mercy, but his feet tangled and he fell to the ground, his sight going hazy as the thing from the storm loomed over him.

# CHAPTER 8

They didn't talk very much on the drive back to town.

Liam turned the truck's heater on high, but it didn't fully warm him through his soaking clothes. He didn't know if he just needed to get dry or if the chill he felt had to do with what he saw at the Shevlins'. Several times he glanced at Dani, but she didn't meet his gaze. Instead, she stared out the windshield at the rain-slicked road, her fingers playing with the edge of her T-shirt.

When they reached town, he began to turn the truck in the direction of her hotel, but she put a hand on his arm as he did.

"Could we go to your hotel instead?"

He nodded and headed for the south end of town, the darkened eyes of shop windows watching them as they passed by.

When they reached his room, he offered her a pair of his sweatpants and a clean T-shirt. She thanked him and headed for the bathroom. After a few minutes, he heard the shower start, the patter of water matching the din of rain on the roof above. Twenty minutes later, Dani emerged from the bathroom just as he shut the door and walked past her carrying an almost-scalding pizza box.

"What's that?" she asked, following him to where he set the pizza on the desk beside the bed.

"This is a pizza," he said, grinning over his shoulder. She swatted at him, and he dodged it, nodding toward a bin of ice containing a six-pack of beer. "Thought you might need one of those," he said, pulling a piece of sausage pizza onto a paper plate for her.

When he looked up, he saw Dani's eyes focused on him, a strange look on her face. "What?" he asked, holding out her plate.

"How did you know this is what I needed?"

Liam smiled. "I didn't. I just like pizza and beer."

She laughed and sat on the bed as he cracked two of the bottles open and handed one to her.

He sat on the floor while they ate with relish, and he surprised himself by how many slices he consumed. He hadn't felt this full or satisfied by food in a long time. He began to trace through his memory for a better-tasting meal and stopped, content to enjoy the moment.

"You know, if it wasn't for a crazed lunatic running free, this town would probably be okay," Liam said, finishing off the last bite of his pizza. He waited and looked at Dani out of the corner of his eye.

A begrudging smile played at the corners of her mouth, and when she saw him looking at her, she shook her head.

"That's a little dark," she said.

"The best humor always is."

"Terrible."

"Why are you smiling?"

"I'm not," Dani said, smiling.

"Okay, just saying," Liam said, holding up his hands. Their eyes locked for a split second, and his stomach fluttered like he was on a roller coaster. Dani looked away, her face darkening. "I'm sorry," he said.

"No, you're fine and this is great," she said, motioning to the pizza box and beer. "It's just . . ." She paused, searching for words or courage; he didn't know which. "I've never been as scared as I was tonight at that house. When you went outside, I didn't know what was going to happen or if you'd come back, and I . . . I don't know . . ." Her voice trailed off as she took another sip of beer, looking away.

He saw the glistening of tears and reached out to touch her hand. "I'm sorry. I shouldn't have left you there. I got caught up in the moment and reacted."

Dani nodded, pulling her hand away from his to swipe at her tears. She was quiet for a long time, then she turned to him again.

"Who do you think it was out there?"

"Truthfully?"

"Yeah."

"The killer," he said, waiting for her to cringe. She only nodded.

"What do you think he was doing?"

"I'm not sure. That's what I've been going over in my head. I don't know if he saw me or if he was just on a little reminiscent tour or what."

"That's so creepy."

"If it's any consolation, I was scared out of my mind too."

"Yeah, it gives me great confidence that the guy with the gun was just as terrified as I was." Dani's eyes sparkled, and in that moment he couldn't think of anything more beautiful.

"Listen here, I was just saying that to make you feel better. I wasn't actually scared at all," Liam said, sniffing and turning his eyes to the ceiling.

"Umm-hmm," Dani said with a mocking nod. She shifted on the bed and turned toward him a little more. "Why do you have a gun with you if you aren't a cop anymore?"

"I asked myself the same thing when I grabbed it to bring with me," Liam said. "Call it a premonition, I don't know. I just brought it out of instinct."

"Well, I'm glad you had it tonight."

"Me too."

He felt his eyelids growing heavy, the crushing exhaustion no longer held back by adrenaline or his frantic thoughts. He yawned, stifling it with the back of his hand. Dani finished her beer and stood, setting the empty bottle on the table nearby.

"I should go," she said, glancing at the digital clock. "It's almost ten."

He nodded, wanting anything but to agree. "If you want, you can stay here."

The words came out before he had time to think, and he nearly clapped a hand over his mouth. Dani didn't move from the foot of the bed and gazed at him through a few locks of damp hair.

"I mean, you can stay if you want. I'll sleep on the floor. I don't sleep very well anyway. I just thought you might not want to be alone. I didn't mean—"

Dani smiled at his discomfort. "Thank you. I would like to stay, if it's really okay with you."

"It's fine, yeah, absolutely," Liam said. "Let me just rearrange a little."

He busied himself arranging a few blankets and a pillow on the floor while Dani went to the bathroom. When she returned, he was already on his makeshift bed. She moved across the room and shut the last lamp off, throwing everything into shadow, cut only by the faint glow of the single parking lot light behind the hotel. He heard the soft swishing of her clothes against the blankets as she climbed into the queen-sized bed. He lay with one arm crooked behind his head, listening to her even breathing. They were quiet for a long time, and just when he thought she might be asleep, she spoke.

"Liam?"

"Yeah?"

"Would you sleep up here with me? I'm not coming on to you, but . . ." Her voice trailed off into silence.

He rose from his place on the floor, snagging a blanket and pillow as he went. Dani lay on the far side of the bed, her face turned toward him, although he couldn't make out her eyes.

The River Is Dark

"Sure, I'll sleep on top of the covers."

He lay down and threw the blanket over himself, making sure to keep a polite distance between them. The last thing he wanted was her thinking he was taking advantage of her unwillingness to be alone. After he settled and all was quiet again, he waited for the weight of sleep to fall upon him, praying he wouldn't have an attack now. How would he explain it to her? The thought of telling her made his insides squirm. He would just breathe and wait. Maybe he would be calm enough in a few hours to get some sleep.

Dani moved beside him, and he heard her hand slide across the space between them. Her fingers touched his bicep and carefully traced down his arm to find his hand. The grazing sensation of her delicate fingers on his skin sent a wave of goose bumps across him, wholly unlike the earlier prickling of his skin at the Shevlins'. He grasped her hand and heard her sigh, a small sound, content in a way that thrilled him.

He lay savoring the softness of her hand and resisted the urge to caress it. She needed comfort, nothing else. His muscles began to relax, and to his surprise, a wave of serenity spread over him, a blanket that smothered the tension his body had held all day without his full awareness.

Liam yawned again, apprehension attempting to blossom in his guts, but no vision appeared behind his eyelids when he shut them. And without knowing it, he fell into a dreamless sleep.

The cell phone vibrated beside his head, and his eyes snapped open in the dark of the room. Reluctantly he let Dani's hand go, both their palms now covered in sweat, and snatched the phone off the bedside table. The screen showed a number he didn't know and the time: 2:17. Liam hit the answer button and pressed the phone to his ear, standing from the bed.

"Hello?"

Panicked breathing met his ear, along with a hoarse curse.
"Hello?" Liam asked again, moving toward the bathroom, not wanting to wake Dani.

"Liam?"

"Who is this?"

"It's Nut. God, man, there's been another one!"

"What? Another murder?"

"Yes! Oh Lord, I think I'm gonna pass out."

"Nut, slow down. What happened?" Liam stepped into the bathroom and swung the door shut.

The other man sounded as though he were having a conniption.
"God, I've never seen anything like that in my life!"

"Nut, calm down, start from the beginning." Liam set an edge
to his voice, the tone gentle but commanding. It was the voice he'd
used when interviewing suspects or getting a statement from someone shaken by a recent crime.

"Okay, Lord, okay. I was . . . I was on my way to Lenny's place
on the south end of town. He's got a little nook out of the weather,
and he told me to stop by sometime tonight. I was on my way and
took the boardwalk by the river, past the park, since it's the fastest
route. I fucking stumbled on him, right there on the rocks!"

"Who? Who did you stumble on?"

"I can't be sure, but it looks like that big shot from Colton."

"Are you sure he's dead?"

"God, yes! He's . . . he's . . ." Nut made a choking sound. "You
just have to come see."

Liam straightened in the darkness of the bathroom, indecision
tilting him one way and then another.

"Where are you?"

# CHAPTER 9

The headlights of the Chevy shone off the wet blacktop, turning the road into a glazed onyx river.

Liam drove fast, but not so fast that he couldn't spot the parking lot he searched for. Soon, he came to the turn and swung off the deserted street, pulling into a space at the rear of the machine shop's lot. He reached into the glove box and grabbed the small flashlight from where Dani deposited it the night before. He turned in his seat, searching for any other signs of life before exiting the truck.

Apprehension wormed through him, and he nearly stopped in his tracks after only a few steps. This was the worst possible scenario he could put himself in at the moment. He was already on the BCA's radar, the sheriff had entrusted him with sensitive information, and now he was going to investigate a murder scene before notifying the authorities. If someone saw him here—he didn't even want to consider it.

He moved down the sidewalk, the business fronts giving him accusing looks as he passed by. He stayed in the shadows until he saw the sign for the turnoff to the park. With a quick glance over his shoulder, he bolted through the pools of light from the streetlamps and into the welcoming night of the unlit walking path leading to the river.

The air smelled fresh and clean, the rain having washed all other competing scents from it. He could still see the occasional flicker of lightning in the eastern sky, the retreating bank of clouds a swollen form of condensed darkness. The reality of what he was about to do made his stomach flop, but he pushed on, knowing that if he didn't do it now, he would lose his chance to inspect the body and crime scene.

He moved as quietly as possible down the path, his ears hypersensitive to any sounds besides his own heartbeat and the soft rasp of his shoes on the tar. The open space of the park widened before him, and he stopped, raking the darkness with his eyes. He could hear the river now, a soft shush of flowing water straight ahead. He moved in that direction, still following the path, trying to position in his mind the area that Nut described over the phone. Soon the path began to curve, the river on his right, its waters swollen between the shoulders of the banks. Liam stopped and turned to the left, stepping onto the large chunks of rock embedded in the ground between the path and the grassy hills of the park. A shadow unfolded itself from a sitting position and he froze, his hand going to the handle of the Sig at his back.

"Nut?" he whispered.

"Yes, God Almighty, who else do you think it would be?"

Liam moved across the rocks, their uneven surfaces trying to throw him off balance in the dark. "Where?"

The vagrant's face was drawn and constricted, and a faint smell of booze hung in the air around him. The older man raised one arm and pointed to a small depression a dozen yards from where they stood. "He's there. I went to cut across the stones and meet up with the path where it curves again, and fucking almost tripped over him."

Liam said nothing and moved past him, being careful not to fall and skin a knee; he didn't need his DNA discovered at a murder scene. As they reached the bowl in the ground, Liam began to make out the lines of a body.

"You didn't touch anything, did you?" Liam asked.

"Uh, no, like I said, I almost stepped on him. Took me a second to get my bearings, but then I called you."

Glancing once more around the area, Liam bent his knees and flicked on the flashlight. Nut cursed under his breath, and Liam blinked, taking the scene in.

The body lay spread-eagle, its chest as well as its feet bare. A thin pair of sweatpants covered its legs. The skin was white, all of the blood that wasn't splashed on the stones surrounding it having pooled at the lowest point. Liam played the light from the corpse's feet to its thickly muscled chest, noting several puncture wounds in the abdomen, and stopped where its face should be.

The man's head was crushed flat beneath a large stone.

Gore and graying brain matter lay on the rocks around the body's ruined skull like splattered mud. The stone that sat amidst the shattered mess was nearly a foot wide, resembling a rough triangle. Liam could make out no features of the man's head. From the chin up, everything was pulverized. He moved the light lower until it shone on the corpse's right arm, wrist bones glistening in the glow, the hand missing.

Liam stood and circled the body, careful to avoid any blood spatters and loose rocks. Kneeling next to the dead man's other side, he examined the amputated wrist more closely. A deep groove ran around the arm's circumference before the bloody stump, a white rut still indented from earlier pressure.

"They cut off his hand before they brought him here," Liam murmured. "Tied a tourniquet around the stump so he wouldn't bleed to death."

"Why the hell would they do that?" Nut asked in a hushed voice.

"So they could torture him." Liam shifted the light to the deep holes gored in the dead man's stomach. "They wanted something from him," Liam said, more to himself than to Nut. "And I bet they got it."

"If they attacked him at his house, why the hell did they bring him all the way down here?" Nut asked. "The place he was rentin' has to be almost a half mile upriver."

Liam stood and swept the light in a little circle, and then snapped it off. "To send a message. This is a display."

"Well, it got through to me. Don't go out at night anymore, that's the message I got."

Liam moved around the perimeter of the corpse's outstretched limbs, looking for anything that might have been dropped or left behind. A sound that raised the hair on the back of his neck met his ears, and he looked up, searching for its source.

A car pulled into the park and cruised down the drive toward them.

"Go toward the path. Don't hurry and don't fall," Liam said.

Nut cursed again and moved away, a quiet clack of rocks marking his retreat. Liam stood for another ten seconds, studying the shape of the car, before he followed. He saw no light bar above the cab, and he doubted a small town like Tallston would have an unmarked cruiser. Longing to stay and investigate the area, Liam hurried away from the approaching vehicle and managed to stay clear of its sweeping headlights. Nut waited on the opposite side of the path, crouching low and watching the car, with wide eyes.

"Listen to me," Liam whispered. "You don't breathe a word of this to anyone. In a few hours, if the body hasn't been discovered, I'll call it in anonymously. I'll contact you later."

Nut jerked his head up and down, his wild mane bouncing with the movement. Liam watched him turn and scurry away down the path until it met a grove of trees, where the vagrant veered off and vanished into the shadows.

Liam moved in the same direction, his eyes locked on the car that was now parked in the lot before the playground. The dome light inside the car flared as the headlights went out, and Liam saw two teenagers inside. The driver was a boy wearing a dark coat, and the girl was blond, a giggle splitting her mouth into a grin as they opened their doors and stepped into the night.

"It'll be fun," the boy said.

"Danny, we can just do it in the backseat, we don't have to go down by the river," the girl chided.

"I don't want your dad catching us again, he's crazy."

"But that's what makes it exciting."

Liam lost their conversation as he left the path and felt a solid coating of dew soak his shoes. He glanced over his shoulder as he headed in the direction of his truck and saw the two teenagers making their way across the playground with what looked like a blanket draped over the boy's shoulder.

Liam crossed the street and could just make out the shape of his truck when he heard the girl scream at the top of her lungs, and he knew he wouldn't have to call in the murder after all.

———

Liam eased onto the bed beside Dani and studied her face in the dim light of the room. Her hair fell in tangles across her cheek, and he could hear the light breaths that she pulled in between her parted lips. He lay there, imagining a life that wasn't his, of early mornings just like this, listening to her breathing, knowing that when she woke he could make her breakfast in their kitchen. He saw the morning light playing off her face and her eyes coming open with the touch of his hand. Her smile. He imagined not looking at the closet where his gun rested, not thinking thoughts of darkness that clouded his days gray. He thought of happiness.

And then her face came back to him.

She was pretty and young, and had dark hair that curled near her shoulders. She stepped out of the doorway, and for an instant he saw a smile on her lips before she turned her head, her hand resting on the curve of her belly.

He sighed and forced the image away, the fantasy of Dani crushed beneath a reality already in place. It was his; he owned it and he had to carry it. Happiness was a foreign concept meant for others, not him. Not him.

———— ————

Hours later, Dani stirred. She smacked her lips and slid a hand out from beneath the covers to rub her sleep-stained eyes. Liam stopped staring at the ceiling and sat up, his face impassive as she looked at him and blinked.

"Hi," she said.

"Hi."

"Were you able to sleep?"

"A little."

"Was I snoring?" The disgust in her voice made him smile.

"No, but there's been a development."

Dani propped herself up on an elbow and studied his face. He began to speak, telling her of his dealings with Nut and the call he received during the night. As he told her the details of the murder scene, her face became quizzical and she began to bite at her lower lip. When he finished, he waited, glancing every so often at the brightening window behind her.

"That was a huge risk," she said.

"I know."

"Someone could have seen you."

"I know."

"Do you think you can trust a drunk hobo?"

"I have to since he's my only other source of information besides the sheriff."

"And you don't think Nut had anything to do with it?"

"No."

"How can you be so sure?"

"Because I've interrogated hundreds of suspects. I know when someone's lying. Nut's a fool and a drunk, but he's telling the truth."

Dani pursed her lips. "Forgive me if I'm not a hundred percent convinced."

Liam smiled. "You're forgiven."

"Just don't put too much faith in him, okay? You don't know him at all."

"Noted."

Dani ran her tongue over her teeth and grimaced. "Pizza-and-beer breath."

"Mmm, my favorite," Liam said.

She shot him a look of dismay and got out of bed. He liked how she looked in his clothes, small but strong in her own way. She caught him staring at her, and he dropped his eyes to his socked feet and began to pull at a loose string near his ankle.

"So what do you think it means?" Dani asked, looking out the window.

"The murder?"

She nodded without looking at him.

"I think somehow everything's connected to the Colton project across the river. There's too much coincidence with Jerry Shevlin and the company rep being murdered. It's obvious that someone doesn't want the project to go through."

Dani turned to him and leaned against the table beneath the window. "But killing someone to stop an industrial project? Isn't that extreme and, overall, not very effective? I mean, won't they just get someone else to head up the development?"

"You're right, but I'm thinking that the person or persons we're dealing with aren't thinking lucidly."

"Really?" Dani said, raising her eyebrows.

"I mean, they're obviously psychopaths, but this isn't the way to stop Colton from proceeding if that's what they're trying to accomplish. Nut told me there was a group opposing the project in town. I want to speak to them at some point today, but there's something else I want to do first," he said, rising from the bed to look past Dani out the window.

"What's that?"

"I want to go across the river."

# CHAPTER 10

They ate breakfast at the café where Liam met Nut on his first day in town.

As they dined on sausage and pancakes, Liam couldn't help but feel the normality of the moment. There were several other people in the restaurant, even with the early hour, their conversations muddled into a dull but comforting hum of humanity. People living, thriving, and enjoying one another. Liam caught himself listening to the din, the clatter of spoons and forks, instead of eating. He felt the beginnings of a smile forming on his lips as he watched Dani take a too-big bite of her pancake and struggle not to look unladylike while chewing it.

After paying for breakfast, they left the café and headed to the local funeral home, two blocks down. The building stood by itself, separated by alleys on either side that, no doubt, led to the rear, where they loaded and unloaded the bodies set for burial. The exchange with the funeral director lasted an hour and a half. He was a stocky man in a black suit who nodded the whole time, speaking to them in a low, comforting voice. After they gave the director all the necessary information, he assured them that he would take care of the details and all they needed to do was tell him when they would like to hold the funerals. Liam and Dani agreed that a single service would work best, and Liam referred the director to his brother's lawyer for burial-versus-cremation preference, though he mentioned that most likely only Suzie's body would be fit for an open casket.

After the time spent inside, the fresh air tasted sweet and light compared to the stuffy interior of the building tainted with grief and sorrow. They both left their windows down as they rolled through the growing heat of the day, the morning smelling of clipped grass and warming tar.

Liam took the street that he had driven only hours before and squinted through the glaring sun at the park, slowing the truck as he looked. He could see a small portion of the clearing from the road, but the light reflected off a dozen vehicles behind the trees was easy to discern. A sheriff's deputy blocked the entrance to the park with an angled cruiser, and glanced at them as they drove by.

"Looks like it's in full swing," Dani said.

"Yep."

"And you're sure you didn't leave anything incriminating behind?"

"I'm sure. There's no finding footprints on rock. Even if they did find a track, I can just say I was there earlier, which I was."

They followed the street to its end, where it terminated in a T that shot left and right. Liam turned left, and after passing several quaint homes, they spotted the river flowing at the base of a public water access and turnaround. A ramshackle bait store with dirty windows and sagging siding stood on the bank, overlooking the brown water. Liam parked the truck in one of three empty spaces, and they both hopped out, their feet crunching on the gravel in front of the shop.

The smell of dead fish met Liam's nose as he pulled open the rickety screen door and stepped inside the shop. A long row of minnow tanks lined the left wall—dark, shifting schools of twitching tails and fins twirling in the bubbling water—and Liam steered away from the overpowering smell that emanated from them. The floor was concrete, with a single stained rug leading to a pitted counter, where a scruffy middle-aged man sat reading a paper. He was skinny and had large lips and a long nose, which he wrinkled every few seconds beneath the bill of a torn Green Bay Packers hat. His brown eyes didn't look up from the paper until Liam and Dani stopped on the other side of an ancient cash register.

"Howdy, folks, what can I do for ya?"

"Well, I saw that you have a guide service listed in the Yellow Pages," Liam said, trying to sound as touristy as possible.

"We sure do. You two wantin' to catch a few walleyes?"

Liam smiled. "Actually, we're just looking for a ride across the river. There's some hills that look like good hiking a few miles down, and we'd like to check them out."

The man behind the counter tipped his hat back and scratched at his forehead. "You just want a ride across the river?"

"Yes," Liam said.

"Why don't you just drive over the bridge down south—it's only a few miles out of the way. There's a nice road that runs into the state land you're talkin' about."

"Yeah, we know, we just want to spend as much time in the woods as we can. Our time's limited, and we don't want to drive all the way around to find the entrance."

The man's eyes floated over them both before he shrugged. "Sure, we can give you a lift. I'll have my son, Tom, float you over. Whereabouts you guys want to land?"

Liam pointed straight across the river. "Just over there, if that works."

The man nodded. "Tom's just gearing up the boat for the day. I'll let him know, and he can bring you across right away."

"Perfect," Liam said. Dani stood smiling next to him.

The bait-store owner nodded and went through a door covered by a black curtain behind the counter. He returned after only a minute and stepped up to the cash register, tapping at the stained, unmarked keys with his index fingers.

"That'll be forty dollars for the ride over and back. What time would you like Tom to pick you up?"

"Oh, around one should be just fine," Liam said, looking at his phone.

The man nodded and accepted the cash Liam handed him over the counter. He directed them outside the building and down an unsteady walkway that led to a short dock extending into the river.

A remarkably new and clean Lund fishing boat bobbed in the current, and a boy with the same long nose as the man in the shop greeted them. He was no more than sixteen, and was polite and helpful as he got them situated in the boat before casting off and firing up the motor. Liam pointed to a spot beneath some overhanging trees on the far bank, and Tom piloted them to it. Liam and Dani hopped out of the boat and onto the riverbank's slick edge, beveled by yesterday's rain into a sheet of brown muck that looked solid but wasn't. Liam frowned as he felt his tennis shoe slide into the wetness of the bank, and saw Dani smile as she jumped over the spot to drier land.

Liam pushed the boat free into the pulling flow of water, and Tom called that he would be back to get them at one. Liam checked his phone again, noting that they had a little under three hours before they had to be back to this spot. They moved up the incline of the bank until they crested a small rise, which sunk back down and became tangled with growths of hazel brush. Reed grass slithered against their shins and, in some places, their thighs. Liam managed to find a pool of standing water and cursed as his sock went from damp to sopping.

They climbed to higher ground, where the tangled nettles of wild raspberries dissipated and the trees grew taller, blocking out the sun with a canopy of intertwining leaves and branches. Liam stopped and surveyed the surroundings. He could still see the river on the left. Birds flitted between trees overhead and called to one another in snippets of song.

"It's beautiful out here," Dani said beside him.

He glanced at her as she popped a wild raspberry into her mouth. "Yes, it is." Liam picked a long piece of grass and began to split it into sections. "So did you ever get back together with him?"

"With who?"

"The boyfriend you broke up with right before the wedding."

Dani looked down and smoothed a bit of hair behind one ear. "Yeah, we did. Didn't work out, again, and we broke up a few months later. I should've known better, trusted my instincts the first time."

"It's tough when you're young, and in love."

Dani shook her head, her eyes far away. "How about you?"

"I didn't get back together with my boyfriend. I totally deserved better."

Dani laughed and tossed a twig at him as they continued walking. "Seriously."

"Oh, you know, cop works all the time, married to the job, can't commit, that old story."

"That old chestnut."

"Yeah."

"It's funny, I thought you would've been happily married with a family by now."

"Ditto."

"Guess we're both losers."

"Speak for yourself."

Dani smiled and they walked in silence for a while before she asked, "What do you think we'll find at the foundry?"

"Probably nothing, but I want to walk the land myself, see if anything sticks out."

They moved southeast, keeping the river in sight while winding between tall stands of birch and the occasional towering oak. After a half hour, Liam saw a flat slant of gray emerge through the trees ahead. Gradually the rest of the building came into view, and when they finally stepped free from the forest into the clearing, Liam paused to observe the structure.

It was two stories tall, just as he'd estimated the first time he spied it from across the river. It was rectangular, divided into what he assumed were two different eras of building. The front, the most recent construction, was sheet metal with a base made of cinder block. It ran for two hundred yards or more until it met the edge of the river, where a large overhead door stood on its end, a system of decrepit rails extending from the loading dock to the edge of the river. Some sort of trolley system for exporting its product onto ships, he assumed. A bank of dirty windows, some broken and with yawning teeth of glass, sat twenty feet above the ground at the front of the building, but other than that the walls were smooth and unbroken.

The rear of the foundry looked to be the original building, much older than the newer construction. It was made of brick, stained a deep brown with time and moisture. It stretched back into the trees, which grew uncontained against its sides, reclaiming the ground man once cleared, the creep of nature slow but inevitable.

"Wow, it's huge," Dani said after a few seconds of silence.

Liam nodded. "Wonder if we can get inside."

He stalked forward, heading for a door cut into the otherwise unblemished side of the building. When he touched the rusting doorknob, he knew it wouldn't turn. He tried anyway, the rough steel flaking off beneath his twisting hand as it held firm. "Locked," he said, stepping back. Liam rubbed the rust away from his palm, his eyes watching the way it stained the skin red.

"Let's try the older part," Dani suggested.

They walked through the tall weeds, which only grew higher the closer they got to the brick portion of the building. Liam felt a few nettles scrape through his jeans, and he batted away a flurry of mosquitoes.

"I'm totally getting Lyme disease out of this," he said. He heard Dani giggle behind him. "I think I'll let you cut the path from here on out," Liam said, half smiling over his shoulder.

"Sorry, it just seems like you're not much for the outdoors."

"I went hunting all the time with my dad when I was a kid, thank you. I just happen to have feet that are attracted to puddles. I'd be the guy you'd want with you in the desert. No water? Here, let me walk around, I'll fall in some."

Dani laughed again, and Liam smiled. Her laugh was warm and unique in a way that he was sure she would call "annoying," but he could have listened to it all day.

As they moved beneath the ceiling of trees leaning against the building, the weeds became sparser and the walking easier. A few windows with rusted latches lined the brick ten feet above their heads, and Liam saw an archway farther down, its recesses filled with darkness and waving cobwebs. They headed toward it.

The doors set within the arch were solid steel. An iron crossbar secured with a padlock the size of a baseball stretched across their centers, and Liam didn't bother yanking on the handles, knowing it was futile.

"Let's try the other side, and maybe poke around along the perimeter of the woods," he said, motioning to the closest corner of the building. He took a step in that direction and stopped, smelling something rank in the air.

"God, what is that?" Dani asked behind him.

It took only a moment of scanning the area to see what caused the stench. Several piles of human feces grew up from the ground, forming small pyramids. A fresh splatter of waste coated the top of the closest pile. Liam wrinkled his nose.

"We found a regular hot spot," Liam said. "But where's the newspapers and Charmin?"

"Wow, that's a lot of shit," Dani said. "This must be a homeless hangout."

Liam nodded and began to inspect the foundry again. Suddenly, an earsplitting shriek pierced the serenity of the forest, and adrenaline dumped into his veins. One hand whipped to his back and drew the Sig, his other arm reaching for and finding Dani's fingers without taking his eyes off the corner of the building.

"What was that?" Dani asked, her voice so low he almost couldn't hear it over the pounding of his heart.

"I don't know," he whispered. "Sounded like steel rubbing on steel."

Letting go of Dani, he motioned for her to follow and stepped around the end of the brick, leading with the barrel of the gun. The back wall was flat, made of unremarkable brick. Liam swept the edge of the woods with the pistol and continued on, trying to keep his eyes everywhere at once. The screech came again, and now he knew it was the grating of metal, unused and unoiled, against something equally rusty. Checking to make sure Dani was close behind, he sped up and neared the next corner of the building, stopping before swinging clear of it.

The last unexplored side of the structure was almost the same as its counterparts, save for a long row of bushes extending into heavy vines that snaked into and through the cracks in the brick. Two more overhead doors sat at the far end, both featureless and caked with the grime of disuse.

Liam waited, letting his breathing slow while keeping the firearm outstretched. After nearly a minute, he lowered the gun and turned to Dani, who leaned closer to him.

"Do you think it was something on the roof? Maybe the wind—"

The snapping of twigs in the woods cut her words off.

Liam spun toward the sound, raising the Sig, and saw a growth of small trees rattle with the passage of something near the ground.

"Come on," Liam said as he began to run.

They entered the shade of the forest, and Liam spotted a small trail leading away from the foundry. The sounds of breaking sticks came sporadically, and he took a moment to determine their direction before setting off. Branches and leaves slid over his arms and face as he moved. Dappled sunlight coursed through the canopy of trees in patches, but most of the woods sat in green shade, all the birds silent or departed from their perches.

Liam saw movement ahead—a swinging branch whipping back into place with the recent passage of something. He ran toward it, drawing a bead on the spot in case someone waited for them. He heard Dani close behind him and waved her to slow as they reached the place where he'd seen the movement.

They stood in a shallow ditch that dropped a few feet and then climbed a miniature bluff on its other side. He waited, breathing as quietly as he could, straining his ears for a sound. One came from his right, and then another from the left. He looked both ways, seeing a trail of grass recently trampled to the left and a crow take flight from a treetop on the right.

"There's two of them," Dani said.

"Fuck," Liam said, and made a decision. "This way." He ran to the right.

They followed the bluff until it receded into the ground and they could climb out of the little gorge. The sound of footsteps rasped ahead, and Liam pelted onward, praying that Dani would keep up with him. He saw something through the thick brush growing fifty yards from where he ran—an odd shape and the flash of white skin. It was there and gone before he could see more.

He poured on the speed, fighting through the tangles of grass and gripping thorns of wild cucumbers. When they met the solid wall of brush, Liam stopped, searching for a way through. The sounds of retreat were subtler, and he wasn't sure if the person they pursued was farther away or if the architecture of the forest distorted the acoustics.

There was a break in the brambles to his left, and he fought his way through to the other side, where a more formidable trail began. Its surface looked beaten and well used, almost like a hiking path or a popular animal run. He paused, listening for telltale sounds. The woods were silent, still. He looked into and through the cascade of greenery, trying to spot a shifting branch or swaying fern. Nothing moved.

"Where'd he go?" Dani said behind him.

Liam shook his head, looking for a signal of their quarry's location. He walked forward, his senses over-heightened, the colors of the woods too bright, the scratching of a beetle crawling across a dead leaf too loud. A pressing sensation filtered through his skin and sunk into the lowest part of his guts. He stopped and waited, knowing exactly what the feeling was.

"We're being watched," Liam whispered. He was about to step over a rotting log blocking the path when Dani grabbed his arm.

"What's that?" she asked, pointing to a bend in the trail.

Liam studied the spot, at first dismissing it as a leaning tree. But then he saw the flutter of yellow in the light breeze that chilled the sweat on his skin. They moved toward the bend in the trail, and soon he realized it was not a tree at all.

The cabin listed to one side, its Lincoln Log corners parting to reveal blackened mouths between their joints. The roof was mostly gone, perhaps collapsing beneath a past snowfall or surrendering to the rot of the furry moss that covered the majority of the cabin's surface. It was small, no more than two rooms, a single open window beside the canted front door, like a canvas painted in motor oil. A circle of yellow material hung from a bent nail beside the door, the bright color tainted by a speckling of dark stains.

They approached the shack, and Liam left Dani at the front while he circumvented the structure to make sure there wasn't anyone behind or inside it. When he looked through another glassless window on the back side, he saw that the interior was one room with several sticks of decayed furniture rotting into indistinguishable combinations of wood and stuffing. The floor was dirt, and he saw the decapitated head of a doll sporting bedraggled hair—which once might have been blond—in a corner, its eyes covered with mud.

When he rounded the last side, he saw Dani standing with her hand over her mouth, her eyes full of tears.

"What is it?" he asked, looking to where she gazed.

She raised a hand and pointed at the circle of yellow material. "That's Suzie's headband."

Liam pushed the Sig into its holster and moved closer to the cabin. The headband swung in the breeze, giving him a better look at both its blood-splotched sides. A small blue flower stitched into the band stood out amidst the burgundy drops. A shiver tried to course through his spine and he shut it off, turning in place to examine the woods around them. He could still feel eyes pressing, prodding from somewhere nearby, a force that changed as he pivoted. He needed to get Dani out of here, now.

"Let's go," he said, taking her by the arm.

She bit her lower lip and nodded as they made their way back down the path, away from the collapsing shack and its yellow flag.

# CHAPTER 11

"I think you should leave town."

Liam didn't look at her when he said the words, instead favoring the wall of the bait store through the Chevy's windshield. He knew she was staring at the side of his face, and could imagine her incredulous expression.

"What? Why?"

"Because this is getting too dangerous."

"And it wasn't the other night at the Shevlins'?"

Liam squeezed his eyes shut. "They saw our faces today." He finally turned to her. "They know what you look like." He watched the anger in her eyes recede, but then her lips formed a solid line.

"No. If you're staying, I am too."

He sighed. "Dani, please—"

"No. You asked me for help and now you want me to leave? No. End of story."

"I'm kicking myself right now harder than you know for bringing you into this, but you can still go away." He stared straight into her eyes, begging for her to see the reason in his argument.

"Sorry, bud, not gonna happen." Dani tilted her head and gave a look that asked him to challenge her.

He turned back to stare out of the windshield. "Dammit."

"Yep. So what's next?"

He rubbed his forehead and pressed his fingers into his eye sockets, trying to crush the weariness that coated them. "Coffee."

Dani laughed. "And then what?"

Liam dropped his hands from his face. "We go to the sheriff, tell him what we saw. Maybe he can get a search warrant for the foundry property." He was about to make another, more tactful attempt at urging her to leave town when his cell phone buzzed in his pocket. He fished the phone out. A blocked number came up, and he answered without hesitation.

"Sheriff?"

A pause. "No, this is Agent Phelps. Mr. Dempsey, we need you to stop by the station in town to ask you some questions."

Liam's heart missed a beat, then fluttered into action again. "You have me on the line now—go ahead."

"I'm afraid I'll need to see you in person."

"Do I need my lawyer present?"

Another pause. "That's for you to decide, Mr. Dempsey. As soon as you can make it, we'll be here."

The line went dead, and Liam pulled the phone away from his ear and set it in the center console, his hand barely shaking.

"Something went wrong," Dani said.

"Yes. I think it was a mistake to go to the park last night."

After dropping Dani off at her hotel amidst her protests, Liam parked in front of the sheriff's station and went inside, feeling like his steps were those of a man walking death row, last rites only minutes away. Someone must have seen him and Nut. Identified his truck pulling away from the area? Pulled a shoe print from the walkway? He tried to calm himself as he made his way to the partition and smiled at the female deputy behind the glass. Before he could say a word, the door to his left opened and Phelps's face appeared.

"Mr. Dempsey, thanks for coming down right away. Come in."

Liam walked through the door, which Phelps held open for him without a word. The door to a room directly to the right stood open. A man younger than Phelps, with a neatly trimmed goatee, sat behind a small table. He wore a black dress shirt and tan slacks. He stood as Liam entered the room, and held out a hand.

"Mr. Dempsey, I'm Special Agent Lee Richardson."

Liam shook hands with the agent and noticed a white stripe of scar running down the left side of his head and disappearing behind his ear. Phelps shut the door behind Liam, and he felt his insides go cold. This was it. They'd tell him they had him dead to rights at the Haines murder scene, and what could he say? He had been there, but they would never believe it was after the man had been killed.

"Have a seat, Liam," Phelps said, rounding the desk to sit beside Richardson.

Liam sat in a chair at the table and glanced at the corners of the room. No cameras, but that didn't mean anything.

Phelps set a digital recorder on the table amidst a few papers and hit a button. "Do you have a problem with us recording our conversation?"

Liam licked his lips as a strange calmness came over him. If this was it, why panic? "That's fine."

"State your name, please," Phelps said.

"Liam Patrick Dempsey."

"Mr. Dempsey, these questions are concerning the recent murders of your brother, Dr. Allen Dempsey, and his wife, Suzanne Dempsey. Now, can you tell me where you were on the night of the murders?"

Right to it, then. "I was at my home in Nexton."

"Was anyone with you?"

"No, I live alone."

"When was the last time you saw your brother and sister-in-law alive?"

"Two years ago, at my father's funeral."

Phelps flipped through a stack of papers while Richardson watched him, nodding with each answer. "Mr. Dempsey, are you aware that Suzanne left you a considerable amount of money in the form of a life-insurance plan?"

"I wasn't until yesterday morning."

Phelps glanced up from the paperwork. "You're saying you knew nothing about the insurance policy?"

"That's right," Liam said, holding the agent's gaze. Phelps closed a folder and sat back in his chair.

"I find that hard to believe."

"It was a shock, that's for sure," Liam said, trying to keep his teeth from clenching in anger. "I'm not keeping the money, if you're insinuating that I killed them because of the policy. I'm researching a charity to give it to at this time. You can also speak to my brother's lawyer. I think he would give a statement regarding his opinion on whether or not I was aware of Suzie's policy."

Richardson's eyebrows rose slightly, but Phelps remained motionless.

"Were you romantically involved with your brother's wife, Liam?" Phelps asked.

And there it was, the trip wire that he was supposed to blunder into. Liam's spirits rose. They didn't have anything but the insurance policy. "No, I wasn't. Suzie was a great person, very kind, compassionate. I believe, since my brother and I didn't see each other very much, she wanted to make sure I'd be taken care of if something ever happened to them."

"That's it?" Phelps grunted.

"As far as I can see, that's it," Liam said, his eyes boring holes through the other man.

Richardson sat forward, placing his elbows on the table. "Would you be willing to show us the documentation when you finalize the donation?" His voice was low and even, his eyes imploring. This man didn't suspect him in the least.

"Absolutely," Liam said. He saw Phelps glance at the other agent and then shift back, examining him before punching the button on the recorder between them.

"That's all we needed from you, Mr. Dempsey."

"I'm free to go?"

"Unless there's anything else you'd like to add," Phelps said in a mocking tone.

Liam felt the edge of very thin ice beneath his feet, but couldn't stop himself. "Have there been any developments in the case? I heard rumors about another murder this morning."

"Where did you hear that?" Phelps asked, his voice an ice pick.

Liam shrugged. "Café, people talking."

Phelps stared at him, the agent's jaw muscles flexing inside his cheeks. "We have a suspect in custody, that's all I can say."

Liam nodded. *Who?* his mind asked, but he wouldn't let the word slip out. He had chased two people through the woods this morning; whom did they have in custody now? He stood and turned toward the door, but Phelps spoke as Liam touched the knob.

"Mr. Dempsey, just don't leave town quite yet, yeah?"

Liam glanced at him over his shoulder. "My brother's and sister-in-law's funerals are two days from now. I don't think I'll head out until after that."

Without another look back, he swung the door open and stepped into the hall. Farther down the corridor, he heard a lock opening and the shuffling of feet. He waited, hoping it was the sheriff. When two

men entered his field of vision, one in handcuffs and the other following closely behind, his eyes opened wide against the fatigue that
had stalked him all morning.

A sheriff's deputy pushed a ragged-looking man through the
entry and into the holding area, and Liam saw Nut's eyes find his
before the door swung closed and blocked him from view.

# CHAPTER 12

Liam sat in his truck in the Brenton's Hardware parking lot, his gaze unfocused and bleary, the image of Nut being led into the cellblock replaying over and over in his mind.

Something had gone wrong, that was apparent. Nut had to have touched something in the park before he arrived. Would the older man crack and mention his name?

Liam tried to convince himself that the latter question wasn't more important than finding out why Nut was in custody, but the tension created by the thought of his cell phone ringing with a blocked number again was almost too much to bear.

He drummed his fingers on the steering wheel, trying to break the repetitive loop in his mind. He looked across the street and watched a gaggle of teenagers meander along the storefronts. A woman in a ratty sweatshirt, the hood pulled up obscuring her face, passed them in the opposite direction. A news van rolled into view, a jumble of unfamiliar station letters scrawled across its side. It was a circus now, three-ring, with a sideshow to boot, and he was in the center of it all. The news of another murder would travel fast, and there would be no hushing it. Tallston would become a playground for the broadcasters.

Liam sipped the tall coffee he'd picked up from the drive-through at the end of the street. He didn't flinch at the scalding brew as it slid in a line of fire from his mouth to his stomach.

His cell phone chirped a text message, and when he picked it up, relief swept over him at seeing Dani's number.

*Are you ok?*

He typed *yes* and that he would call her soon. What he wouldn't give right now to go to her hotel and pick her up for lunch, where they could discuss something normal over a drink. Normal—what would that even feel like?

He shook his head. He couldn't let his focus drift away now that everything had gone from bad to worse. He drummed his fingers once more on the steering wheel, then fired up the Chevy's engine.

He found the community center only a block from his hotel. It was a one-story brick building fronted completely with glass. The lobby breathed against him with its air-conditioning as he searched the wall of pamphlets and corkboard, avoiding eye contact with the elderly man at the help desk. Words like *Parenthood* and *Group Therapy* jumped out at him in bold letters. He saw advertisements for weekly cribbage clubs, an announcement for a fishing tournament that was three weeks past, and two homemade fliers offering lawn-mowing services. At the very end of the wall, a leaning plastic stand stood on a table amongst a flurry of business-card holders. The faded title at the top of the printout snagged his eyes: *Citizens for Conservation (The Colton Incorporated project and the ecological impact).*

Liam scanned the paper covered with a few bold statistics and facts until he found a small pyramid of text at the very bottom, consisting of a woman's name, phone number, and address for group meetings. Liam folded the paper and walked out of the empty center, nodding once at the old man, who watched him go.

The address on the paper led him to a blue Victorian house at the
north end of Tallston. A picket fence lined the immaculate front yard,
and a newer Ford Explorer rested in the paved driveway. The gate
between the fence newels was open, small-town trust at its best, an
invitation to walk right up to the front door—which was exactly what
he did. After knocking, he heard movement inside the house—a
squeaking floorboard and a loud dog bark followed by muffled words
of scolding. The door opened, and a tall woman in her sixties stood
inside the screen. A stack of gray hair curled away from her head, with
two black sticks poking from it. A thin pair of black-framed glasses
perched on her nose, behind which two wispy blue eyes studied him.

"Yes?" she asked.

Liam caught movement behind her, and an immense Great
Dane with a gray coat meandered to her side, its wide head cocked,
matching its owner's stare.

"Are you Grace Fitger?"

"Yes. Are you with the police? Because I already spoke to those
two agents this morning."

"No, I'm not. My name is Liam Dempsey, I—" He paused, seeing the abrupt change come over the woman's face, a storm cloud
washing her features.

"Oh God," she said, bringing a hand to her throat. "You're his
brother—you look just like him."

Liam mimicked the Dane's movement, tipping his head. "You
knew Allen?"

Grace pursed her lips and nodded. "I worked for him for almost
twenty years."

She showed him inside and closed the door behind them, shutting out the brightness of the day. The dog stood in the doorway of
the living room until Grace pushed past him, rubbing the Dane's ear
affectionately as she went. Grace and Liam sat in two chairs angled
before a tall fireplace in the center of the room. As he got comfortable,

the dog came straight to him, their eyes level with each other, and sat so that his head rested on Liam's thigh. Liam put a hand on the dog's huge head and rubbed his right ear just as he saw Grace do earlier.

"He's a big baby," Grace said. "I got him for protection, and I think he came home with me for the same reason."

Liam smiled. "What's his name?"

"Ashes."

"You're a good boy, aren't you, Ashes?" Liam said, scratching the dog's ear harder as the Dane began to swish his long tail back and forth across the hardwood floor.

"I'm very sorry about Allen and Suzie," Grace said.

Liam looked up from the grinning dog. "Thank you."

"I don't know what the hell's happening in this town, but it's terrifying, to say the least."

Liam sat back in his chair, and Ashes slid awkwardly to the floor, pinning Liam's feet beneath the dog's body. "That's actually what brought me to you."

Grace sighed. "Would you like some coffee, Liam?"

"I'd love some."

She returned to the room a few minutes later and handed him a steaming cup before returning to her seat. "I suppose you'd like to know about my time at Allen's clinic?"

Liam sipped the coffee, noting its excellence. "Actually, what I'm interested in is the ecological group you started."

Grace's eyes narrowed. "Why's that?"

"I don't know if you've heard or not, but there's a rumor around town that Donald Haines was killed last night. He's the project—"

"I know who he is," Grace said. "If you came here to make the same accusations that those two agents did this morning, I'll have to ask you to leave, Allen's brother or not."

"I'm not accusing you of anything, I just want to ask you some questions." He took her silence as consent. "Why did you start the group?"

Grace hesitated before answering. "Because I care about nature and despise huge corporations like Colton. I grew up in this town, lived here all my life. I've canoed the river more times than I can count, climbed the hills that border Wisconsin until I knew every foothold and path. Hell, I've even gone cliff-jumping with people a third of my age over at Corner Bluff." She leaned forward, cupping her mug in hands that looked worn and used, the skin cracked here and there with cuts and scrapes. "Colton is going to destroy that land across the river, clear-cut the trees, tear the ground up, and salt the earth. It'll be a barren waste instead of the nature it is now." A tremor of emotion ran through her voice, and Liam realized that it wasn't her first time giving this speech, but it wasn't something she rehearsed.

"How many people are in the group?"

Grace sniffed. "Not enough. This town's a bunch of hypocrites when it comes to some things. 'Oh, look at the jewel of Minnesota! We love our wilderness! You want to put a huge pulp plant across the river and cut down all the trees? More money into the community you say? Go right ahead!'"

"You're very passionate about this," Liam said, taking another sip of coffee.

"I wouldn't have lost my job if I wasn't."

Liam stared at her. "You lost your job?"

"Yep. I was a nurse for your brother for nearly twenty years. I applied for the job shortly after he opened up the clinic. I was working at Fairview in Dayton before that, a half-hour commute every morning. Allen hired me on the spot and treated me well, up until Colton came to town."

"How was my brother involved with Colton?" Liam asked, already guessing the answer.

"His best friend was Jerry Shevlin. Jerry owned the land that Colton purchased across the river—made a fortune on it, I'm sure, like he needed any more money. Those people were rolling in it. I mean, they made a donation to the clinic every year for over a hundred thousand dollars."

The picture on Jerry Shevlin's desk appeared in Liam's mind like a dealt card on a poker table. "Was there a grand reopening for the clinic that the Shevlins were a part of?"

Grace finished the last of her coffee and set the cup on a table by her chair. "Not really a grand reopening, but an expansion. I have no idea how much the Shevlins donated for that endeavor, but about two years after Allen opened the clinic, he expanded from six rooms to twenty-four. He hired four more nurses and another doctor, not to mention purchased a bunch of equipment that cost a bundle."

"Why were the Shevlins so generous when it came to the clinic?" Liam asked.

Grace frowned. "I suppose it had something to do with the loss of their child."

"What happened?" Liam said, sitting forward and disturbing Ashes from his nap.

"It was before I started working at the clinic, but from what I gathered, Karen wanted to do a home birth and Jerry was dead set against it. Well, she had her way, and wouldn't you know, there were complications. The baby died, and I think the donations were Jerry's way of raging against his son's death. It might've been a little slap in the face to Karen too, although they stayed together and always looked happy whenever they went gallivanting around town."

"You don't seem to be a fan of the Shevlins. I mean, even outside of the Colton issue."

"They were rotten people, Mr. Dempsey," Grace said with a chilly voice. "I knew it the first time I saw Jerry throwing rocks at a raft of ducks in the river when he was nine. Same with Karen. She showed up when she was about fifteen, an air about her that she was better than everyone else. I'm sorry they're dead, but much sorrier for their son, Eric. A kinder boy you couldn't find."

"So why did you lose your job?" Liam saw Grace's mouth tighten at the question.

"I spoke my mind, said I didn't agree with the sale of the land and what it was going to be used for. I made the mistake of saying it around Allen, and he had words with me one afternoon when we were alone. He told me in no uncertain terms that if I wanted to remain in my position, I would keep any opinions on the matter to myself." Grace sat a little straighter in her chair. "I quit the next day and put in my notice to run for a seat on the city council."

"And you won."

"Damn right I won." Her head dipped a bit as she rubbed her callused hands together in her lap. "Not that it will do any good when we vote. The other members are friends of our asshole mayor, and if he wants it to go through, it'll go through. In fact, we're having a special assembly two days from now to decide if the scheduled meeting to vote on the project will stand despite the recent events . . . and it will." Her hands clenched into fists, and her gaze extended beyond the room they sat in. "If I were made of stronger stuff, I'd go to the mayor right now and tell him if he didn't shut the project down, I'd slip a note to his wife about all the excursions he makes up to his cabin with one of the city interns."

Grace came back to herself and glanced at Liam. "I'm sorry. Here I am blabbering about the town's dirty laundry."

"It's quite all right."

She studied him for a moment before speaking. "I always wondered why Allen and you didn't have anything to do with each other, but I never asked."

"He never spoke of me, did he?" Liam said, hating the flame of hope that flickered in his chest.

"No, but I found a little picture of you and your father in his desk drawer one day when I was looking for a prescription pad. All of you looked alike."

Liam felt the flame waver and die. "Yes, we did."

"What did you really want to know?" Grace said.

"You've actually answered all my questions."

"No, you mentioned Donald Haines being murdered and wanted to scope out the leader of the hippie squad as a suspect—am I correct?"

Liam appraised the woman across from him. She was as sharp as a tack. "I was curious, yes, but I didn't think you were the one writing *lies* on the Colton signs."

Grace shrugged. "There's a couple of our members who are a little young and a lot stupid."

Liam nodded. "Anyone who might go so far as to—"

"Murder that man? No. There's only five of us in the group, Mr. Dempsey, and I've known them all since they were babies."

"Please, call me Liam. And I really appreciate your help—you've been great," Liam said, standing. Ashes rose from the floor and almost knocked him back into the chair with a nudge from his head.

Grace followed him to the door, and stopped him with a touch of her hand on his shoulder just as he was about to step into the sunlight.

"Do you think they'll catch whoever did this?"

Liam eyed her for a moment before squeezing her hand. "Yes, but keep him close," he said, motioning to the Dane. "Because I think someone else is going to die before they do."

# CHAPTER 13

When he climbed into the Chevy, a text message waited on his cell phone's screen with only the words *Call soon*, sent by a number he didn't recognize.

He dialed it, apprehension building within him as the other end of the line rang.

"Liam." The sheriff's voice, low and conspiring. "What in the fuck did you do?"

Liam waited, weighing his options. "Nut was keeping me informed."

"Yeah?" Barnes prompted.

"He found Haines early last night on his way to the boardwalk. He called me right away."

"And you went down there first." It wasn't a question. "God Almighty, boy. Where was your fucking head at?"

"Listen," Liam said, his voice beginning to rise with anger. "You called me into your office and handed me information along with the go-ahead to help, not the other way around, so don't criticize my tactics when you asked for them." The line went silent, but he could still hear the older man's breathing. "How did they pin this on Nut, by the way?"

The sheriff grunted. "They found a shoe print in a muddy spot outside the rocks, as well as an empty rum bottle with Nut's fingerprints on it a hundred feet away in some weeds. When they hauled him in, he had a gold necklace on him that belonged to Haines."

Liam closed his eyes and leaned his head back against the seat. "Dammit."

"Yeah," Barnes continued, his voice growing closer to a whisper. "And you better hope to hell that bum doesn't breathe a word to those agents about talking to you. If that happens, I know nothing about those documents you have, and I'll hang your ass out to dry if it comes to that."

"Gee, thanks, Barnes, so glad I could help out your little bumblefuck community."

Barnes's voice rose an octave. "Listen—"

"No, you fucking listen!" Liam said, his voice taking on an edge that silenced the sheriff. "They have the wrong man, and you know it. I chased two people through the woods this morning outside of the foundry. Suzie's headband was hanging on a little shack out in the forest. Now, you need to get a search warrant and go over there with a full team of forensics to see what you can find—not tomorrow, today."

"I can't."

"Why?"

"Because I got a call from both the mayor and a man named Ian Black with Colton this morning. This project is going through. Both of them said it in no uncertain terms, and with the BCA arresting Nut, what can I say? That you went trespassing and someone ran from you in the woods? They'll fucking lock you up."

Liam seethed, wanting to pummel something. He raised a fist but resisted smashing it into his dashboard, opting instead for his thigh, which burned with the impact.

"Someone's trying to stop this thing from happening, Sheriff, and they don't care how they do it. You can't just wash your hands of it, retiring or not." He heard the other man swallow and waited, hoping his words were enough.

"I'm sorry, Liam, I am, but there's nothing I can do."

Liam rubbed his forehead, his exhaustion chased away by the rage that burned inside him. "Then let me talk to Nut."

Again, a pause. "Okay, but just for a few minutes. He's not supposed to see anyone. I'll let you in the back."

"I'll be there in five minutes."

Liam hit the end button without waiting for a reply, and spun the Chevy around, casting dirt and pebbles across the street as he sped toward the station.

When the back door of the sheriff's station clicked open after Liam knocked minutes later, he didn't even try to meet Barnes's gaze; his anger was still too much to contain. Barnes didn't say a word and turned away, retreating to his office as soon as Liam stepped inside the building. Liam moved down the row of bars until he came even with the only occupied cell. Nut sat slumped like a half-empty sack of potatoes on the edge of a cot, his stringy hair hanging over his face as he stared at the floor. He didn't look up when Liam stepped close to the bars and gripped one in each hand.

"I'm sorry, Nut."

The vagrant shifted just enough to look at him through a tangle of gray hair, his face rutted with new wrinkles, his eyes beyond bloodshot. "Ain't your fault."

Liam glanced up and down the hallway. "What the hell were you doing with that man's necklace?"

Nut glowered further, and he began to resemble an aging hound dog. "I took it from around his neck. Looked like something I could hock at the local pawn. Didn't think about it."

Liam opened his mouth to cuss at the man but realized there was no point. The vagrant was lower than a well digger's shoes. Why should he make him feel worse? The question that came out of his mouth next surprised him. "What's your real name?"

Nut looked up at him, the sallow skin around his eyes pulling tighter. He blinked, as if trying to remember. "Perry. Perry Collins."

Liam nodded. "Why do they call you Nut?"

"'Cause I love Skippy."

Liam smiled wanly at the joke. Nut sighed and hoisted himself off the cot. He turned and looked out of the window in his cell, which was no more than six inches square.

"Had a family when I was very young. Wife, boy, and girl. Had a little place out on a county road not too far from town. It wasn't much, but we were happy." Nut swayed as if he was still intoxicated, but Liam wondered if it wasn't the power of the memory throwing him off balance. "Used to smoke, couple packs a day. Jeanie tried to get me to quit so many times I lost track. Loved her, but I guess the old nicotine was a little too much for me to give up. I fell asleep in my chair one night, smoking in front of the TV. Woke up in the hospital with my lungs on fire. My hair was gone, and they had to take one of my toes on my left foot since it was so badly burned."

Nut turned to Liam, and he saw the desolation on the older man's face. This was where Nut lived most of his days, in his mind, waiting for the booze to file the edges off the pain.

"They burned away in the fire, my sweet babies and my beautiful wife. They died because of me. And the firemen told me that they died of smoke inhalation, never felt the flames that turned them to ash. But I know they were lying—I could see it in their faces." Nut lowered his eyes to the floor and shuffled back to the cot and sat. "I know because I heard them screaming. Can still hear them."

Liam closed his eyes. "My God. I'm so sorry."

Nut nodded. "So they call me crazy, and for a while I was, till I learned to self-medicate when the memories and guilt get too strong." He pressed the heel of one hand to each eye, squashing the tears out of existence. "I didn't mention your name, if that's what you came here for. I threw the phone I used to call you in a pile of trash when I saw they were coming to get me."

"Thank you. I'm going to get you out of here, Perry. They will not hang this on you."

Nut raised his freshly reddened eyes to meet Liam's. "They got me, son. I have no alibi, even if I mentioned I was helpin' you."

Liam knelt at the edge of the cell, crossing his arms on the inside of the bars. "If I said the word *monster* to you, would that mean anything?"

Nut squinted, working his jaw up and down for a few seconds, as if chewing on something. "What do you mean?"

"The Shevlin kid, in his phone call to 911, he said, 'A monster is killing my parents.'" Liam pulled himself closer to the bars and lowered his voice further. "This morning I went to the foundry and chased two people into the woods. I caught a glimpse of one of them through the trees, and he looked . . . strange."

"Strange how?" Nut asked.

Liam ferreted in his memory for the image. *The forest's undergrowth concealed the figure except for the general shape, its head oblong, its back twisted and humped.*

"He looked deformed." Liam watched Nut and saw him weigh something out in his mind. "What is it?"

"People see things from time to time," Nut said in a voice so quiet Liam could barely hear it. "Just talk mostly, of something in the woods. A few hunters have mentioned that they feel like they're being watched, some see something moving through the forest, but no one's ever gotten a clear look." Nut paused, brushing away the coarse hair from his face, and stared at Liam.

"Go on, I believe you," Liam urged.

"In the toughest winters, more pets go missing than usual. Cats, dogs, and whatnot. About five years ago, an acquaintance of mine from the shelter disappeared one night. We went looking for him at a little lean-to that he'd built down on the river's edge. It was empty, but there was a set of footprints leading away from it across the river. The guys I was with said he musta got drunk and walked the wrong direction, got lost, and either broke through the ice and drowned or wandered off into the woods and froze." Nut slid to the closest end of the bench. Liam smelled the reek of old booze and sweat coming from the man. "But I saw those footprints leading away through the snow. They were too big for the man we were looking for, and too deep, like whoever made them was carrying something heavy."

Barnes's door opened with a creak, and Liam jerked away from the bars in spite of himself. The sheriff leaned into the hallway.

"You need to get going."

Liam raised his chin once in acknowledgment before looking again at Nut. "I promise, I'll get you out of here."

Without waiting for a reply, Liam stood and made his way down the corridor, leaving Nut to stare after him from the confines of the cell.

———

"This isn't good," Dani said, setting down her fork. Her Greek salad sat before her partially eaten, along with an almost-empty glass of red wine.

Liam nodded from across the small table they shared, which overlooked the flowing river. He turned his beer bottle in slow circles as he looked across the water toward the deepening shadows that hung within the trees on the far shore. His attempt at eating a cheeseburger lay on his plate with only a few bites missing.

"What are we going to do?" Dani asked.

Liam glanced at her and then returned his gaze to the trees. "I still want you to leave town."

"We went over this already, I'm not going anywhere."

"I don't want you implicated in this thing, and I'm a hair from being pulled into the meat grinder myself. I'll be lucky if I get out of this unscathed."

"God, you're stubborn."

"Really? I could say the same thing about you."

"I mean it."

"Me too."

"You're impossible."

A smile tugged at the corner of his mouth. "My dad used to say the same thing."

"Well, he was right. Anyway, don't you think something at Haines's house will exonerate Nut? Some kind of forensic evidence?"

Liam considered it. "If the killers were sloppy enough to leave a trace, yes. But I doubt they did. My guess is they came inside, hacked his hand off, and then tortured him. Then they dragged him outside and carried him the half mile or so to the spot where he was found."

Dani shivered. "That's bold."

"Bold with balls on it," Liam said, then glanced at Dani. Her expression looked caught between dismay and laughter. "Sorry," he said. "Old saying of my dad's—it just slips out sometimes."

"He was really special to you, wasn't he?"

Liam nodded. "He was the kindest, smartest man I ever knew. There's a weird hole left when one of your parents dies. I think it's the fact that you're always trying to live up to their expectations, whether good or bad, and when they're gone, you realize you're truly on your own. There's no one else to answer to."

They were quiet for a long time before Dani broke the silence. "I'm sorry that the three of you weren't closer."

"Me too." Liam sipped his beer and stared at a formation of geese paddling soundlessly in the current. "I always hoped that the rift would close. I didn't know how to fix it since I couldn't bring my mom back, and I think that's the only thing that might've made a difference. Allen was an adult by the time I realized he hated me, and what could I do? Everything was set in stone already. He was my big brother, and I was his worst enemy."

"That's not fair."

Liam laughed without humor. "With family, it never is."

Dani made as if to say something further, but stopped and pushed a piece of lamb around her plate instead. The sun glittered once more across the water before making its exit for the evening behind the serrated horizon of treetops. They paid for dinner and left the little restaurant, riding in silence to Dani's hotel. When Liam parked beneath the awning and turned to say good night, she surprised him by touching his hand, her eyes searching his face in the twilight.

"What are we going to do?"

"I'm going to speak with the agents in charge of the case tomorrow, see if they'll tell me anything. Maybe you're right, and they picked something up at Haines's house and Nut'll be released."

"And if he isn't?"

He frowned. "Then I'll go to the council meeting and tell them they need to hold off on the vote until the real killer is caught."

She stared at him for a long time before gripping his hand tighter. "And you won't do anything stupid?"

"That's a tall order for me."

"I mean it, please don't take any chances. I know you feel responsible, but if Nut hadn't taken the necklace, he probably wouldn't be in jail right now."

"Yeah, and if I hadn't enlisted his help, he wouldn't be there either."

Dani released his hand. Liam wanted to reach out to her again, to feel her skin against his own. He wanted to slide closer to her and finally attempt the kiss that hung in anticipation between them. But he didn't. He let her open the door and step into the evening.

"Just be careful," she said, and shut the door.

He watched her move to the hotel lobby and disappear inside.

Why was it always this way? Why did he always end up opposite of what he really wanted?

"Because you're an asshole," he answered himself, and put the Chevy into gear.

As he drove through the quiet town, he tried to unweave the myriad clues that prodded his mind like a rock inside a boot. He felt no closer to finding those who were responsible, and the frustration burned in an internal wash of acid. He arrived at his hotel, and was deep in thought when the desk clerk stopped him as he walked toward the stairway.

"Oh, Mr. Dempsey?"

Liam angled toward the counter. "Yes?"

"Someone left this for you."

The clerk set a dingy envelope on the counter, Liam's name barely legible on the front. He picked it up, staring at the unfamiliar, looping script.

"Who sent it?"

The clerk shook his head. "I'm not sure. I went to the bathroom a couple of hours ago, and when I came back, it was sitting on the desk."

"Thank you," Liam said, moving again toward the stairs.

When the door of his room clicked shut behind him, he pulled the straight razor from his pocket and slid its edge beneath the envelope flap. The blade cut through the envelope with a hiss, and he returned it to his pocket. A single folded piece of paper lay inside. He opened it and read the few words scrawled in the same hand that graced the front of the envelope.

*I stopped by but you weren't here. Meet me at Allen's tonight at ten. I have something to show you. —Barnes*

The flaring anger that had plagued him all afternoon when his mind turned to the sheriff lessened. Perhaps he'd found something of importance, something that would help free Nut if used correctly.

Liam traced the pencil lines with a fingertip, then glanced at the clock beside his bed. It was almost time.

# CHAPTER 14

The Chevy's headlights cut through the night surrounding his brother's house and lit up the front windows in shining squares.

Liam guided the truck to a stop before the garage and put it in park. He checked his rearview mirror and then looked at the dash. The sheriff's car was nowhere in sight, but he was a few minutes early. He waited in the cab, the garage doors awash in the Chevy's low beams. He reached for the stereo knob, but listening to music was the equivalent of whistling in a graveyard, and he let his hand fall to his lap. His mind began to spool through the facts again, and he wondered if he'd missed something within the house. Maybe that was what the sheriff wanted him to see.

Liam snapped the keys backward and shut the truck off, a vacuum of sound rushing into his ears. He opened the door to dispel the discomfort, letting the distant chirping of frogs and the rustling of leaves take its place. The pale light within the truck extinguished when he shut the door, and darkness overtook him. The breeze that caressed the trees felt good against his face, cool in contrast to the heat that cloaked the daylight hours. He gazed up at the sovereign blue of the night sky and saw a half moon hanging amidst the glow of light pollution from the town below. The moon looked cancerous, eaten away by the unforgiving space around it.

Liam moved to the front door, rummaging in his pockets until his hand closed over the house keys. He unlocked the door and slid his hand along the wall until he found the light switch, illuminating the room with a flick of his finger. Everything was the same as the day before. He moved deeper into the house, letting his mind roam as the intuitive side attempted to take over and shut out a voice that kept speaking to him in buried tones of the past.

He walked around the bloodstains, and saw his brother driving away from their father's house in his beaten-up car. It was before Allen opened the clinic, and their father had handed him a thousand dollars they couldn't spare as he left. Liam remembered watching Allen drop the money on the floor and shrug off his father's attempt to hug him.

He moved down the unlit hall to the master bedroom, turning on the light when he got there. The bed where Allen and Suzie had slept looked comfortable and just right for the space. *Suzie.* He thought about her face, up close as he danced with her at the wedding. How happy she looked in the DJ's flashing lights. She'd laughed as he twirled her, her gown billowing out in a cloud of opal and pearl.

Liam turned the light off and moved to Allen's study. He stood in the black of the room, smelling the leather of the books on the nearby shelf; the dryness of paper; something tangy—old wine, maybe. The weight of residual life crashed upon him, pushed him down until he realized he was on his knees near his brother's desk. There were tears on his cheeks but he couldn't remember crying them. The moon looked in at him through a high window, and he wished it would leave him be. He wanted to sleep on the floor where his brother once moved and loved and lived. He wanted a part of Allen that he'd never been able to touch or know for himself. His brother was gone, erased from a negative spot in his life that Allen possessed only as a ghost while alive. And now, it was as if he had never existed at all.

He heard the faint sound of a door closing in the living room. The sheriff.

Liam swiped at his eyes and sniffed, inhaling a last odor of his brother's study, and got to his feet. He couldn't let the sheriff see him in this state; Barnes would think he was unfit to continue investigating. Liam stepped out of the office and walked down the hall, his feet padding on the carpet without a sound. He heard a click in the kitchen just as he came into the living room. He stopped, looking around for Barnes.

"Sheriff?" His voice sounded odd, and for a moment he wondered why, the niggling instinct in the deepest part of his brain beginning to awaken.

He stepped into the kitchen, its floors and counters awash in the spill from the living room's lamps. Barnes wasn't there either. Liam walked to the windows lining the living room and peered into the night, cupping his hands around his face.

The sheriff's car was nowhere to be seen.

The lights went out.

Liam froze, the muttered warning in his mind becoming a screaming cry of fear. *Trap.* How foolish had he been to follow the directions of a letter without checking it first? Dani's earlier question echoed in his head. *You won't do anything stupid?* Too late.

His hand found the grip of the Sig as he tried to control his breathing. He would call for help, but his phone was in the Chevy. He could go right out the door and jump into his truck and run away, or he could face the ones that had spilled his brother's blood on the very floor on which he stood. It wasn't even a choice.

Liam crouched, making sure the safety was off with only the touch of his fingertip, and closed his eyes to force his pupils to expand faster. He listened, waiting for a sound of movement from the kitchen. Nothing. When he opened his eyes, the shapes of the furniture around him became malignant hiding spots, and he resisted the urge to cover the spaces they concealed with his weapon. He knew where he had to go.

The garage.

Since the house was one level and he knew no one was at the end where he had come from, there was only one place they could be. Liam sidled into the kitchen, glancing again at the counter and the empty area behind it. His heart surged into his throat and battered his eardrums as he moved toward the door to the garage. It was closed, but he could feel life behind it. Someone waited for him on the other side in the darkness, someone who was banking on him not running away. He exhaled and blinked, trying to clear his eyes of excessive moisture. He wanted to kick the door in, but he remembered it opened toward the kitchen, not away from it. With one hand, he reached out and grasped the knob, feeling it slip in his sweaty palm. He mentally counted down, tensing every aspect of his mind and body. *3 . . . 2 . . . 1 . . .*

With a jerk of his hand, Liam tore the door open and thrust the gun forward, first to one side of the doorway and then to the other, his senses firing faster than his thoughts. The garage was even darker than the house; two sloping shapes took up the bulk of the space, his brother's SUV and a lower car on the far side. The last stall was empty.

He waited, listening as he panned the gun back and forth across the garage. He smelled something, a briny stink of sweat and feces. Liam stepped toward the Escalade, careful to keep his feet away from the underside of the vehicle. Dropping to his haunches, Liam put one hand on the floor and squinted at the space beneath the SUV. He saw no deeper shades of darkness there and stood again, turning both ways before reaching out to pull the door handle of the Cadillac. The handle moved without releasing the door. Locked.

He heard something, and for a moment he thought it was only leaves skittering across the apron outside the doors. But he listened harder, concentrating on the sound as his mind identified it.

Whispering.

It was low, the words indiscernible, but there. He tried to get a lock on where it came from, but immediately it ceased, leaving the garage in a quiet that almost hurt his ears. Crouching again, he edged around the front of the SUV, keeping low enough so he wouldn't present much of a target. When he reached the passenger side of the bumper, he poked one eye around the corner. No one stood in the gap between the car and the Escalade. He listened, hoping to hear a soft inhalation or the scratch of a shoe on the concrete floor. The garage was silent save for the breeze outside that licked at the bases of the three overhead doors.

With the Sig held out before him, he duck-walked between the vehicles to the car's door, put a hand on the handle, and pulled.

The door to the kitchen slammed shut.

Liam jerked around, moving to aim over the Escalade's hood, but the darkness in the garage was complete. The meager light provided by the open door was sealed away from him, and the garage was now a tomb. Scraping footsteps ran away from the door, and he fired in their direction. In the muzzle flash he saw a short figure duck toward the rear end of the Cadillac as a shadow detached itself from the front of the car to his right and lunged toward him.

Liam spun and cried out, trying to step back as he aimed. Something hard struck his gun hand, making his fingers burn as he squeezed off another shot. The gun flew free of his grip and over the car's roof. He heard the Sig clatter to the floor on the opposite side. In the bullet flare he saw an impossible face oozing with deformity, head much too large, eyes full of hatred. He fell backward and landed hard on his ass, sparks of impact popping behind his eyes in the darkness. A whooshing sound filled the air above his head, and something collided with the door of the SUV beside him. He heard the rending of metal and saw flashes of steel biting through paint and aluminum.

Scrambling back, he nearly collapsed with the pain of his hand, aware that the other person was behind him. With a rolling motion, he flipped his feet back over his head, kicking out with his right leg. His shoe connected with flesh and he heard a grunt of pain as the assailant behind him fell back and bounced off the garage door. Liam kept his momentum and turned fully over so that he landed on his feet. The hulking mass in between the cars lurched, and the shriek of steel on steel filled the garage as the weapon sprung free of the Cadillac's door.

Liam rolled to his right, onto the car's trunk. As he twisted away, he heard the same rush of air, and a jagged line of fire streaked across his exposed back. He screamed as the pain hammered his brain. There was nothing else besides the burning in his back. He gagged under the weight of it and tried to catch his breath as he crashed to the floor, his arms almost dropping him onto his face. The concrete tilted beneath him, and he bit down on the side of his cheek, knowing he would be dead if he passed out now.

Heavy footsteps rounded the rear of the car, and he crawled forward, his knees skinning open through his jeans against the rough floor. He heard the now-familiar sound of the weapon cutting air and tucked his legs close to his body. A hollow crack of steel meeting concrete resounded in the close air of the garage, and Liam felt chips of the floor pelt his pant legs. He crawled forward again, wetness running down his back, into his jeans, and around his sides. His hand fell on the polymer handle of the gun, and he tipped onto his shoulder, firing as he did so.

The garage flashed into brilliance, and he heard the whining song of a ricochet and saw a shower of sparks a few feet in front of him. He pulled the trigger again, the muzzle spitting fire, and caught a glimpse of the hunched form skittering toward the kitchen door. A rage, distilled enough to cut through the pain in his back, encompassed every inch of his body. He thrummed with its energy and flung himself to his feet.

Rounding the end of the Cadillac, he saw the smaller figure dive through the door into the kitchen. He jerked the trigger twice, sprinting forward, the empty cases flying past his face and over his shoulder. An animalistic sound barreled up from within him as he leapt through the door. The two figures sprinted across the living room toward the picture window. He fired again, shattering the glass, and the attackers jumped through the falling shards.

The window exploded into the night, catching moonlight on each edge as it fell in a million pieces around the two bodies. Liam tried to run forward but stumbled, his vision dipping unnaturally. He caught himself on an easy chair and raised the Sig again. The two people were only outlines now, running full speed for the safety of the woods. Liam braced the pistol with both hands, concentrating on the larger figure, and fired twice more before the gun locked open, empty. Smoke hung in the air, and cordite burned his nostrils as he stepped to the window and searched the yard, hoping to see a slumped form at the edge of the woods. The light of the moon revealed nothing as the floor surged again beneath his feet.

Liam steadied himself on the empty window frame and took a few deep breaths, willing his vision to stabilize. When it did, he moved to the door and flung it open, the outside air molding to the beating pulse in his face. He jogged to his truck, yanked the door open, slid into the seat, and twisted the keys in the ignition.

The moon guided him down the side of the bluffs, his headlights sometimes wandering to the high grass beside the road and then across the centerline. It was years and only minutes before the parking lot of his hotel came into view. With a last rallying effort, he focused on the parking space near the entrance and slid the Chevy to a stop, keying the engine off without putting the truck in park.

The air inside the cab throbbed in time with the wound on his back. He sat in a sticky wetness that reminded him of falling into a mud puddle as a child. His hand groped for the door handle, but it eluded his aching fingers. He felt himself tip back until his shoulder met the center console.

Liam grabbed at the steering wheel, but it was too far away now. The phone. He could use the phone to call for help. His fingers twitched along the console until they found the familiar rectangular shape. Just as he raised it in front of his face, it slipped from his grasp and slid away at almost the same time as his consciousness.

# CHAPTER 15

Sunlight pried its sharp fingernails beneath his eyelids.

Liam tried to move an arm to block the offending rays, but it felt as if his body was encased in quicksand. He blinked instead, and rolled his eyes away from the eastern sky, where the sun, an inferno of orange, hovered. He studied the roof of his truck. Why was he here? He squeezed his eyes shut and worked his mouth, feeling the sticky paste of dried spit on his gums. What the hell was going on? He tried to sit forward, and a stripe of pain more intense than the morning light bloomed across his back.

Liam opened his mouth to release a moan, and the night before came rushing back. The letter, the trap, the attack in the garage, his hazy drive back to the hotel. Reaching out, he managed to grab the steering wheel and tried to hoist himself from his slumped position. A Velcro sound filled the cab, and for a moment he wondered how a dozen fishhooks had become embedded in his back. Reality took over a second later—he was glued to the seat with his own blood.

Liam settled back into his original spot, his shoulder thudding with the renewed pressure against the console, his fingers alive with pins and needles.

"Holy. Shit." His voice came out in a croak. Nausea wormed its way through his guts, and he refused to make more of a mess than he already had. Clamping his teeth together, he strained against his dried injury and felt the sickening pull of the seat separating from his body.

*"FUCK!"* he yelled, sitting up straight. A trickle of heat traced the channel of his spine, and he almost passed out again. "Fuck that shit, you piece of fucking—"

Grabbing the door handle just in time, he half stepped, half fell from the cab of the truck. His head felt like it was full of Novocain, his limbs not much better. When he attempted to shut the door, he realized the fingers on his right hand wouldn't open or close all the way, their joints swollen so much that his digits resembled cooked sausages.

Retrieving a light, long-sleeved button-up from the backseat, he strained to put it over his shoulders, his back screaming in agony the entire time. After steadying himself against the truck for another few minutes, he picked up his phone and hobbled into the hotel and past the front desk, giving the clerk as much of a smile as he could muster.

In his bathroom he stripped both shirts off, his T-shirt coming away in a crackling layer, pulling one last time at the wound. He closed his eyes and turned just enough so that he faced the mirror in the corner of the small room, his back exposed to another mirror behind him. He opened his eyes.

A saw-toothed gash ran in a horizontal line beneath his shoulder blades. Dried blood coated most of his back, interspersed with a few dripping lines from where the truck's seat had pulled the scab free. The wound was fairly deep and almost a quarter inch wide. When he moved, he felt the snagging pain of the cut, but the muscles beneath didn't seem to be damaged.

Reaching back with one arm, he tried to touch the area, but only got close to one edge. He sighed and turned to lean against the sink. He couldn't disinfect it himself.

"Shit," he said to his haggard reflection, and walked to the table, where his phone lay.

When he stepped out of the shower twenty minutes later, he heard knocking at the door. Liam wrapped a towel around his waist and considered putting on a shirt, but knew he would only have to take it off in a minute. When he opened the door, Dani's eyes widened a little at the sight of him in a towel.

"Always answer the door like this?" she asked, stepping past him.

"Only for beautiful women and the pizza delivery guy," he said, shutting the door. "You didn't bring any pizza, did you?"

Dani started to say something but caught sight of his back when he turned away from her, and she let out a small gasp.

"Oh my God, Liam! You're bleeding! Are you okay?"

"Well, that's what I was hoping you could tell me." He smiled and went to sit in a chair close to the bed. "I had room service bring up some antiseptic and a little gauze. I figured you could play nurse." He looked up and saw her raise her eyebrows. "You don't have to put on an outfit or anything."

Dani laughed and shook her head as she positioned herself on the bed behind him. "What happened?"

He relayed the story as she began to clean the wound. She paused to listen as she dabbed hydrogen peroxide. At times he forgot to continue speaking, the feeling of her delicate fingers moving gently over his flesh nearly sending goose bumps outward from the gash. When he finished talking, Dani sighed behind him.

"That was really stupid."

"I know."

"*Really* stupid." Dani punctuated her words with an extra, cold dousing of peroxide across the cut, which made him stiffen.

"Yeah, I know. I don't need you to rub it in. The part about me being stupid, not the antiseptic. You can rub that in."

"Can you be serious for a second?" Dani's voice was shrill, and she stopped cleaning his back.

"Sorry," he said, and turned his head toward her. "I'm sorry."

Her face softened, and she returned to wiping the gash clean. "What the hell did they cut you with?"

"The murder weapon—some sort of sword or piece of jagged steel. I couldn't see anything in the garage."

"But you were able to see enough of the guy's face for an ID?"

Liam recalled the image of the monstrous head above him in the muzzle flash, bulbous growths bulging beneath the skin like tumors. "Yeah, pretty sure I could ID him."

"Could you describe him enough for me to do a sketch?"

"I think so."

"Good." She applied a bandage and smoothed the medical tape along his back. "God, you are so lucky."

"I know. As soon as we're done, I want to go back up to Allen's and see if I hit either of them. I have a feeling I missed, but I want to be sure."

"No, you need to leave that to the BCA. Call them and have them go up there to check it out."

"Dani, I—"

"No, you listen." Her voice sapped the argument from him, and he fell silent. "You almost bled to death last night. It's a miracle you didn't. I know you want to catch these people, but there's a line between seeking justice and being reckless."

Liam opened his mouth to respond, but a sharp knock on the door cut him off. He stood and crossed the room, glancing at Dani over his shoulder.

"Who is it?" he asked, putting his hand on the doorknob.

"Agents Phelps and Richardson. We need to ask you some questions, Liam."

Liam clenched his jaw and stared at the ceiling before pulling the door open. Both agents stood in the hallway, Phelps with his hand on his belt and Richardson sipping from a coffee.

"I was just going to call you guys," Liam said, sweeping an arm toward the hotel room.

"That so?" Phelps said, moving past him.

"Yep."

"And why's that?"

"Oh, just this," Liam said, shifting so that both agents could see his back and the white bandage spanning it.

"How did that happen?" Phelps said, leaning against the wall as he eyed Dani on the bed.

"I was attacked at my brother's place last night by two people."

"Attacked?"

"Yes, attacked. I found them in the garage, and one of them cut me with a weapon of some kind. I managed to fight them off, and they escaped through the living room window."

Phelps stared at him like a wax sculpture. "And why didn't you report this last night?"

"I barely made it back here and passed out in my truck. Dani was just helping me clean the wound. I was going to call you in a few minutes," Liam said, adjusting the towel tighter around his waist.

Richardson spoke up. "We got a report this morning from a sheriff's deputy out on patrol that he saw a broken window at your brother's house. When he went to investigate, he said there were signs of a struggle and blood on the floor. We came up here to find out if you knew anything about it."

Liam nodded. "Guys, I think the people in my brother's place last night were the real killers. I think you've got the wrong man locked up." Liam watched the agents' reactions. Richardson squinted at him, his eyebrows knitting together, while Phelps stared across the room without blinking. Liam glanced at the table covered with the case files and then back at Phelps.

"Have you been drinking, Liam?" Phelps said.

Liam followed his gaze and saw the empty beer bottles from his and Dani's dinner two nights before. "We had a few beers a couple nights ago."

Phelps turned his gaze back to him. "What were you doing at your brother's house?"

Liam ran his tongue along his bottom row of teeth. "I was reminiscing. Why? Is there a problem with me having access to the house?"

Anger flared and then receded in Phelps's eyes. "No, but I'm wondering if you didn't have a little too much to drink and broke the window yourself, causing the injury on your back."

"I didn't do this to myself, I was attacked. The suspects are still at large, and this community is not safe. Whoever's doing this doesn't want the project across the river to go through, isn't that obvious by now?"

"This investigation is none of your concern," Phelps said, stepping into Liam's space.

"I'd like you to comb the area around the house in case one of them cut themselves jumping through the window," Liam said, locking eyes with Phelps, and then swinging a glance at Richardson. "You find only my blood out there, fine, but if there's someone else's—"

"We don't need you to tell us how to do our job, and I'll thank you to stay away from that crime scene from now on, as we'll have a patrolman stationed there. You can notify the sheriff for an escort if you need access to the house. We'll be in touch if we need anything else."

Phelps spun away from him, bumping Liam with his shoulder as he went. Liam's body tensed, but he resisted the urge to form a fist. Richardson looked as though he wanted to say something, and even opened his mouth, but he shut it and followed his partner out the door, closing it as he left. Liam shoved his palm against the door as hard as he could and locked the dead bolt. He stalked back to where Dani sat, and grabbed a clean set of jeans and a T-shirt from his bag.

"See how much help they are? That egotistical fuck can't see past the end of his nose, and it's going to mean someone else's life. The only upside is that he didn't spot the paperwork across the room."

Dani dropped her chin to her chest, then stood and looked up at him. "We should go to the hospital, you probably need stitches."

"I don't have time," he said, moving toward the bathroom.

"You need to rest, you lost a lot of blood."

"Last night was the most sleep I've gotten in a while, I'll manage," Liam said, pausing at the bathroom door. He looked at Dani and gave her a half smile.

"I can't—"

"I know," Liam said, and felt his heart bend at the sight of a delicate teardrop sliding down her face. "I know. Call me if you need anything else before the funeral, and please don't go out at night."

She nodded and wiped the errant tear from her chin as she tried to move past him. He reached out and stopped her with a hand on her forearm. She brought her eyes up to his, and she was so close it made his pulse double its pace. He could smell her shampoo and see the tear-track glistening on her skin.

"Promise me you'll be careful," he said.

Her breath brushed his bare skin, and he felt the air grow tight between them, a magnetic field straining to bring them closer. Her eyelids fluttered, and she stepped away, dropping her gaze to the floor.

"It's not me you need to be worried about," she said, moving past him and out the door.

# CHAPTER 16

For the remainder of the day Liam studied the case notes from the sheriff, leaving his hotel room only twice, the first time to grab an orange juice and two protein bars from a convenience store and the second to pick up a bottle of whiskey and a burger from a local fast-food joint called Cliff's.

Each time he exited the hotel, the sun sat behind a thick blanket of white clouds, a cataract in the sky. He saw a few news vans parked in front of the sheriff's station and wondered if Phelps was giving them an announcement about the case.

When he returned to his room the second time, the door barely closed behind him before he spun the cap off the whiskey and drank three swallows straight from the bottle. He cleared his throat as the liquor splashed into his stomach and exploded in a satisfying ball of warmth. He devoured the burger standing, glancing every so often at the paperwork spread out in piles across the table. As he finished the last bite and tossed the wrapper away, he hoped, for what seemed the hundredth time that day, that he hit one of the attackers the night before—and wished against it. If one of them caught a bullet, the other would make sure they got away or would bury the body somewhere no one would find it. If that was the case, then the remaining suspect would most likely disappear and there would be no way to exonerate Nut. If he'd hit neither of them, they would be free to kill again, unchecked.

Liam sighed, moving the papers around into a Go Fish pile, their edges overlapping one another, and tried to sort the information in his mind as he picked up a pen and sat at the table.

The Shevlins' murders made sense being tied to the land purchase and their involvement with Colton. He wrote *Colton* in the center of a blank piece of paper, drew a line to the right, and scribbled *Shevlins*. Donald Haines also fell in with his theory, especially with the display of his body in such a public place. He drew a line to the left and wrote *Haines*. Then he drew a line straight up and wrote Allen's and Suzie's names, circling them. They were the only ones that didn't fit. What connected them to Colton besides knowing the Shevlins? He stood and paced the room, murmuring to himself, the whiskey turning the glow of the lamp on the desk into a soft halo of light.

"Allen and Jerry were friends, but Allen didn't know Donald Haines." He turned, walking back to the desk to glance at the simple connection chart.

"Grace and her group are opposing the project, but they aren't responsible either." He couldn't fathom the elderly woman organizing something as insidious as the murders, even if she loved the outdoors as much as she said she did.

"And Suzie wasn't supposed to die."

He walked away from the table and came back to stare at the paper again. Picking up the pen, he drew a line connecting the Shevlins and Allen. The answer lay between the two families, he could feel it.

Staring out the darkening window at the river beyond, he went over his options for finding what tied his brother to the wealthy couple. He didn't want to chance another visit to the Shevlins' house since Phelps might have a patrol there too, and there wasn't anything at Allen and Suzie's. He tapped the pen against his forehead and then paused, an idea forming in his mind.

He grabbed his phone and dialed Grace's number, glancing at the time to make sure it wasn't too late to call. She answered on the second ring.

"Hello?"

"Grace, it's Liam Dempsey."

"Liam, I've just heard. That poor man they call Nut—Perry, is it? I can't believe it was him."

"That's because it wasn't," he said, sitting on the bed. Quiet hung on the phone line, and he waited, trying to gauge her reaction.

"You think he's innocent?"

"I know he is, because two people tried to kill me at Allen's place last night."

Grace inhaled a sharp breath. "My God, are you okay?"

"I'm fine, but I do need to know two things from you."

"What's that?"

He paused, figuring out the best way to ask without having her hang up on him. "First, I want to know if the special meeting tomorrow is open to the public."

"Yes, it is. It's at one o'clock at city hall. Why? Are you coming?"

"I am. I'm going to try to dissuade the rest of the council from going ahead with the vote. I think that might mean saving someone's life."

"Lord," Grace breathed.

"And the second thing is asking a lot of you."

"I'm in it up to my waist already, Liam, go ahead."

"I think there's another connection between my brother and the Shevlins that's at the center of all this." He waited a beat. "Would you have any way to gain access to Jerry's and Karen's medical records at the clinic?" He cringed and waited for her to berate him or simply hang up, but neither happened.

"Liam, that *is* asking a lot of me."

"I know, but I think it might mean the difference between saving the next victim's life and not."

He heard Grace moving around on the other end of the line and a single loud woof from Ashes. "Why should I trust you, Liam?"

"Because your dog loves me."

Her surprised laughter filtered through the phone in warm waves. "You definitely have something Allen didn't."

"What's that?"

"A sense of humor."

Liam waited, knowing they stood upon a cliff together.

"One of my dearest friends still works as a receptionist at the clinic," she said after a moment, and Liam closed his eyes, relieved. "I'm sure she would let me borrow her keys. What would you like me to look for?"

"Anything to do with the Shevlins. If you could find their doctor visits, see if Allen had anything stored in their files that he might not want to keep at home, where Suzie might've seen it."

"When do you need this by?"

"The sooner the better," he said, rising off the bed.

"I'll do what I can, but I'll need a little time. It will most likely have to be tomorrow night at the earliest."

"Okay, that'll work." He picked up the whiskey bottle and stared at the amber liquid. "Thank you, Grace. I wouldn't ask if I didn't think it was crucial."

"Just come bail my old ass out if I get caught and we'll call it even."

"It's a deal."

"Good night, Liam. I'll see you tomorrow."

"Good night."

Liam ended the call and took another long pull from the bottle. It burned again, but this time he barely felt it. He wedged a chair under the doorknob after locking both the dead bolt and the security bar, then sat and reloaded the Sig's empty magazine. His eyes hung level with the opaque window, his fingers sliding the rounds in one by one. When he finished, he took a last drink of whiskey before capping the bottle and setting it aside.

The bed felt luxurious save for the blinding pain in his back when he lay down. He grimaced, rolling onto his side until the blazing slice beneath his shoulder blades receded to a manageable throb in time with his heartbeat. He closed his eyes, letting the liquor draw him away from the pain and occasional sound from outside his room. He tried to recall the feeling of Dani's hands on his back, how gentle her touch was and the softness of her fingers. He thought about the pull he felt when she was close to him, like he stood at the door of an airplane with no parachute, wanting only to feel the sensation of falling without the worry of the ground below.

Just as he was about to drift away completely, he heard pounding footsteps on concrete, those of him and the man in front of him. The man's lank, dirty hair hung over his shoulders and onto the mechanic's coveralls he wore. Liam's stomach swung in a sickening way as he watched the man spin, a crazed grin cut in his pasty-white face. The gun leveled at Liam, its muzzle the only thing he could see. It encompassed everything, the world shrinking into a tunnel, until the flash of his own weapon perforated the silence, morphing from a gunshot into a woman's scream, then into his own as he sat up in bed, his eyes flicking around the room.

The dream's resonance hung over him, and he felt sweat bead and then fall from the end of his nose. Rubbing his forehead, he slumped sideways onto the bed and breathed, trying to force the images out of his head.

Gradually his heart returned to a normal speed, and the lingering effect of the whiskey drew his eyes closed once again.

---

Tallston's city hall stood in the center of town, a monolith of brownstone mimicking the towering bluffs that ringed the city's edge. No traffic moved on the street as Liam pulled into a parking space in the building's shadow, its intricately carved façade resembling a medieval stronghold more than a municipal center. He climbed out of the Chevy and into the scorching heat of the day, stretching his limbs while taking care not to put too much tension on the skin of his back lest he open the scabbed gash there.

The morning had come much too early, and he spent the predawn hours poring over the case notes again to see if there was anything else to glean. Nothing stood out to him, so he dedicated the rest of his morning to what he would say to the assembly at the meeting.

A secretary on the first level of the building directed him to the third floor, where the meeting would take place. He climbed the stairs, a small amount of trepidation spreading through him at the thought of the scene he was about to make. The doors to the meeting room stood wide open, revealing a large space with high ceilings. Several rows of chairs sat in a half-circle formation before an opposite-curving bench of seats elevated a foot higher than everything else in the room. A bank of floor-to-ceiling windows ran behind the council's bench, and a simple wooden podium with a snaking microphone attached to its top stood off to one side of the public's chairs.

People filled less than half of the seats, and several sets of eyes turned to him as he entered the room. He searched the faces and nearly stopped in his tracks when he saw the petite form of Shirley Strafford beside her dour-looking cameraman. The reporter spotted him at almost the same instant, and she smiled, making her face look plastic and false. The cameraman's lip curled in a similar fashion, and Liam stared at him until the other man finally looked away.

Liam chose a seat close to the door, only a few paces behind the podium. Several of the city council members already sat behind the long desk, and after a moment he caught Grace's eye. She nodded at him and winked once. A high-backed chair to her right was empty, and he saw a triangular nameplate on the desk that read *Harley Jefferson—Mayor.*

Liam glanced around the room once more, noting the time. It was two minutes after one. Allen's and Suzie's funerals were set for three o'clock, and he hoped the meeting wouldn't run overly long since he still needed to get back to his hotel room to change into the black slacks and dress shirt he'd brought for the inevitable function.

His train of thought dissolved as three more people entered the room and strode behind the desk at the front. Two were women, and the other was a man, surely the mayor, dressed in a three-piece suit made of shiny gray material that looked gaudy under the fluorescent lighting. He had a strong jaw and dark hair with just a touch of gray at the temples, above the body of a high school linebacker gone to seed. Liam noted the alarming tension on the mayor's suit-jacket buttons being applied by his ample belly beneath the fabric.

Harley Jefferson and the two women seated themselves, and the mayor nodded to the rest of the council on either side. The members all lowered their heads and shuffled a few papers before adjusting their respective microphones into place. The mayor glanced around the room, smiling briefly at a pretty brunette woman half his age sitting before a laptop at the far end of the room. The woman waved at him before turning back to her computer. The mayor cleared his throat audibly and then scanned the crowd before speaking.

"Good afternoon. I hereby call this special city council meeting to order. Roll call for attending members."

Harley rattled off a list of names that each of the six people on the bench claimed. The room fell silent again, and Harley looked up from the desk.

"We are holding this special meeting due to the terrible recent events that have taken place in our city. First off, I would like to extend my condolences to the family and friends of the victims. We lost several fine members of the community in the last two weeks, and they will be sorely missed."

Harley shuffled a few papers and cleared his throat again. "As I was saying, there was some concern raised in light of the crimes, and we were tentative as a governing body to proceed with our scheduled meeting on Monday of next week, out of respect and in accordance with the law enforcement's investigation. Therefore, this meeting's sole purpose is to decide whether or not we will gather on Monday to vote on that meeting's proposals."

A few mutters filled the public seating area, and Liam looked at the people to try to gauge their reactions. Most sat stoically, but a few leaned forward in expectance or anticipation.

"Before the council votes, we will entertain any questions or comments from the public. If you have something to say, please step to the podium, state your name and address, and then feel free to speak on the issue."

Liam felt all the eyes in the room rest upon him as he stood and walked to the podium. The faces of the council members and mayor gazed at him as he placed his hands on the cool wood and licked his lips, which suddenly felt too dry.

"Good afternoon, my name is Liam Dempsey, my address is 1400 Wayward Drive, Nexton, Minnesota." He ran his eyes over each face, pausing just a second longer on Grace's. "My brother was Dr. Allen Dempsey. Some of you might have known him. Suzie, his wife, was also very involved in the community here. They were murdered in their home early this week, and I have reason to believe that their deaths have something to do with the Colton project across the river."

A few hushed voices exchanged words behind him, and Harley leaned forward, his dark eyebrows lowering so that they hung as bushy ceilings above his squinting eyes.

"Sir, I'm very sorry for your loss, but this is not a court of law and we aren't—"

"Hear me out," Liam said, holding up a hand. The mayor's mouth tried to churn out more words, but Liam continued before the other man could speak. "As you may all know, Donald Haines, the project manager for Colton Incorporated, was murdered two nights ago." More mumbling from the public. "This is not a coincidence, this is a pattern. The people responsible for the murders do not want this project to go through."

"We were told that the authorities have a suspect in custody," a balding man in a gray sweater said from the mayor's left.

"Exactly," Harley said, spreading his hands out in a calming motion. "I was told yesterday by a reputable source that a man has been arrested and that the reason for concern is over."

"I was attacked two nights ago at my brother's house," Liam said. His words cut through the din that was building in the room and left silence in its wake. "I fought off two individuals, and was nearly killed doing so. The man that is in custody right now is innocent, and the killers are still free."

Loud conversation broke out in all parts of the room. Liam watched the mayor lean forward and ask for order, but people kept talking. Grace caught his eye and nodded again. This was okay—he had people talking. Maybe even a few of them would listen.

"We need to quiet down! *Quiet down!*" Harley yelled. His baritone voice reverberated in the large space, and the cacophony of speculation receded to a few muted whispers. When he looked satisfied, the mayor shifted his eyes back to Liam and pointed a finger in his direction. "You need to sit down, sir, before I have you removed from this meeting."

Liam opened his mouth to respond, but Grace spoke before he could.

"Actually, Harley, he has a right to speak just as anyone else does, and we need to hear him out."

The mayor's upper lip curled, revealing a set of even teeth. He stared at Grace for a few moments, and when it appeared that she wasn't going to drop her gaze from his, he turned back to the podium and spoke through clenched jaws. "Proceed, but please tell us what this has to do with today's meeting."

Liam nodded. "Like I said, I believe the murders are somehow tied to the Colton project, and the people responsible do not want that plant to be built. They'll be watching the outcome of this meeting, and if you decide to go ahead with the vote on Monday, I think that will be all it takes to provoke them again." Liam leaned forward, metering his words into the most powerful syllables he could. "If you proceed with the vote, I believe someone else will die."

Harley waved a hand before his face, but another voice cut him off.

"Why should they believe someone as unstable as yourself, Mr. Dempsey?"

Liam turned to face Shirley Strafford, who rose from her seat and took a few steps toward him.

"Ma'am, this is unacceptable, and this isn't the place to have a discourse. In fact, this isn't the place for either of you," Harley said, motioning to the brunette he had smiled at earlier. "Tracey, get Security up here, please, and have these people escorted out."

Tracey nodded and stood from her chair, but paused when Shirley spoke again.

"Oh, we'll go of our own volition, but I thought you should know you're being preached to by a man who killed a pregnant woman."

There was a collective intake of breath in the room, and time slowed. Liam watched the newswoman's smile widen as her triumphant, large eyes twitched to his face. His heart reversed directions and he felt his limbs grow cold, his tongue thickening into a block of frozen meat. He knew his mouth was hanging open but he could do nothing about it, the reporter's sentence rebounding inside his mind until it was all he heard.

"He shot a pregnant woman while on duty as a homicide detective in Minneapolis ten months ago," Shirley continued, in the confident tone of someone at ease with speaking to a large audience, the facts rolling out of her mouth like poisonous honey. "He was decommissioned and is still under investigation by the Minneapolis Police Department. Oh, and the baby died too."

Liam wanted to weed out the lies, to try to defend himself, but he couldn't speak or move. His stomach roiled, the creeping unease of nausea rising with each second. His legs wobbled, and he put out a hand to steady himself against the podium.

"If I were any of the council, I wouldn't listen to another word from this man. He's unbalanced, and I heard today that the altercation he referred to earlier was nothing more than a drunken fit."

The room broke into raucous babble, a roar in Liam's ears. The rush of blood pounded inside his head, and he turned to look at where the council sat. Several of them gesticulated and tried to be heard above the commotion, while Harley hammered his fist against the desk and yelled for Security. Liam's eyes found Grace, who sat motionless in her seat, a rock amidst a frothing sea of movement. She looked stricken, and her skin wasn't the same shade as before.

He knew he had to get out of the room, out of the building, out of this town. He couldn't stay here anymore; he needed the solitude of his farmhouse, the wind pushing against the windows and the sun on the floor of the kitchen. It was a mistake to come here, to think he could help or even function properly. Vomit rolled up the back of his throat, and he gagged. He spun on his heel to flee from the room, but pulled up short.

Dani stood near the doorway, one hand clasped over her mouth.

Her eyes found his, and she blinked, her head jerking in a small movement. He didn't know whether it was a shudder or an admonition. Liam felt a delicate strand of something within him break.

Already tenuous, it held a weight heavier than he had realized, and when it let go, the falling sensation was too great.

He ran.

Pushing past Dani, he didn't wait to see whether she reached out to him or shrank away. The shafts of sunlight streaming through the windows outside the room were razor blades that shredded his sight. He tripped when his feet met the stairs and nearly fell, his legs beyond rubber. Stumbling, he covered his mouth and stifled back the puke that yearned to tumble out. The stairway went on forever, switching back until he became dizzy and sure that he was underground, that the stairs continued into hell and he was almost there.

Liam burst through the doors to the outside in a stumbling haze. A raging storm of static buzzed in his head, and the memory of holding the gun, aiming at the man in the alley, tried to filter through it all. He gasped and finally threw up on the sidewalk, drawing repulsed comments from a nearby family passing behind him. He lurched to his truck, his eyes puddles of tears, wiping the sick from his mouth with one forearm as he searched for his keys with the other hand.

Then he was inside the cab, his fingers turning the keys, the engine purring to life. Without bothering to look over his shoulder, he backed up, eliciting a honk from a minivan that slammed on its brakes to avoid him. He shifted into drive, the tires leaving twin black strips on the pavement as he tore into the shimmering day.

# CHAPTER 17

Liam meant to leave town, but instead, he drank.

He took the first swig just to rinse the taste of bile out of his mouth and to steady his shaking hands as he packed his bags in the hotel room. The second and third were because the first helped. Within twenty minutes of leaving the city hall, his room was clean and he was drunk. The defiling afternoon sun slid across the bed, so unlike the rays that filtered into his farmhouse. How could the sun be so different here? He responded to its touch with a yank to the heavy blinds, and the room became layered in shadow. Each time the reporter's words replayed in his head, he took a sip of whiskey. Each time he saw the abhorred expression on Dani's face, he took another. It was a drinking game of the most lethal kind, no cards or dice needed, only the hitching whir of his mind to signal a turn. He floated in a pool of despair, not awake and not dreaming. The room rotated at an even pace, and after what felt like hours, he closed his eyes.

He and Allen stood on the edge of the bluffs outside Allen's house. It was almost sunset, and the river below leached the dying light from the sky like it would never see the sun again. A bird made a forlorn call in the woods, and he wondered why it was so sad, how anything could be so sad looking at the view beyond.

"It's beautiful," he said to Allen. His voice had a paper sound to it, one-dimensional and lifeless, so adverse when compared to their surroundings.

"Yes, it is," Allen answered. Liam glanced at his brother, who had his eyes closed, his lips parted as if he was drinking the clean air in. "The river is dark, and the night isn't something to swim in."

Liam gazed out at the vista and wondered if night could ever truly fall over the evening before them. He thought it might last forever.

"Let her go," Allen said.

"Who?"

"Sacrifices are necessary and prudent. Triage the soul and you'll be successful."

Liam watched Allen turn away from him and step closer to the edge of the bluff. "Why didn't you love me?" Liam asked.

The sound of rain began to beat against his eardrums, and he glanced at the horizon, where a tumorous cloud advanced toward the vanishing sun. Veins of lightning coursed down its bloated sides, and its belly broke loose and began to flood the land beneath it with blood. The red rain ran in streams, meeting the river and tainting it. Liam watched the scarlet tendrils extend and consume the water until it flowed like an artery within the banks. The salty smell drifted to him, and he looked at Allen again, wondering if his brother had heard the question.

"If you forget yourself, no one will remember you," Allen said, his voice so low it sounded like the growing wind before the storm. He turned his head, and Liam saw that his eyes weren't closed anymore.

They weren't there at all.

Two sunken pools of ichor swirled in his eye sockets. Allen smiled horribly and then stepped off the bluff into the open air.

A moan escaped his lips as he rolled off the bed and caught himself on the floor. The room was pitch-black, and he felt awash in its swimming motion. He felt with a hand until he found the foot of the bedside table. He stood and wobbled, the whiskey still wreaking havoc in his skull. The digital numbers of the clock told him it was close to 7:00 p.m. He slid his foot right until it nudged the bed, and he sat.

He'd missed the funerals. Dani knew about him, as did the city council and probably the rest of the town by now. He had to leave; there wasn't anything else he could do. Liam stood again and fumbled with the lamp on the table until it clicked on, the light making him wince even with its dim wattage. He went to the bathroom and drank several cups of water. After brushing his teeth, he stowed away the last of his things in the duffel bag and stood in the center of the small room.

Just as he was about to snap off the light, he heard the sound of footsteps in the hallway. He listened as they slowed and finally stopped before his door. He waited. At last, a soft knock. The Sig sat on top of a folded shirt in his bag, and he retrieved it, flicking off the safety. As he moved to the door, another knock came, this time louder.

"Who is it?" he said beside the door, his hand on the knob.

A pause. "It's me."

His stomach rolled. Putting the gun back into the bag, he snapped on another light and went to the door. He pulled it open, revealing Dani, who stood in the hallway. She wore a plain black dress that came to just above her knees. A clasp pulled her hair tight at the back of her head, and she clutched a small black purse with both hands. He waited, staring into her face. He noted the tearstains, both new and old, in crooked lines on her cheeks. Her mascara ran in a few small streaks, which only made her eyes look more luminous.

"You didn't come," she said, shifting on the low heels she wore.

"No," he said, looking at the floor.

"It was a nice service, as nice as a funeral can be. I think the whole town was there." He nodded, still not looking at her face. "Liam, I—" He raised a hand toward her. "You don't have to say anything. You didn't even have to come. I understand. I'm leaving here in a few minutes." When he looked up, he saw the crumpled expression, the helplessness, the confusion, and something else.

"I'm sorry," she said.

"For what?"

"For everything that's happened to you." She reached out and took one of his hands in hers, squeezed. He let her hold it but didn't return the pressure.

"Thank you."

"Can I come in?"

He glanced at her again, wondering what she wanted. "I don't—" He shrugged, shaking his head.

"Please?" She squeezed his hand again.

They sat on the bed after he poured them drinks. Dani sipped at hers and then held it between her legs. Liam perched next to her, enough distance between them so that he couldn't feel her warmth, but not enough to escape the smell of her perfume. Something about the smell reminded him of his front porch, of early spring, but he couldn't say why. The silence stretched out between them until he broke it, his words almost too loud in the room.

"They're going ahead with the vote, aren't they?"

Dani sighed. "Yes. Six to one. Grace voted against it."

He chewed at his lip and stared into the depths of his whiskey. "I knew they would, but I had to try."

"You spoke well."

He glanced at her and then away, still not able to bring himself to look her fully in the face. "You heard everything."

"No, not the whole truth, just what that horrible woman said."

155

"She was right."

"About everything?" He sat still, not even breathing. "I didn't think so." She reached out and laid a soft hand against his arm. "Tell me."

The thought of relating the story was like an exponential wall in front of him. With every second it gained altitude, soaring higher and expanding wider. The memory was a pulsing, infected scar, just waiting for him to speak to spill its septic touch across his mind, to immerse him in the moment that he would regret until the last beat of his heart and beyond.

Her grip tightened on his arm, as if she knew he was slipping away. "I don't hate you. You can tell me."

Liam swallowed the lump in his throat, surprising even himself as he began to speak. "I was on a death investigation. A man involved in a narcotic ring had been murdered. It was like several I'd been on before—no witnesses, nothing to go on. I got a tip from the deceased's cousin. A guy called Abford used to run a lot with the victim, so my partner and I went to his apartment to ask him a few questions.

"We knocked, and when he asked who we were and we told him, he shot straight through the door, caught my partner in the stomach. I fired back and then kicked in the door, but Abford was already out the window and halfway down a fire escape. My partner was holding his own in the hallway and already had an ambulance coming. He told me to go, and now I wish to God I would've stayed with him. Just a few seconds and everything would be different."

Liam stopped to drink from the cup he held, the whiskey coating his bone-dry mouth. He felt Dani's eyes on him but didn't look at her, sure that if he did, he wouldn't be able to continue.

"I went down the stairs and out an emergency side exit. Abford had just jumped from the last rung of the fire escape and was running down the alley between the apartment building and a business complex. I ran after him, and I remember how his hair bounced on his back just before he started to spin around." Liam paused, his eyes burning through the floor at his feet.

"All I saw was the muzzle of the gun, and I stopped and took aim. I remember my vision narrowing until all I could see was him aiming back at me. At the last second, right before I pulled the trigger, she stepped in front of me." He swallowed again, his spit thick and acidic. "She was coming out of a beauty parlor. I found out later she'd just gotten her hair cut. It was her and her husband's eighth wedding anniversary the next day, and she wanted to look nice, I suppose. Her name was Kelly."

Tears coated his eyes and began to drop, one by one, onto his pant legs. "My bullet hit her in the neck, clipped her carotid clean in two. She didn't even have time to scream or make a sound. She just fell down, and that's when I first really saw her. In that split second, I knew everything would be different for the rest of my life. I knew it when she hit the ground and all she could do was hug her stomach."

He glanced at Dani, wiping away his tears so that he could see her crying beside him. "She was seven months' pregnant, a boy. The doctors said if I'd hit her anywhere else, they might've been able to save him, but she bled out so quickly he didn't have a chance. I learned all this later, because the moment she fell, I emptied my gun at Abford and killed him too."

"Oh God," Dani whispered. Liam waited for her hand to leave his arm, but it didn't.

"Every day, I wake up and the first thought is of her. About her husband raising two little kids alone without his wife, wondering what his son might have looked like. The second thought is of putting my pistol in my mouth and pulling the trigger. And you know the only reason I don't?" He tilted his head to the side, his mouth a line of anger and trembling grief. "Because I don't think I deserve it. I feel like I should have to suffer with this on my conscience every day, carry it with me at night when I can't sleep, because it's nothing—nothing—compared to what I took from that family."

"It wasn't your fault," Dani said, her voice watery with tears.

"Why? Because the department ruled it an accident, a righteous shooting? Because they closed the book on it? Ho-hum, let's move on with life. Sorry, Liam, but you just need to hoist yourself back up and continue on!" His voice rose, and he stood, shaking. "They're not the ones who can't sleep at night without drinking half a bottle of booze! They're not the ones who wish for death and then deprive themselves of it! They're not the ones who made the mistake!" He thrust a quaking fist into his chest. "It was me . . . it was me."

Sobs rolled through him, unbidden and unlike anything he'd ever felt before. His emotions lay exposed, skinned and bleeding for anyone to see, but there was only this woman, who stood from the bed and came to him.

He jerked back at her first touch, not because he wanted to get away from it but because he longed to collapse into it. Dani's fingers grazed his neck and caressed his wet cheek. He felt her come closer, her body only inches away from his. He turned his head away, and her gentle hands guided his face back. He vibrated with the urge to pull her close but kept his arms at his sides as she looked up at him, her breath hot on his face. Her perfume was everything; it surrounded him, and now he remembered why it was so familiar. There was a lilac bush that bloomed white petals every spring beside his porch, the warm scent like sugar in the air. He held on for one second longer, one beat, and then broke.

His lips found hers, barely touching at first; the subtle glide of her lipstick sending a tremble through him. Instantly he was transported back to Allen and Suzie's wedding night, his arms around Dani, their kiss bridging the years between then and now. She moaned as he drew her close, her body sealing to his, without even air between them. His hands found the back of her head, releasing her hair so that it fell onto her shoulders, as he pressed his lips harder against hers. Their clothes were only burdens, and he undressed them both with a fluidity that seemed dreamlike. He laid her gently on the bed and covered her with himself, a blanket of flesh, and caresses that he couldn't stop, nor did he want to. Then they were one, moving together, the force restrained before now locking them in union. Everything was sound and flesh and a burning pleasure that rose from his depths until time meant nothing and an undeniable heat blossomed in both of them, shuddering, shaking with the power of it as she cried out and arched against him.

They floated flat on the bed, neither moving, only holding each other and whispering not to let go.

After a time, they slid beneath the covers and lay still, his heart a bass drum beating in slow motion. Liam felt her face against his chest as he breathed, letting the sensation of liquid sunlight coast through every inch of him. He tried to say something but couldn't, so he relented and closed his eyes to the dark room as Dani rubbed his chest with one hand.

Immediately, the panic began to grow as sleep tried to pull him down. His breathing quickened and he spasmed, the potential anxiety building within him. *Not now, not after this.* He tried to move away from her heat, but she grasped him and rubbed the side of his neck.

"It's okay, it's okay." Her voice was serene and comforting. The anxiety tried to ratchet up a notch, but lost its grip on him as Dani kissed his shoulder, still stroking his neck. "You're okay."

Liam closed his eyes again, waiting for the accustomed relapse into the memory, but it didn't come. His breathing slowed, his heartbeat returning to normal as the room melted around him in a soft darkness that enveloped everything with the smell of lilac.

# CHAPTER 18

Liam woke to dancing reflections of sunlight from the river on the ceiling above him and the sound of the shower running.

He rubbed the sleep from his eyes and yawned, his jaw cracking with the effort. His body felt wonderful save the snagging pain in his back. Sitting up, the sheets slid against his skin and he realized he was naked. The previous night came back to him in freeze-framed shots of anguish and pleasure alike. Had it all really happened?

Looking around the room, he saw the bedside clock—it was past eight in the morning. He stared at the time, letting the reality of it soak into him.

He'd slept for more than ten hours.

He laughed.

It slipped out accidentally. A sense of restfulness that he hadn't known in almost a year tightened his muscles and made every thought clear. He felt reborn.

The door opened to the bathroom, and Dani emerged in a wash of steam, dressed in khaki shorts and a light T-shirt. Her hair hung in auburn ripples, and he had to restrain himself from going to her just to run his fingers through it.

"You're awake." She smiled at him and came to the side of the bed.

"Yeah, can't believe I slept that long."

Her face lost some of its brightness. "How long's it been since you got a full night's sleep?"

"I don't remember. A long time." He smiled at her. "Last night was . . ." He shook his head.

"It was great," Dani said, leaning toward him.

Liam felt the dampness of her hair on his face as she kissed him. Instantly he was aroused, and he didn't break away from her until a thump issued from the door.

He got out of bed and slid on a pair of boxers before opening the door. The hall was empty, but when he looked down, he saw a rolled-up newspaper near his feet. A similar roll rested in front of every room. Liam picked up the newspaper and returned to the bed, unfolding it as he went. Trepidation of what the headline might be crept into his chest. Did someone die last night?

Nut's photo headlined the top of the page. "'Suspect arrested for recent slayings,'" Liam read. He shook his head and scanned the articles below it. "'Council moves forward with plans to vote tomorrow in light of arrest.'"

"Well, we already knew they were going ahead with it, right?" Dani asked.

"Yeah, but this was just about the worst thing they could do," he said, flicking the paper with a forefinger.

"What's that?"

"Announce it like this." Liam dropped his head and leaned his elbows against his knees. "They're asking for another murder." He wanted to break something. How could everyone be so nearsighted? "If it wasn't for Nut, I'd leave right now, let them deal with it on their own and be a hundred miles away when the next killing happened."

"You couldn't do that," Dani said.

He glanced at her and then looked at the wall. "No, I couldn't. I'm just pissed off." He thought for a moment before grabbing his cell phone from the table.

"Who are you calling?"

"Grace. I'm just hoping she's still willing to go out on a limb for me."

As he found her number and dialed, his doubts increased. The final ring went unanswered, and Grace's voice mail picked up. "Grace, it's Liam. I'm sorry for how things went yesterday at the meeting. Not everything that reporter said is true. I've been cleared of all charges for the shooting, and I wasn't drunk when I got attacked. She's just angry because I wouldn't give her an interview." He paused, choosing his words carefully. "Grace, I still need your help. Please, please trust me."

He ended the call and sat back, looking at Dani. "That's all we can do for now."

The phone rang in his hand, startling him. Without waiting for the caller ID to come up, he answered. "Grace?"

"No, it's Barnes," the sheriff's voice growled from the other end.

Liam frowned. "Yeah?"

"Listen, Liam, I'm sorry for the other day. I heard about what happened up at your brother's place."

"So you believe me?"

"Yes."

"That makes two of us."

"Look, I don't know how you're handling this. I've heard a lot of rumors flying around this morning about a scene at the meeting yesterday. Sounded like that blond reporter shouted your business to everyone."

Liam stood and paced to the window. "Yeah, that's about it."

"Like I said, I don't know what your plan is, but something just came up and I thought you should know."

Liam's guts constricted. *There was a killing last night, it was just too soon for the papers to report it.* "What is it?"

"It's the Shevlin kid."

"God, did he die?"

The sheriff paused. "No, he woke up late last night."

The drive to Fairview Hospital in the neighboring town of Dayton was mercifully short, and Liam was glad because the air-conditioning in the Chevy couldn't keep up with the mugginess of the morning. The miles flew by outside the window, as the land smoothed out and became flat fields lined with green rows of waving corn and endless bushels of wheat.

"So what did the sheriff say about us visiting the boy in the hospital?" Dani asked as the first signs of Dayton came into view on the horizon.

"Just that the BCA questioned him earlier this morning and then left, so we shouldn't bump into them," Liam said, wiping a bead of sweat from his temple. "Apparently, they showed him a picture of Nut and he told them that Nut hadn't been the one in the house that night."

"So are they going to release him?"

"No, they think that the kid's still in shock and doesn't remember. They're going to try to hang this whole thing around Nut's neck."

Dani unfolded a mid-sized notebook she'd grabbed from the desk in his room, and scribbled a little at its top with a pencil. "Describe the guy that attacked you in the garage."

Liam shot her a glance, and when he saw she was serious, he began to speak. Racking his brain, he strained to recall every detail that he saw in the bright flash of the muzzle. When he looked at Dani's sketchpad, he was surprised to see a lifelike drawing taking shape on the paper. She worked with short, precise movements, accented with long, wide shading as she laid the pencil on its side. By the time he guided the truck past the first stoplight in Dayton, the picture was nearly done.

"Wow, are you sure this is what he looked like?" Dani asked, holding up the pad.

Liam looked at it and then back at the road before nodding. "Yes, more or less, that's about it."

Dani lowered the sketch to her lap and stared at the deformed face she'd drawn. "But what would cause someone to look like this?"

He shrugged, searching the left side of the street for the three-story building that the sheriff had described to him. "I don't know, an accident possibly? Some sort of chemical?"

Dani continued to work on the drawing, and he finally spotted the hospital, its awning supporting the rounded letters of its name. He found a parking spot amongst the crowded lot, and they stepped out into the heaviness of the day.

The air-conditioning inside Fairview put the Chevy's to shame, and Liam felt the accumulated sweat on his body cool in an instant. An elderly woman wearing a green vest with the words *Fairview Volunteer* stitched in black thread on the left breast sat behind a reception desk a few yards opposite the entrance. When Liam stepped up to the counter, she smiled, her face wrinkling.

"Hello, how can I help you?"

"We're here to see Eric Shevlin," Liam said. "Can you tell us which floor he's on?"

The woman picked up a phone from the desk and dialed a number, still smiling as she said something into the receiver. After a moment, she pulled the phone away from her mouth, her eyes narrower than before.

"Are you law enforcement?"

"No, we're friends of the family," Liam said. Dani caught his eye, and he gave her a little nod. She smiled at the woman behind the desk.

"Okay, let me check," the receptionist said, and turned away from them. Finally, she set the phone back in its cradle. "He's on the third floor, but he may be sleeping. Check with the nurses' station when you get there—it'll be straight ahead from the elevators." She pointed with a bony arm at a bank of silver elevator doors on the left wall of the lobby.

"Thank you," Liam said, moving away from the desk.

"How are we going to pull this off? We're not friends of the family," Dani said as soon as the elevator doors shut.

"I'm his godfather's brother, that's got to count for something," Liam said as he punched the button marked *3* on the panel.

The doors slid open a minute later, revealing a rounded counter staffed by three women in multicolored scrubs. A hallway ran straight past the nurses' station and to the left, opening every few feet in wide doorways. A nurse holding a chart in one hand and a Styrofoam cup in the other smiled at them as they approached.

"We're looking for Eric Shevlin's room," Liam said.

The nurse eyed them. "I'm not sure if he's awake, and I don't know if the officer guarding the door will let you in."

"We just want to talk with him for a minute. My brother was his godfather."

The nurse shifted her gaze between them and then nodded. "His room is down the hall at the very end," she said, pointing directly ahead.

"Thanks so much," Liam said, moving past the desk. He could feel the nurse's eyes on his back as they walked away, but he focused on the officer sitting in a chair outside a closed door at the end of the corridor. The cop sat with his legs wide apart, his cell phone held before his face. He looked to be about twenty-five, with two days' growth of stubble on his cheeks. When they were still a few steps away, he looked up and then stood, tucking his phone out of sight.

"What can I do for you folks?"

"Hi, we're here to see Eric. Is he awake?"

The officer shot the nurses' station a look before focusing again on Liam. "Uh, did they say it was okay at the desk?"

Liam nodded. "Yeah, they said if he was awake, it would be fine."

"How do you know him?" the cop asked, still not moving from in front of the door.

"My brother was his godfather. I just wanted to say hi to the kid, let him know someone's thinking about him." In the back of his mind, he cursed himself for not picking up a stuffed bear to bring with him; it would have been more convincing.

"You two have ID on you?" the officer asked.

"Sure," Liam said, and motioned to Dani, who drew out her billfold from her purse. They held up their licenses as the cop inspected them. After a second, he nodded.

"I'll have to pat you down, and miss, you'll have to leave your purse out here with me."

"That's fine," Liam said.

The officer ran his hands around Liam's waist, and he was infinitely thankful that he left his gun and razor at the hotel room. After swiping down his pant legs, the cop stood and motioned them forward as he opened the door to the room.

A few windows in the far wall were covered by thick sets of blinds that all but blocked out the glow from outside. Electronic whirs and beeps filled the room with their soft noise, and after a moment of letting his eyes adjust, Liam made out the bed and its occupant in the center of the room.

Eric Shevlin lay propped on three or four pillows, his lower half beneath several blankets. His upper body looked small in a blue gown that he swam in. His hair was dark and hung toward his eyes, which were barely open. Liam glanced at the boy's right arm, which ended just before the elbow in a wrap of bandages.

"I'm going to leave the door open," the officer said behind them. Liam nodded and walked to the side of the bed.

The boy's eyes opened a bit more, and Liam saw a slight glaze of drugs on their surfaces that Eric struggled to see through. "Who are you?" he asked after looking at both Dani and Liam. His voice was rough, as if he had a sore throat, and Liam realized it was from barely speaking for almost two weeks.

Liam leaned forward, keeping the distance between them small so he could lower his voice. "My name is Liam. I'm Dr. Dempsey's brother."

Eric's gaze ran from Liam's forehead down to his chin and back again. "You look like him," he said at last.

Liam smiled. "This is Dani. We both came to see how you were doing."

Eric raised his remaining hand off the bed in an attempt to wave at Dani, but the IV inserted in his arm and the blood-pressure cuff prevented him from moving more than a few inches.

"Hi, Eric," Dani said, stepping closer to the bed. "How are you feeling?"

Eric tried to shrug. "Like I've been asleep too long." He swallowed and turned his head to the right. "Could you open my blinds just a little?"

Liam walked to the other side of the bed and twisted a hanging plastic rod until the shades yawned wide enough for a few shafts of sunlight to fall onto the bed. "That okay?" Liam asked, returning to his position. Eric nodded and began to flick at a tag on one of the blankets with his fingertips.

"Do they have good food here?" Liam asked.

Eric shifted his gaze to Liam's face and then back to the tag. "Not really. I had a feeding tube until last night when I woke up." A stricken look crossed his young features.

"Do you remember why you're here?" Liam said as gently as he could. Eric nodded, his hair scratching against the pillow behind him. "Do you want to talk to me about it?"

Eric bit his lower lip and looked toward the window, a slat of light coating his face. "They didn't believe me," he said after a while.

"Who didn't?"

"The guys who were here this morning. They asked me all kinds of questions, and when I told them, I could see they thought I was lying or something."

Liam came closer and placed his hand on Eric's exposed bicep, where there were no tubes or needles. "I'll believe you." The boy turned his head and studied Liam's face, as if searching for a hidden joke there.

"My mom and dad are dead." It was a statement, and Liam was grateful it wasn't a question. "I remember almost everything from that night, but it's kind of like a dream too."

"Just tell us what happened if you can," Liam said, squeezing his arm. Eric nodded and closed his eyes.

"It came through the door, and Champ ran right at it. But it had this thing in its hands, a big piece of pointed steel, and it hit Champ with it. My dad—" Eric stopped, and his eyelids scrunched closed further, as if he could shut out the vision inside his head. "My dad ran at it, and it stabbed him. That's when my mom made me run. She started screaming to run away and hide, so I did."

Tears leaked from beneath his eyelids, and Liam felt Dani nudge his arm. He glanced at her as she shook her head. He didn't like it any more than she did, but they needed Eric to keep talking.

"What did you do then?" Liam asked.

"I ran," Eric whispered. "I ran upstairs and I heard my mom screaming and it was roaring something . . . something like—" His tearstained eyes opened, his eyelashes coated in moisture like pine boughs after a rain. "I can't remember what it said. I hid under Mom and Dad's bed and called 911. It came looking for me, and it pulled the bed away from me. It knew I was in there." Eric's frame quaked beneath the blanket, and Liam willed the boy's nerves to hold. "I saw it raise the sword, and then that was it until I woke up here."

Liam licked his lips. "Eric, you say 'it.' It was a man, right?"

The boy's eyes got very large. "It was a monster."

"If I showed you a drawing, would you be able to tell me if it looked like the monster?"

Eric nodded. Liam motioned to Dani, who opened the sketchpad and turned it to the correct page before facing the picture toward Eric.

Immediately the boy stiffened, and Liam heard the quiet beeping of the heart monitor begin to pick up speed. "That's it," Eric gasped. "That's it." His eyes sought out Liam's. "Why do you have a picture of it?" The fear in his voice was palpable.

"Because I saw it too," Liam said.

Eric watched him for a long time. Finally, he nodded and frowned. "Why aren't Dr. Dempsey and Suzie here?"

Liam grimaced internally. The boy didn't know yet. He studied his young face and knew the kid couldn't possibly weather another two deaths of people he cared for. "They couldn't come, but we came instead," Liam said. He saw the boy's gaze flit to the picture Dani held and then back. "What is it, Eric?"

"When it looked at me, I could see—" Eric squirmed in the bed, the heart-rate monitor beginning to chirp again.

"What could you see?" Liam asked, leaning forward.

"In its eyes, it hated me."

Liam squeezed Eric's arm one last time before withdrawing his hand. "You're safe now, Eric. No one's going to hurt you, you have my word."

Liam took the sketchpad from Dani and grabbed a pen from a desk in the corner of the room. After scribbling his cell number on a page, he tore it out and folded it into Eric's hand. "If you need something or want to tell me anything else, you call me, day or night, okay?"

Eric nodded, and Liam smiled at him as he and Dani turned away.

"I lost one of my arms," Eric said in a hushed voice, stopping them just before the doorway. "I like to play baseball, and now . . ." He trailed off and glanced at the distended bandages around the stump to his right.

Liam leaned against the doorjamb, looking at the boy. "You ever heard of Jim Abbott?" Liam asked. Eric shook his head. "He was a pitcher for the Angels, the Brewers, the White Sox, and the Yankees. He threw a no-hitter against the Cleveland Indians, and you know what?"

"What?"

"He only had one hand." Liam smiled at the expression of wonder that crossed the boy's face. They waved at Eric one last time and left the room. After Dani retrieved her purse from the officer by the door, she grasped Liam's hand and pulled him close to kiss him on the cheek.

"What was that for?" he asked as they neared the elevators.

"For hope," she said, and stepped through the doors as they opened.

# CHAPTER 19

They stopped for lunch at a small Italian restaurant in the center of Dayton and ate at a table outside, in the shade of an enormous umbrella.

As Liam finished the last of his chicken primavera, he noticed Dani studying the drawing on the pad.

"You're very good, I meant to tell you that earlier," he said.

She looked up at him through a few strands of loose hair. "You're just saying that."

"No, really, I don't know anyone else that can draw a mutated murderer any better." Balling up a used napkin, she threw it at him. "But seriously, you have a ton of talent—I mean it. I think you should start selling prints online or something."

"Of this?" she asked, tapping the face on the paper.

"Well, it might appeal to some people. I know I'd buy a few for the house." She laughed as the waitress came to take the credit card he'd set on top of the bill. "I think you could do well," he continued. "This is your real passion, right?"

"Yes, but it won't pay the bills—not right away anyhow, but someday maybe."

Dani's eyes became wistful. He imagined them sitting across from each other at the table in his house just as they were now. The rightness of the image caught him off-guard, and he looked away from her toward the street.

"So what's next?" she asked after the waitress thanked them and moved away to clear a nearby table.

"We go back to the hotel and start over," Liam said, scratching his signature onto the receipt.

"With or without clothes?" Dani said, and laughed at the way his mouth opened.

He shook his head as they started walking to the Chevy. "Incorrigible" was all he said before climbing inside.

The air seemed to thicken as they neared Tallston. The weight of it pressed through the vents of the truck with coils of humidity the air-conditioning couldn't disperse. He tried to dispel the feeling by turning the fan up another notch, and wondered if it was the weather or something else that hung over him, the sensation of being crushed beneath an unrelenting, invisible rock.

As they pulled through the small town, Dani turned her head toward the passenger window and stared out at the sun-drenched streets. "Wouldn't it be wonderful if we could just go swimming or something? Go for a boat ride on the river without this hanging over our heads?"

"It would be great," he agreed. "I haven't been on a vacation in years."

The thought of a carefree trip was so enticing it was the equivalent of a starving man being shown a steak dinner just out of reach. The relief of telling Dani about his past was an immeasurable burden laid on the ground after carrying it for so long; at least, it felt that way in her presence. But the thought of a vacation on which he could actually enjoy himself was still too sweet to consider. Just as he began to imagine what it would be like, the building where Kelly's husband lived with his two surviving children bloomed across his inner eye. The rough brick beneath his knuckles, Kelly's last name near the buzzer, the feeling of the plastic button's surface under his finger.

"Liam, look out!" Dani yelled.

He came back to himself just in time to stomp the brakes and avoid the woman crossing the street in front of the truck. The Chevy's hood came up almost to her shoulders and obscured most of her from view. His heart felt as if it were trying to pry itself from his chest. The woman turned her head beneath the dark shawl she wore to give the truck and its occupants a fleeting look before continuing on her way across the street.

"Shit! Where did she come from?" Liam asked as he let the truck roll forward again.

"I don't know, she was just there all of a sudden."

He gave the woman a last glance over his shoulder, noting the shabby look of her pants and the stained shirt she wore. "Must be a homeless person."

"That's what I thought too," Dani said.

They parked in front of Liam's hotel, and the unyielding heat tried to crush them as they walked inside. Only a minute had passed after shutting Liam's door when a knock brought him back to the hall. A kid no older than eighteen dressed in a tan uniform stood outside the door holding a bouquet of white lilies and a large envelope.

"Yes?"

"Are you Mr. Dempsey?"

"Yes."

The kid handed him the flowers and envelope. "Here you are, sir."

"Thank you," Liam said. The heft of the envelope surprised him. He turned it over as he walked back into the room but could find no markings on its outside. The card suspended within the flowers said, *Sharing in your sorrow.* Liam tore the envelope open and pulled out documents obviously made on an old copy machine.

"What is it?" Dani asked, looking over his shoulder.

"The Shevlins' medical files," he said, shuffling through them. "Grace came through—everything's here. I knew her dog loved me."

They cleared the table and stacked the case notes in a pile at one corner before spreading out the new information. It was an ocean of white with several blurry photocopied images of x-rays mixed in.

"Let's find the earliest visit, shall we?" Liam said. They slowly searched through the pages, comparing dates, until they narrowed it down to a single document.

"A death certificate?" Dani asked.

"Yes, for their first son, Peter."

Liam scanned the paper. Seeing the date of birth and death as the same day was off-putting, but he continued on, noting the signatures of both Jerry and Karen on the left-hand side beneath the title *Relatives*. On the right, his eyes fixed on his brother's name under the heading of *M.D.*

"Allen signed off on the death." He read out loud the text written in his brother's swooping and almost illegible hand. "'Cause of death: Breech birth leading to nuchal cord strangulation. Infant was born immotile and unresponsive.'"

"That's terrible," Dani said.

Liam nodded, setting the page down. "So that looks like the first instance they were involved with one another. Everything else is just checkups, random colds . . . and it looks like Eric broke his arm when he was seven, the same arm he lost."

"Maybe there's no connection between them other than being friends," Dani said, sitting back from the table to stretch. "Maybe the donations were just like Grace said, a little reminder to Karen that they should've had the baby in a hospital, not at home."

Liam tapped his forehead. "Maybe."

"You don't sound convinced."

"I'm not." Liam glanced at the death certificate again, and something hooked his attention. He brought the page close to his face, turning it over several times.

"What is it?" Dani asked.

"There was another document attached to this page," he said, pointing to the two negative images of small staple holes in the upper left corner. "But it was removed."

He dropped the certificate onto the rest of the pages and shuffled through them. After some time, he sat back again, looking out the window at the thick afternoon sunlight. "There aren't any other loose pages here that are torn or show signs of stapling. That means it either got thrown away or it's somewhere else."

He stood and moved to his bag, retrieving the holster from inside, the Sig nestled within the leather.

"Where are we going?" Dani asked.

"I'm going back to the Shevlins' to look in the file cabinets we didn't get to go through the other day."

"I thought you said it was too risky to go back there since they'd have a patrol watching the place."

Liam strained to fit the holster into the back of his pants. "Don't have a choice now. I need to put this together, give Phelps something he can't deny, before someone else is killed. I'm guessing they're more concerned with watching Allen and Suzie's at the present, not the Shevlins'. Plus, we didn't give them any reason to think we'd been out there."

Dani watched him latch his belt in place and make the final adjustments to the holster. "Don't even think you're leaving me here while you go back there, 'cause it isn't happening."

He sighed. She looked so beautiful, outlined by the window behind her; even the defiance on her face pulled her features into something becoming. "I'm going alone, and I don't care if you get mad at me or not. I won't put you in harm's way again. I was stupid to do it in the first place."

"You can't tell me what to do."

"No, I can't, but I can make you understand." He crossed the space between them and grasped her by the shoulders. "I don't know what would've happened the other night if you would've been with me at the house."

"I might've been able to save you from almost getting skinned."

"Yeah, and you might've gotten killed too," he said, with more force than he intended. Dani tried to shrug his hands away, but he held her tight. "Dani, I care about you, a lot." She shifted in his grip but looked up at him and chewed on her lip. "I won't endanger you again. I won't."

He let her go and moved to his bag, reaching inside for the second of the three magazines he'd brought for the Sig. He almost grabbed the third one but opted against it, not knowing where he would carry it comfortably.

"You can't live this way, you know," she said quietly.

"What way?"

"Like everything you touch is glass. You can't live like it all could break at any moment—no one can."

He was about to refute what she said, but stopped, knowing anything he tried to say would be a half truth or less. "I'll drop you off at your hotel if you want," he finally said.

Dani looked at the floor. "I'll walk."

He opened his mouth but then shut it, unwilling to push her any further than he already had. "I'll call you soon," he said, moving to the door. When he heard no answer, he left the room. The last he saw of her was her back as she turned away.

# CHAPTER 20

The backdrop of sky was no longer heated cobalt but overcast gray as he drove toward the Shevlins'.

A clotted wall of clouds lined the western horizon, their battered hides stolid in the late-afternoon air. The gnawing ache from leaving Dani angry wouldn't go away, no matter how many times he told himself that her safety was more important. A new thought floated to the forefront of his mind as he neared the small road they had parked the truck on before: what if everything turned out all right? If they were able to stop the killers and clear Nut, what then? He saw the same scene in his mind, he and Dani at his kitchen table, and mentally shoved it away. That was such a long shot it wasn't even worth day-dreaming about—nonetheless, he let it play out one last time.

Liam parked the truck behind the copse of trees and shut it off before climbing out. The day still held the oppressive humidity, and moisture began to adhere his T-shirt to his skin. The quick pace he set as he walked down the road and into the Shevlins' driveway didn't help either, and by the time the house and river came into view, sweat slicked nearly every inch of his body. He stopped and waited at the crest of the hill, making sure no one followed him and nothing moved below. When he was satisfied, he jogged down the slight hill and onto the porch, glancing through the dark windows as he turned the key in the lock.

The house was even more ominous alone. Liam stood on the threshold, tracing the path Eric took the night his parents were slaughtered. Now, he could see the boy's panicked face racing away from the kitchen and up the stairs, only to wait for the footsteps to follow, to find him cowering beneath his parents' bed.

Liam strode through the shadowed linings of the house, toward Jerry's office. The sun was already behind the interlaced branches of the forest outside, throwing scarecrow shapes across the yard as it dipped even lower. After entering the office, he pulled the flashlight out of his pocket, illuminating the picture of his brother on the desk before turning to the file cabinets.

He went through the files methodically. The first cabinet contained Jerry Shevlin's financial undertakings—land acquirements, personal stock exchange notes, and deeds to three buildings within the city limits. He sifted through these until he found the folder he searched for. Drawing out the thick layers of paper marked *Colton Inc.*, he laid them on the floor of the office and began to examine the pages one by one. Most of the legal documents meant nothing to him, but the final packet he opened revealed the selling price of the land the foundry sat upon.

"Three million dollars," Liam said to the empty room. He shook his head at the sum, and searched for his brother's name within the text but saw nothing except Jerry's and Karen's signatures.

Gathering up the piles, he folded them just as they had been and placed them back into the filing cabinet. The second cabinet's drawers contained tax information for Jerry's trading company, and with a sigh, Liam flipped through each page, determined to find a connection within the mind-numbing jargon, perhaps a systematic pattern of money being transferred that would point him in the right direction, but he saw nothing. It was only after he closed the last folder that he realized what was missing: the donations to Allen's clinic.

He flicked back through several pages of prior years' taxes to affirm his suspicions. Nowhere had Jerry Shevlin reported the donations in his paperwork. Liam frowned. Why would a sharp businessman such as Shevlin not cite the amounts if they were as considerable as Grace had mentioned?

Looking at the cabinet, he realized that he was on the last drawer; there weren't any other folders to go through. Another dead end. "Shit," he said, and stacked the papers back into a semblance of order. He sighed and rubbed his lower back, noting over three hours had passed since his arrival. Without bothering to fully tuck the pages properly, he dropped the bloated folder back onto the hanger within the cabinet and was about to slam the drawer shut when something caught his eye.

A few sheets of loose paper lay flat beneath the suspended folders within the drawer.

He could barely see their corners, the two vampiric holes in their white skin causing his heart to speed up as he reached inside and drew the papers out into the beam of his flashlight. His eyes opened wider upon seeing the clinic's symbol on the letterhead, his vision snagging on two words near the top: *Test Results.* Flipping to the next page revealed an array of numbers and columns, each corresponding to another by a dotted line. At the top, the patient's name, slanted in italics, read *Karen Shevlin.* Circled at the very bottom was a section set apart from the rest of the data.

"Alkaline phosphatase," he said, tasting the words to see if they meant anything to him. Alkaline levels were a mystery to him, although he once dated a woman recovering from cancer who swore by an alkaline diet. Liam tapped his finger against his temple and searched the rest of the page for anything else of significance, but nothing stood out.

He rose and set the papers on the desk, clicking off the flashlight as he did so, and pulled out his phone. But before he could dial the number he intended, the display lit up with an incoming call. The number wasn't familiar other than the area code of Tallston, and after a hesitation, he answered it.

"Hello?"

Quiet breathing from the other end, along with a muffled beep.

"Hello?" he asked again, stepping into the doorway of the office.

"Mr. Dempsey?" The voice was young, and all at once the background noises made sense.

"Eric?"

A pause. "Yes."

"Eric, is everything all right?"

"Yeah, I was sleeping and I had a dream."

Liam leaned against the doorjamb, glancing out the darkening windows. "I'm sorry, was it a bad one?"

"Yes, it was—" A hitching breath. "It was about that night."

"Dreams can be really scary, but they're just dreams, they can't hurt you. You're safe now, Eric, but I'm really glad you called me. Are you feeling a little bit better now that you're awake?"

"Kinda. Was that the truth about Jim Abbott? Did he really have only one hand?"

Liam smiled. "Yes, and he was a very good pitcher."

"Do you think I'll ever be able to play again?"

"I have no doubt in my mind that you'll play again, Eric. You're going to be just fine."

Liam listened to the humming equipment in the boy's room and wondered if anyone else had visited him. He hadn't thought to ask at the hospital, and Grace didn't mention any other close family. If there wasn't anyone else, that explained why the boy had called him.

"I remember now."

The words snapped him out of his reverie. "Remember what?"

"I remember what it was yelling that night—it was in the dream."

"What was it, Eric?" Liam asked, his skin beginning to tingle with anticipation.

"It was screaming, 'Momma, look at me.'"

Liam found the shovel in the steel building on the other side of the driveway. It only took two blows from the heel of his shoe against the door for the lock to give way. The shovel stood beside various other garden tools, which looked brand-new against the inside wall, and he spared no glances for anything else within the building once he had the spade in his hand. Heat lightning did a soundless, stabbing jig in the clouds to the west, and a bank of fog hung in patches of floating gossamer across the river. Evening tipped toward night as the sun slid behind the horizon, the last warm glow fading from the land.

Liam moved across the yard, his thoughts shrouded in a buffeting haze of confusion, much like the opposite shore of the river, an almost-impossible answer trying to be heard above the din. He stopped before the stone, not bothering to check his surroundings, and plunged the steel tip of the shovel into the dirt. The soil was soft and pliable; each time he raised the tool up, it bit full mouthfuls from the ground, leaving an ever-growing hole in its wake. The angel on the headstone remained with its face averted, and as he dug, he imagined it was more from the desecration taking place before it than from mourning. Sweat pooled at his armpits and ran in a stream down his bent spine, stinging the wound on his back. The weight of his exertions pleaded with him to rest, his muscles crying out for a break, but he took none. A crow cawed once, hidden somewhere in the trees as he labored on, the pile of dirt increasing beside him, growing even as he stooped lower and lower into the ground.

The shovel's tip struck something at almost five feet down. His hands slid a few painful inches on the handle, and he froze, the hollow sound echoing in his ears. With careful motions, he cleared the remaining dirt away, widening the small hole as he did. After several minutes, the stained oak of a casket lid began to emerge through the grit. He'd never seen such a small coffin, and the sight of it shocked him. *Infantile* was the word that came to mind, and he nearly brayed insane laughter at the appropriateness of it. He scraped more soil away and saw that the wooden box was only two feet long, almost square.

Setting the shovel beside the hole, Liam reached down with both hands and grasped the lip of the lid, not knowing how it was designed. After a moment of tugging, the entire casket began to shift, and he tried to heave it out of the grave. The top came completely free, the hinges having rusted away in the span of twenty years. The bulk of the box dropped back into place with soft *whump*, the earth accepting its gift once again, and he was left holding the lid in his hands, so light he thought he could sail it away like a Frisbee.

Browned silk, once the color of ivory, draped the inside of the coffin. A pillow no larger than a pincushion sat at one end, slanted from his encroachment. A musky smell of turned earth was the only thing that met his nostrils as he squinted into the choking gloom of the hole.

The casket was empty.

# CHAPTER 21

The Chevy's engine screamed as the truck rocketed down the back road.

Liam punched in Grace's number for the second time and let it ring until the voice mail picked up. Cursing, he ended the call and focused on driving, his knuckles flares of white beneath the layer of dirt. The pressure he felt earlier when coming into town with Dani was tenfold now. It constricted his lungs like a python killing its dinner.

Gritting his teeth, he took a corner too fast and barely missed a car traveling in the opposite direction. The honk of the other driver's horn blared and faded as he pressed his foot back to the gas pedal. Turning north, he sped up the street until he saw Grace's house, and breathed a sigh of relief at the sight of lights on inside. Liam skidded the truck to a stop in front of her garage and swung out of his seat, barely pausing to snatch the keys from the ignition. As soon as he reached it, he started hammering on the front door, not stopping when Ashes began a tirade of deep barks loud enough to feel through the door frame. Soon Grace's pinched face peered out at him through the window beside the door, and he saw her frown before dropping a curtain back in place.

The door opened a few inches, and the old woman's face appeared in the crack. "What do you want?"

"I need to come in, please, Grace. This is important."

The urgency in his voice didn't move her, and she glanced at the soiled knees of his jeans and the sweat stains in his T-shirt. "What happened to you?"

"Please let me in and I'll tell you everything. I need your help."

She wavered a beat and then licked her lips. "I've done all I can. I'm sorry, but I can't associate with you anymore."

Before he could open his mouth to reply, she shut the door, and he heard the dead bolt turn. His eyes flashed back and forth across the door's surface, then he leaned forward and called to her, his voice rebounding back to him. "The Shevlins' first son isn't dead."

Liam waited, sweat running down every inch of his body, the rest of the street silent and still. The door opened again, wider this time.

"What did you say?" Grace asked, her mouth not closing after she spoke.

"I said, the Shevlins' first son isn't dead. He's alive, and he's the one killing people."

Grace's mouth finally closed, and she swallowed, her eyes wide and shining. "Come in," she said, and stepped to the side.

Ashes met him amidst a fury of licks and shoves with his large head. Liam petted his neck, partially to calm the dog and partially to calm himself, as he watched Grace shut and lock the door behind them. When she turned to face him, her features looked harder than he'd ever seen them. Worry lines he hadn't noticed before stood out beneath the glow of the overhead light.

"You listen to me, young man. I went out on a very thin limb for you getting that paperwork. My friend almost didn't give me her keys when I said I couldn't tell her what it was about, and now you show up here covered in filth and spouting off about a ghost?" She straightened and placed her hands on her hips. "Explain yourself."

He nodded. "I went to the Shevlins' tonight to see if I could find anything linking them and Allen together, any other business dealings or a paper trail leading to an exchange of money, but there was nothing except this." He unfolded the two sheets of paper with Karen's test results and handed them to Grace. She took them and shot him a strange look before examining the pages.

"These are just standard tests—bone density, x-rays, blood work," she said.

"What is alkaline phosphatase?"

Grace studied the circled words at the bottom of the page. "It's an enzyme found in all tissues of the body." She squinted and held the paper closer. "Her levels were very high."

"What does that mean?"

She stared at the papers a moment longer and then handed them back to him. "It could mean a lot of things—bone disease, a problem with the bile ducts, liver issues, pregnancy. It's possible she was pregnant with her first son at the time."

Liam shook his head. "The date on the test is January fifth, 1992. Their son was born June eighth, 1993."

"Possibly a miscarriage?" Grace asked.

"Maybe, but there's no record in the files of another pregnancy. Besides, this was stapled to their son's death certificate, the one you included in the envelope, but it was removed and I found it in the bottom of Jerry's file cabinet."

Grace pursed her lips and looked at the pieces of paper in his hand. "Why wouldn't Allen include them in her file?"

"Exactly," Liam said. "I think the bigger question is, why did Jerry hide them?"

"What does this have to do with the murders?"

"I'm not sure yet, but I got a call from Eric tonight and he told me he remembered hearing the murderer yelling something as he ran away to hide. He heard him yelling, 'Momma, look at me.'"

Grace shook her head and shrugged. "But what does that mean?" Her eyes suddenly ran up and down his clothes, as if seeing the dirt and sweat for the first time, before her mouth gaped open and a look of horror crossed her face. "You didn't." It was a whispered plea, a prayer.

Liam stepped forward, holding his palms out to her, and was glad when she didn't retreat. "The casket was empty. There was nothing there."

He watched her try to swallow the information that he gave her, ingesting its implications. After what seemed like an eternity, she looked at the floor, breath heaving in and out.

"You're sure he's still alive?"

Liam nodded. "Yes."

"And what do you need from me?"

"I think the next victim is going to be a city council member. I think the decision to go ahead and vote tomorrow is going to push him to kill again. I need you to call everyone on the council and warn them. Tell them to be extra vigilant—make them understand. I'll call the sheriff and tell him to send someone to patrol around their houses."

She nodded and turned away from him, wobbling a little as she went. Ashes nudged at his thigh again, and Liam stroked his head while he dialed Barnes's number and listened to the ringing, his insides trying to move while he stood still.

"Hello?"

"Barnes, it's Liam."

Silence on the line. "What do you want?"

"I've come across some information, and I think I know who they're going after next."

"Listen, son, I might've made a mistake letting you in on this. I don't think you've fully accepted your brother's death yet."

Liam's hand convulsed and he nearly dropped the phone. "I'm fine, Sheriff, but you have to listen to me. The killers are going to target one of the city council members to stop the vote tomorrow, and I think they're going to do it tonight."

Barnes made a sucking sound. "What makes you so sure?"

"Because it was fucking advertised in this morning's paper. The ones responsible will have seen it by now, and they're waiting for dark to do it, which is . . ." He paused to draw aside the curtains from a nearby window. ". . . in about fifteen minutes."

"Liam, you know my hands are tied as long as the BCA has this. Phelps thinks he's got his man. They're going to transfer Nut up north tomorrow morning."

Liam ran a hand through his sweat-soaked hair. "Just put another couple guys out on patrol tonight. Have them drive past the city council members' homes. It's the least you can do."

The line became very quiet, and he began to wonder if the sheriff wasn't there anymore when the older man spoke. "I'll see what I can do." There was a click, and he was gone.

Liam stared at the phone for a moment. *Better than nothing.* He almost put the phone away, and then pressed Dani's number, seesawing on the edge of the decision. The call went to voice mail, and he wasn't surprised. After her voice told him to leave a message and she'd get back to him, he froze, letting the first few seconds of the recording go by in silence.

"Dani, it's me. I'm sorry about earlier, but you have to see things from my point of view. I did find something out, and I'll tell you about it whenever you can call me back." He hesitated, knowing if he let anything about his whereabouts slip, she might try to come find him. "Stay in your room tonight, please. I'll talk to you soon."

He ended the call and tucked the phone away. In the kitchen, he could hear Grace's voice but the words were indistinct. Ashes laid a wet runner of drool onto the back of his hand with one lick and sat on the floor, his tongue lolling out of his mouth, ears cocked at different angles.

Despite the situation, Liam laughed. "You goofball," he said, ruffling the dog's fur. "Let's take a walk."

Liam set off across the living room and passed through an archway that opened to a back porch. The door leading into the backyard was solidly built and locked tight with a large dead bolt; although, if it were hit with the weapon that he'd seen in Allen and Suzie's garage, it would give. There were no windows in the entry, and when he moved into a small dining room, he saw that the sills of the windows there were a good six feet off the ground. In the next room, he heard the beep of Grace's cordless phone, and a moment later, she came into the room still holding the device in one hand.

"So?" he asked.

"I was able to get ahold of five out of the six other members. I told them that I had reason to believe we were all in danger because of our vote yesterday. They weren't too receptive, but they all said that they'd be careful and keep their phones handy."

"Who weren't you able to reach?"

"The mayor. I called his home and his wife said he was working late at the office, so I tried his direct line and there was no answer."

"Did you call his cell?"

She nodded. "No answer there either."

A wriggling sense of dread began to seep through him, and he looked at the floor for a moment before speaking again. "You said he was having an affair with an intern? The dark-haired woman he was all eyes for yesterday at the meeting?"

"Yes, that's her. Tracey Wilhelm."

"Do you have her number?"

"I could find her home number, I'm sure."

"Do it, call her right now."

Grace walked into the kitchen and returned a few minutes later. "No answer."

"Shit," Liam said, his eyes flitting around the room as if another option would present itself out of the woodwork. He hesitated for only another beat, and then moved past Grace toward the front door, talking as he strode by. "You said he takes her up to his cabin some-times? Where is it?"

Grace followed him, the phone clutched to her chest. "It's on Shallow Drive, up near the Corner Bluffs. If you go north a few blocks, you'll see the road on the right. Follow it for about three miles, and then you'll see a turnoff marked *Bramble Lane*. His cabin is the first driveway on the left."

"Good. Call his cell again—keep calling it." Liam stopped, his hand on the doorknob, and looked back at her. "Do you have a gun?"

She didn't hesitate. "Yes, a shotgun for sporting clays."

"Perfect. Load it and go upstairs with Ashes. Keep the phone close and stay awake as long as you can. If you hear anything down-stairs, call 911 and blow a hole through anyone who comes to your room." He fixed her with a steady gaze. "I don't think you need to worry, though, because they're going to try to kill the mayor tonight."

Without looking back, he swung out the door and raced toward his truck through the deepening dark of the night.

# CHAPTER 22

"What the fuck does she want?" Harley scowled at his phone and flicked the off button, ending the trilling jangle of the ringtone.

"Who was it?"

Harley glanced at Tracey in the passenger seat of the truck. "That old hippie bitch, Grace, that's on the council. God, she's a pain in my ass. The only one that voted against us going forward with tomorrow's decision!"

"Ugh, she's so earthy," Tracey said, making a face. "I bet she doesn't even shave her armpits."

Harley laughed and turned onto Shallow Drive, his heart pumping harder as Tracey placed a hand on his upper thigh. "But I shaved for you," she said, her hand gliding up near his crotch and back down.

He groaned. "You don't know what you do to me."

"Should I tell you what I'm going to do to you?"

"Mmm, go ahead."

"I'm going to take everything off but this when we get there," she said, fingering the solitaire diamond pendant at her throat. She held it up, and he saw it glint in the dim light of the dashboard. "God, Harley, it's so beautiful."

He smiled. Distracted by a bauble. She was great in bed, but oh so dumb sometimes. "You deserve something as pretty as you are."

She grinned and slid closer to him as he rounded a bend in the gravel road. "How much did it cost?"

He knew this part turned her on the most, knowing how much cash he'd dropped on her. Some sort of value issues in her past, he supposed, but he wasn't going to question it. "It was four grand." He heard her excited intake of breath.

"How did you afford that? I mean, I know you make a lot of money, but how did you sneak it past your wife?"

He smiled again. "You can keep a secret, right?"

"Would I be here now if I couldn't?"

"Good point. You know that big shot from Colton that got his head bashed in?"

"Yeah."

"Let's just say he made sure the vote was going to go his way." He felt her hand trace the same path up his thigh and then grasp him through his slacks. The truck swerved and then came back to center.

"You bad, bad boy," she said in his ear. Her head turned for a moment toward the bed of the truck. "Is that camping gear in the back?"

He sighed, feeling her hand draw away from the place he wanted it the most. "Yeah, my oldest boy borrowed the truck yesterday to go camping with some buddies, and he didn't take it out when he got back. He had to use our tent since no one else had one that could hold five teenage boys."

"Oh, I thought I saw it move back there. The tent isn't going to blow out, is it?"

Harley glanced in the rearview mirror, but all he could see was the general bulk of the flaccid canvas in the pale scarlet glow of the running lights. "No, it's fine. There's some stuff piled on it to keep it down."

Harley guided the truck to the right, onto the side road, the Bramble Lane sign barely visible in this year's growth of forest, which seemed to encroach the little drive more every season. His body thrummed with excitement at the thought of a few hours alone with Tracey at the cabin. He barely noted the tendrils of fog lacing the edges of the woods where the truck's headlights scraped the darkness away. As he turned into the driveway of the cabin, he reached over, grasping Tracey's thigh and trying to run his fingers beneath the skirt she wore. With a mocking offended sound, she slapped his hand away.

"Not so fast, big boy. Gotta wait till we get inside."

"Oh, I can't wait to get inside," he growled.

"Just wait until you see what I'm wearing," she said as he coasted to a stop before the modest cabin in a little clearing ringed with fog. He growled again and made a grab at her, but she pulled away, giggling as she opened her door.

Harley flipped the ignition off and jumped out of the truck like a schoolboy released for summer vacation. The headlights stayed on for a few seconds and then winked out, leaving the afterimage of the porch stairs and the cabin beyond burned into his retinas. He heard the opposite door slam and, strangely, the rustling of the canvas in the rear of the truck. Maybe she wanted to do it out under the night sky. The idea thrilled him, but as he rounded the front of the truck, he heard Tracey make a short squeal of pain. *Shit.* Had she turned her ankle in the ruts beside the driveway? He'd been meaning to have them filled in. If those ruts cost him his night with her, he'd have to take double his blood-pressure medication when he got home, not to mention some aspirin to dull the ache in his balls that grew by the second.

As Harley came around the truck's fender, he saw Tracey standing stock-still, an outline beside her door. Hearing a pattering of liquid, he glanced down and saw a pool expanding near her feet.

"What'd you spill?"

A small breeze nudged the trees in the yard and brought a scent to his face: the thick tang of copper. "Wha—"

A shadow rose behind Tracey as she jerked a little and more blood pattered to the ground around her high heels. Harley stared at the thing behind her, thinking it was the tent being raised by the breeze. To reinforce his thoughts, he heard a sound like opening a car window while on the highway.

Tracey's head exploded in a spatter of bone and brain.

Something cut through the top of her skull, cleaving it in two as it sheared down to her neck, stopping just above the shining glint of the diamond there. Harley screamed, but not before he heard some of Tracey's teeth tinkle off the side of the truck. The pitch of his yell was so high, for a second he thought it was from the loons that sometimes swam in the backwaters of the river, their cries like knives to the eardrums. Tracey fell forward and slid off the massive blade still hanging in the air, suspended by the humped shadow in the bed of his truck. Harley made a choking sound, and pain flared beneath his left armpit. The dreaded heart attack that he always imagined stalked him just one cheeseburger out of sight was finally here, and he prayed for it.

He stumbled back, finding the ruts beside the driveway with his own feet. He fell in a heavy pile, his bones remembering instantly the feeling of impact from his high school football days, and he brought his head up and saw the shadow crawl from the bed of the truck. Harley flipped onto his stomach, wheezing out a strangled gasp as he struggled to his feet, the rough rocks near the driveway shredding the skin on his palms. He had to make it to the house, had to get inside, had to call for help. Gravel crunched near the truck as he made it to his feet, angled low like a sprinter coming off the blocks. Before he could launch himself forward, he heard the same howl of air parting behind him.

It felt like being hit by a baseball bat across the ass. There was a split second of numbness and then a searing pain that stretched from one side of his hips to the other. Harley tried to run and found that his legs wouldn't respond. Instead, he tumbled forward, his hands and face colliding with the bottom step of the porch. A hot, running sensation cascaded down the backs of his legs as he reached a shaking hand to his ass, feeling the raw edges of a gaping gash there, like a giant mouth spilling blood freely over his fingers.

"Oh God, please," Harley said, rolling onto his back while trying to inch up the porch steps, his legs nothing more than limp pieces of meat below him. The thing before him stepped closer, and he began to see details in the sparse light.

"Please, no, please, I'll give you anything!" His voice shook and broke as he held up a bloody hand toward the humped figure. "I've got a wife and kids, please!"

It didn't pause at his pleadings. Harley watched the long, heavy weapon spin in the monster's hands, so that it was held like an enormous dagger, the notched tip rising smoothly like the sun he knew he would never see again. Just before the blade came rushing down, a blinding light flashed in his eyes, and he thanked God for taking him away before the thing could hurt him any more.

# CHAPTER 23

Liam swung the truck around a corner and had to brake to miss a deer crossing from the sanctuary of the tree line on the left.

He heard sand spit against the undercarriage as his tires found purchase on the loose dirt near the edge of the road. Looking back down into his hand, he redialed the sheriff's number. The phone rang and rang.

"Come on, come on," he said. A beep sounded in his ear. "Barnes, they're going after the mayor. I'm on my way to his cabin now. I'm guessing you know where it is." He hung up and threw the phone onto the console while focusing on the road.

The sky behind the trees was bruised purple; the leaves and branches stretched and waved their black shapes in contrast. Fog hovered at the edges of the road like milky springs waiting to overflow the ditches, some of it reaching so high he nearly missed the turnoff for Bramble Lane. The back end of the Chevy shuddered as it fishtailed and finally straightened out. Liam tensed his body, seeing the first driveway coming up on the left. With one hand he steered, and with the other he reached back and drew the Sig from its holster. As he turned into the cabin's driveway, he debated whether or not to enter with stealth. He pushed down on the gas, knowing that reaching the mayor was more important than being covert. The truck came over a slight hill, and when the headlights lit up the scene in the yard, Liam's breath caught in his throat.

A woman's collapsed body was beside the mayor's three-quarter-ton diesel pickup, and even in the millisecond that he was able to observe her, Liam saw the damage inflicted to her skull. Ahead of the truck, the mayor lay on his back, partially up a set of blood-drenched steps, his hand raised above him to a humped figure dressed in tattered clothing.

The killer stood with his back to the drive, the curved hunch of his spine pressed against the thin cloth he wore. His head was oblong, just as Liam remembered it from the brief glimpse in the garage. Two knurled arms extended from the malformed body and held what looked like a four-foot chunk of rusted steel shaped like a pointed saw blade. The killer held the weapon above the supine mayor, and as Liam watched, brought it down in a violent, plunging motion.

"Fuck!" Liam yelled as he saw the makeshift sword punch through the mayor's face and pin his head to the step behind. Gore splashed upward in a fountain that caught the Chevy's headlights in a strangely beautiful wash of reds and blacks before splattering down onto the mayor's twitching corpse.

"Dammit!" Liam flattened the gas pedal to the floor, rocketing his truck down the short slope and into the back of the mayor's truck.

The hood crumpled with the impact, and everything that wasn't bolted down in the cab became airborne. Liam jerked forward and saw glass explode in showers of crystal-like pieces. His air bag deployed, but before it blew him backward into the seat, he saw the mayor's truck slide ahead, pushed by the Chevy's momentum, and bash into the humped figure near the stairs.

Liam's ears rang, and he tasted a chemical dust. He shook his head once, opened his eyes, and registered that he still clutched the Sig in one hand. He coughed and fired a round into the air bag. The bag popped with a sound almost equal to the gunshot and deflated, leaving him more room to paw at the door handle until he was able to pry it open and sprawl to the ground. Bright shards of light danced in his eyes, and he wondered if he'd managed to concuss himself with the improvised maneuver. The spangles of light merged and then faded as he stood and aimed the handgun toward the last place he had seen the killer. *Peter,* he told himself, *his name is Peter.*

"Peter! It's over—drop your weapon and put your hands up!" He heard his voice bounce back off the surrounding trees and the front of the cabin, and tried to listen for movement. His vision adjusted more, and he began to make distinctions between the fuzzy objects around him.

The grill of the mayor's truck rested against the mayor, the shining bumper barely grazing the man's bloodied belly. Liam knelt and scanned the underside of both trucks, and then leapt onto the stairs, leveling the gun on the far side of the vehicles. The yard was empty and silent save for the gentle breeze that swirled blankets of fog across the manicured grass.

A scraping thump made him spin around toward the cabin itself. The front door looked intact, and the windows to either side were unbroken. The sound came again, and he realized that it was farther away, around the side of the structure. Liam inched forward and saw that the porch wrapped around the left side of the house. Heat lightning arced in the clouds above, giving a surreal quality to the air, the gaps between the planks he walked on standing out in lines of black against the rest of the wood. He listened, pausing at the corner of the cabin to peek one eye into the open. The porch stood empty.

Liam moved smoothly around the corner, amazed at how the muscle memory of his old job remained within him. He glanced at the ground, which quickly fell away beside the cabin, toward the bluffs thirty yards past the end of the wraparound porch. Yawning darkness waited beyond the bluffs, which could have been the edge of the universe for how much he could see. After another few tentative steps, he reached the next corner and stopped, leaning again around the side of the house to clear the porch. A set of patio furniture rested beside a hulking gas grill. A sliding glass door that led inside was whole, and a bundle of tiki torches leaned against the far railing.

He waited, watching the fog roll in like a quiet tide across the lawn, smelling the air, and listening for even the slightest rustle of a leaf. Nothing moved. An all-encompassing fear began to drape over his shoulders, and his skin slid upon itself, urging him to run. Something wasn't right. Gripping the Sig in both hands, he took one step farther toward the railing, aiming the muzzle down at the spot his instincts told him to look.

The blade shot up between a gap in the wood, cutting a chunk from his shoe and barely missing his stomach.

Liam cried out and fell back onto his ass with a grunt. Pain broiled at the tip of his foot, and he saw a dark stain spread on the planks around it. Leaping to his feet, he fired shots through the floor in bursts, blasting first at where the sword disappeared. He walked in a straight line until he heard and felt a thump beneath the porch.

A hobbling form erupted from the far end of the decking and raced toward the trees. Liam stepped to the railing and squeezed off two more shots. At the second report, he saw Peter flinch and swipe at his left arm before disappearing into the dense woods. Liam spared only a moment to wiggle his toes and make sure they were still attached before hurdling over the railing and onto the dewy grass.

He landed, registering a grenade of pain in his foot before he rolled and then stood again, aiming the Sig at the still forest. Breathing through his mouth, he tried to listen. The sound of branches breaking filtered to him and he began to run. The cooler air of the woods caressed him and almost brought a shiver as it chilled the sweat on his skin. He forced himself to breathe through his nose as he moved, trying to bring his jackhammering heart back into a normal rhythm. Keeping the jagged bluffs close to his right, he pivoted back and forth, combing the dense woods for the hunched shape of his quarry. Leaves brushed against his shirt, and every so often he had to stoop or slide beneath a hanging deadfall.

After almost a minute, the woods opened up and the trees grew farther apart. To his left, Liam spotted a low shape and nearly drew a bead on it before he saw it was only a picnic table. A few campfire pits dotted the ground, and he realized he was now in some sort of campground. He searched the area and stalked ahead, his eyes flitting in every direction. Thick pools of fog filled the dips in the ground and gave an ethereal quality to the landscape. Heat lightning continued to flicker and slash at the sky, giving momentary flashes of clarity.

Liam stopped and turned in a circle, his heart finally slowing enough so that it didn't throb in his vision with each beat. The area was relatively open. Where could Peter have gone? He walked forward, his foot catching on a lip of tar he hadn't noticed until then. A paved path ran from his left and curved along the banks of the bluffs, lined with a wooden fence at waist level. Several more picnic tables stood like sentries near the fence line, their shadows not large enough to conceal a man. He turned again and spotted a massive oak tree growing beside the walking path fifty yards ahead. It was the only place to hide in the vicinity. Liam moved toward it, the Sig outstretched in one hand. As he neared the oak, he heard a soft crackle of bark from the other side. He paused, the gun feeling too large and uncomfortable in his hand.

"Peter, I know you're there. Come out and drop your weapon."

Silence.

Liam moved forward at a half run, his finger tightening on the trigger, preparing for the inevitable recoil. A bank of fog swirled to his right as he rounded the tree—

—and saw that there was nothing there. Confusion became a thousand spiders crawling within his guts as he heard a rustle behind him and tried to spin in its direction.

Peter rose from the ground and stood through the fog that had hidden him, swinging the rusted steel as he moved. Liam felt the blade connect with his gun, and he fired a round that went wild past Peter's shoulder. The massive weapon cut through the air again, and Liam stepped back, firing a second time as the tip of the blade tugged a hole open in his T-shirt. The shot tore bark from the oak's trunk beside Peter's misshapen head, and the other man grunted and swiped at his eyes. Liam aimed the Sig once more, and gaped in horror as the slide locked open, revealing an empty chamber.

Liam fumbled for the spare magazine in his back pocket as Peter closed in, his bulging and twisted arms raising the blade high in the air. Liam felt the flat pockets at the back of his jeans, his throat constricting. He must have lost the magazine near the trucks or jumping over the railing. He backpedaled faster and resisted the urge to hurl the handgun at Peter's face.

Peter advanced, a wheezing coming from his open mouth, his body jerking with a slight limp that made him wobble to one side. Blood dribbled down his left arm where Liam's earlier shot had grazed the flesh.

Liam felt his heels catch on something, and he nearly fell, regaining his balance as he stepped over an open fire pit. Looking around the campsite, he saw nothing he could use as a weapon, and Peter's bulk cut off his escape route back to the mayor's cabin. Peter walked around the edge of the fire pit, raising the weapon to shoulder level, like a baseball player preparing for a home run. Liam lunged forward and kicked the heavy metal cooking grate mounted to the side of the fire pit, and watched as it rotated directly into Peter's shins.

The steel struck his legs with a solid *thunk*, and Peter made a deep, mewling sound of pain as he staggered to the side. Liam took the opportunity and spun away, running as fast as his injured foot would allow him down the walking path. Fog parted around him as he sprinted through it, and he heard uneven footsteps behind him, knowing that Peter was only a few strides away.

The path narrowed, and the tar looped back in a tight curve—the end of the line. Liam saw the wooden fence turn at a ninety-degree angle and shoot off into the woods on his left, but there was a small gap just large enough for a person to walk through. He ran toward it, his ankles trying to turn on the rough ground beneath his feet. Chancing a look over his shoulder, he saw Peter lumbering after him, the serration of his sword like shark's teeth. The fence flew past, and a well-worn hiking trail continued in the shape of a snake's body. Twice he nearly ran straight into a tree or a bramble of bushes, as the path twisted and turned. Peter let out an angry bellow behind him, and he poured on the speed, fueled by how close the killer sounded.

Liam rounded another curve and sensed the trees and brush opening up on both sides. His feet landed on smooth rock, and he pelted on, watching for what he knew must be there. After a dozen more steps, he saw it: a vast void of darkness sheeted with fog. All rational thought told him to stop, not to take another step, but he ran on, his eyes searching the ground, his arms pumping at his sides.

Then it was there, the edge of the bluff, and he flung himself into the yawning darkness, fog ripping past him as he fell. Air howled in his ears, or maybe it was Peter on the cliff's edge, he couldn't be sure. The fall lasted forever and less than a second. He had only a moment to wonder whether his feet would touch water or stone. If he was wrong, he would know instantaneously with the crushing pain of broken legs and a shattered spine before his skull cracked open on the solid rock.

Water swallowed him and slapped against his chest and face, knocking the wind from his lungs in a flurry of bubbles as he sunk deep into the river. The darkness was complete around him as he struggled, the Sig still held in one hand. Some of the bitter liquid flooded his open mouth, and he shut it, kicking toward the promise of air, although he might have been swimming toward the swirling muck of the riverbed instead for how dark it was. The water roared in his ears, and his lungs urged him to breathe, even if it was water, just breathe it in, he had to. As he opened his mouth to comply with the overwhelming need, his head burst into balmy air. Liam coughed, spluttering out water and heaving in oxygen. He'd never tasted anything so sweet in his life.

Feeling the pull of the current, he stroked in the direction he thought was the correct shore, and confirmed it with the flash of heat lightning. He looked up, seeking out the bluff from which he'd plummeted, and in the wash of flashing light, he saw Peter silhouetted there, looking down from the sixty-odd feet that separated them.

Without another glance, Liam swam as hard as he could toward the shore, and sent a prayer of thanks skyward when he felt his shoes touch bottom. After tucking the Sig into its sodden holster, he began to make his way up the rocky shore, toward the sullen glow of Tallston.

# CHAPTER 24

Liam's breath came in ragged gasps by the time he crawled over the rock wall beside his hotel.

His clothes hung from him as though two sizes too big, and he felt a raw blister ready to burst on the bottom of his injured foot. The lighted windows in the hotel looked heavenly, and he jogged toward the front door, relishing the feeling of relative safety.

One thing gnawed at his thoughts, and had since his leap from the cliff: where had the other person been? Peter obviously had an accomplice, but he was alone tonight. Liam threw a glance over his shoulder before pulling the front door open.

If the clerk at the desk thought anything of his bedraggled and still-sopping clothes, he kept it to himself. After entering his room, Liam stripped and re-dressed in dry clothes, the feeling of the soft fabric delicious on his skin. Examining the wound on his foot, he saw that Peter's blade had taken a chunk the size of a dime from between his big and second toes. The hole still seeped blood but didn't look too serious. After he pushed a ball of gauze between his toes, he shoved his injured foot into a sock. He then disassembled the Sig in a few practiced motions and began to dry each part individually. When he felt satisfied, he reassembled the gun, racked the slide a few times, dry-fired it, and then shook it once more to make sure no moisture remained inside.

Slamming his final mag into the butt of the Sig, Liam reached for the phone near his bed but stopped, his hand hanging in midair. His intentions were to call the sheriff, but what if Barnes had taken him seriously and sent a cruiser up to the mayor's cabin? The officer would find his truck smashed near the front door, two dead bodies, and shell casings strewn everywhere. Switching gears, he called Dani instead. Her phone rang several times before going to voice mail. Liam hung up and stared at the wall for almost a minute. If the authorities were already at the crime scene, they'd probably go to Dani's hotel right after they paid his a visit.

Pulling on his still-soaking shoes, he stood from the bed and tucked the Sig into the holster at his back. He needed to get to Dani, tell her what happened, and then figure out their next move. Even Phelps couldn't deny his story now, with two more bodies piled up. It would be an arduous process, but necessary. Nut would be exonerated and Liam would have to endure a rigorous investigation.

Liam left the hotel and jogged onto a back street that ran parallel to the main drag. Despite the ache in his foot, he covered the mile to Dani's hotel in a little less than ten minutes, keeping his eyes peeled for police cars the entire time. Very little traffic graced the roads, and as soon as he turned into the hotel parking lot, he almost sighed with relief upon seeing Dani's Toyota Corolla parked on one side of the building. As he began scanning the rest of the lot for patrol cars, something stopped his search and brought his eyes back to Dani's car.

Her driver's-side door stood partially open.

A frantic plea for his instincts to be wrong echoed inside his head as he made his way toward her car. She just left the door open accidentally, or maybe she ran back inside to grab something. When he got closer, his heart tried to seize. Several dark spots stained the pavement near the driver's side. With the plea still ringing in his head, he pulled the door all the way open.

Drops of blood coated the seat's upholstery, soaked in like old coffee spills. Half a bloody handprint smeared the tan steering wheel with scarlet, and when he reached out to touch it, it came away tacky. Not dry yet. She couldn't have been gone for more than half an hour.

Liam stepped back, careful not to tread in any of the dollops of blood on the ground, and leaned against the car next to Dani's. Now he knew why Peter had been alone at the mayor's cabin. Tears threatened at the corners of his eyes, but he willed them away, replacing the panic in his chest with white-hot anger. She'd better be alive, or no one would walk away from this.

Liam moved away from the car and was about to get out from beneath the overhead light of the parking lot when he spotted something on the ground. Bending down, he saw that it was Dani's cell phone. When he turned it on, he immediately closed his eyes—his earlier call along with his number ready to be dialed on the screen seared all else from his mind.

Swallowing the sickness in the back of his throat, he turned toward the way he'd come and began to run as fast as his foot would allow. There was only one place she could be now, and he hoped he wasn't too late.

# CHAPTER 25

The boat's motor started on the first try.

Keeping the noise at a minimum, Liam tossed away the ropes fastening the boat to the bait store's dock and pushed away from the planking. After angling the craft into the black current of the river, he dug into his pocket for Dani's cell phone and tapped in Barnes's number. The sheriff answered in a hushed voice on the first ring.

"Hello?"

"Barnes, it's me."

"Boy, what the fuck?"

"I'm assuming you're at the mayor's?"

"You assume fucking right." He heard the sheriff curse again and the rustle of clothing. "Where the hell are you?"

"I'm going to the foundry."

"Boy, you're past the point of trouble. This place is a bloodbath, and Phelps is on his way. Once he gets here, all hell is going to break loose, you copy?"

"It's already broken loose, Sheriff." He stopped, steadying himself. "They took Dani."

Silence from Barnes's end. Then, "Suzie's cousin?"

"Yes. I think they took her to the foundry. I'm going there now, and I need backup."

"You got a lot of nerve, son. How am I supposed to believe you with all your shit lying around the bodies here?"

"Oh, use your fucking eyes, Barnes!" Liam half yelled. "Does it look like the mayor and his girlfriend were killed by gunfire?" When he received no reply, he continued. "Look, I have to find her. They took her because they knew she was working with me on this, and they knew I'd come for her. They're trying to end this, Barnes."

The sheriff wheezed. "I don't know what I can do, Liam. Phelps is going to have a shit fit when he gets here, since this is blowing his little closed case wide open again."

Liam steered the boat past the park on his left, where Haines's body had been found. "You know how little I care about how angry Phelps is going to be? I need help, Barnes. Your town needs help. Stand up and do something. Retirement or not, you have an obligation to do what's right." Liam's anger boiled over, and he hit the end button.

His eyes found the darker smudge on the southern shore that was the foundry and piloted the boat toward it, wishing the motor made less noise. Although, it didn't matter; he knew he was expected. Liam swung the boat in on the far side of the decaying pier, which jutted like a mangled tongue into the water. When the boat was a few yards from the shore, he cut the motor and let the momentum carry him onto the soft soil of the bank. After climbing out, he pulled the nose of the craft farther inland and then faced the towering form of the building, its shadow an insurmountable wall in the night. He drew the Sig, making sure the safety was off before beginning to walk. A few strides in, he noticed a crushed area in the long river grass to his left, and when he moved closer, he saw that a small boat lay there, its aluminum belly toward the sky and two oars on the ground beside it. Turning toward the foundry again, he continued on.

The grass rasped against his jeans, whispers of warning that he couldn't heed. Fog hovered in patches of gossamer, with veins extending into the woods surrounding the structure. Liam swung the Sig to the left and right, knowing Peter and his accomplice could be anywhere. The foundry loomed closer, and as he neared the front façade, he veered left and traced the wall as closely as he could, his eyes searching the darkness of the woods on the other side. Soon he came to the large bushes growing from the base of the building's foundation, their viny tendrils snaking into and through the cracked wall. With a blind effort, he pushed into them, letting his right shoulder rub the wall as he moved. After a minute, his outstretched hand touched what he knew must be there—a door.

The steel door was of regular height and width, built out of heavy iron and sitting on a sliding mechanism no doubt hampered by the countless seasons that had attempted to rust the entrance shut. He knew if he tried to move it, the same screech would issue from its track that he and Dani had heard on their first visit. Now the door stood open, a rectangle of utter dark unlike anything he'd encountered before. It waited to swallow him, abysmal, beckoning. Liam paused at the threshold, listening for the soft inhalation of breath but hearing nothing save the clicking of leaves against one another in the nearby trees. Re-gripping the pistol, he stooped low and walked forward, turning left as soon as he entered the building. Something hard struck his shoulder as he sidled into the massive space, and he grunted with the pain that shot down his arm. With one hand, he reached out and felt a flat surface and a cold steel tube that sat at the end of what could only be a worktable.

While he waited for his eyes to adjust to the thick darkness of the foundry, every regret he'd ever had came rushing back in a torrent of sorrow. His brother's face played across his mind, followed by Suzie's. Then it was Abford in the alley, the gun barrel pointing his way, its muzzle looking like a culvert it was so large. Then Kelly, her face obscured by the hair she'd just had cut, unaware that her and her son's lives were seconds from over.

Liam forced his eyes shut, the swimming darkness becoming rolling fountains of color with the pressure. He would not fail again; he would not let her die here alone. When he opened his eyes, he could make out more features of the room he stood in. Innumerable support beams slanted toward the lofted ceiling, which had a long row of skylights. The room itself spanned the entire building, ending in the older portion of the original structure fifty yards to his left, the chipped concrete floor marred by remnants of the work that toiled here half a century ago. Several unnamed pieces of machinery stood a few paces apart near the opposite wall, their purpose shrouded in obscurity by both the lack of light and his ignorance of the jobs that had taken place here. A line of girders close to the sidewalls supported what appeared to be a catwalk with banks of stairs leading up and down at either end of the massive space. Everywhere on the floor were the shapes of I-beams, some only inches long, while others stretched fifty feet or more.

Liam glared into the dark and watched for movement. The soft tick of metal expanding or contracting was the only sound, mocking his vigilance with its shifting resonance. Heat lightning spiderwebbed across the sky directly over the foundry and bathed the interior in a strange red illumination that allowed him to scan his surroundings again. He seemed to be alone.

Liam moved forward, skirting the long worktable, which was coated in dust and grime. A few forgotten hand tools lay on the floor, and he stepped over and between them. The vast space around him stunk of old grease and burned steel, the ozone muted but still there. The place had the feel of a sepulcher, quiet with the waiting of secrets. As he neared a set of stairs leading to the catwalk above him, he stopped, his eardrums straining for a new sound somewhere ahead. It came again, and there was no mistaking it this time.

Crying.

Dani was somewhere ahead, her soft sobs barely audible through the doorway leading into the old part of the structure. She was still alive. A massive chunk of fear fell away and dissolved at the knowledge that he would not find her mangled body amongst the wreckage of this place. Moving even more carefully, he slid up against the old building's rough brick and peered through the doorless opening.

A few candles burned inside on various surfaces, their light paltry but better than the darkness he stood in now. The next room was large but not near the size of the newer section. A conglomeration of broken chairs and piled canvas bags sat everywhere. A few long tables stood in the center of the space, their tops devoid of anything but dust.

Swinging into the room in a low stance, Liam scuttled to the nearest table and knelt beside it, covering his left and then his right with the gun. Nothing moved besides the slow waving of the candle flames. Dani whimpered and sniffed somewhere ahead. He ran fast across the room, leaping over a pile of I-beams and sliding to a stop near a small archway. With his back to the wall, he glanced around, watching the faint outline of the doorway for the darkening of a shadow.

A few cables as thick as his middle finger snaked in tangled lines near his feet and disappeared in a cloak of filth on the floor. In the corner nearest to him, he made out a large pile of canvas arranged like some sort of nest, its center depressed and filled with heaps of blankets. A nearby shelf held several stacks of canned goods along with what looked like large bottles of water. A smell of unwashed flesh and soiled laundry emanated from the corner. The sight disturbed him, mostly because the area looked lived in. Shuffling closer to the archway, he peeked inside the next room.

It was much smaller than the space he stood in now, an antechamber of sorts. It was square and lacked features, measuring fifteen feet across at the most. Candles littered the floor, their meager light illuminating the far wall, where Dani sat with her hands and feet bound together.

Hope surged in his chest, but he resisted the impulse to run to her. This was a trap, but what choice did he have? He leaned farther into the doorway, waiting for the sound of movement or a glimpse of clothing shifting against the backdrop of darkness. Other than Dani, the room looked to be empty. He stood and pivoted inside, the Sig straight out in front of him. His feet made a hollow sound on the floor as he entered, and Dani looked up, her face a mask of fear and matted with blood. When her eyes found him, a look of sheer relief flooded her features, and it nearly broke his heart.

"You found me," she whispered as he hurried forward and hit his knees beside her. With one arm, he hugged her awkwardly, kissing her bloodied temple.

"Of course I did." Liam stood just enough to pull out the straight razor, then crouched again, opening the blade. The bindings at her hands and feet were coils of oily rope. As delicately as he could, he began to slice the strands away from her wrists.

"Do you know where they are?"

Dani shook her head. "Just one attacked me in the parking lot. I think I cut his face, but he hit me with something and I blacked out."

The rope popped free and fell away from her wrists, and he was about to start working on the one locking her ankles together when he heard movement behind him. Liam spun, thrusting the Sig out as he did. Shuffling steps came closer through the darkness, and a shape emerged.

"Stop right there," Liam said, holding the bead steady on the person who stood in the doorway. The figure was small, shorter and much narrower than Peter. "Don't move," Liam said, his voice sounding dead in the enclosed space.

"I'm unarmed, Mr. Dempsey."

211

The voice sent a runner of shock through him, partly because of the grating rasp it contained, but mostly because it was female.

"Who are you?" Liam asked, squinting.

The figure stepped closer, the dancing candlelight revealing two pale hands poking from the arms of a dirty hooded sweatshirt, the cowl pulled forward, shrouding her face from the glow.

"My name is June Harlow."

"What are you doing here?"

"Oh, I escorted Dani across the river. I have to say, young lady, that you are quite the scrapper. You left me with a nasty cut that will forever hinder my good looks." June's white hands drew back the hood, and her face came into view.

Dani gasped.

June's face was lined like that of a woman in her late forties, with crow's-feet extending out from the corners of her eyes. Her dark hair was pulled back in a tight ponytail, and her nose was sharp and prominent, but below that her features became twisted and malformed, as if roughly hewn from a piece of wood. Her jaw sat at an angle, the right side drawn up in a rictus of bulging joints and sinew. Her cheek looked swollen and prodded from within, as if a bag of crushed glass sat inside her mouth. Her chin was wide and sloping, and several teeth stuck crookedly from her smiling lips. A long but shallow gash ran from her left temple down to her throat, and blood still seeped from it.

June cackled, and in the small room it was cold, cruel laughter that raised the hairs on the back of Liam's neck. He responded by pointing the Sig at the woman's deformed face.

"You're going to back up, and then we're all going to walk out of here, nice and easy, okay?"

June chuckled. "Mr. Dempsey, you're just as arrogant as your brother was."

The mention of Allen made him halt as he began to stand. He

kept the muzzle pointed in her direction but lowered it a few inches. "You killed him, didn't you? You and Peter Shevlin."

June sobered, her eyes like two points of flame in the dark. "Oh yes, he died at Peter's hand, as did his wife." She sniffed, her warped mouth tightening. "His wife wasn't supposed to die, but she got in the way. Payment for his sins, I would say."

"Why?" Liam jerked his head around, surprised by Dani's question. "Why would you do this?"

June stepped closer, stopping only when Liam raised the Sig again. "To undo the wrongs of the past, dearie. The sins of the ones across the river run deep, but now they're being cleansed. One by one they fall by a righteous hand."

"This isn't righteous, it's murder," Liam said, finally standing.

"Murder?" June nearly shouted. "You know nothing of murder, Liam." A smile crept onto her face. "But your brother knew it well."

He licked his lips, watching June's hands to make sure she didn't go for a hidden weapon. "What are you talking about? My brother was a doctor, he saved lives."

"He carved a fortune out of the flesh of the weak and helpless!" June roared. "He was the enabler of what's happened."

A semblance of calm spread across her distorted face, and she studied Liam in the flickering light. "You and I aren't that different, Liam. You didn't know the darkness that lived within Allen, but I always suspected my sister had murder in her heart."

"Your sister?" he heard himself say, the answer already forming in his mind before June spoke.

"Karen Shevlin."

Liam heard Dani's surprised intake of breath and glanced at her, then returned his gaze to June. "You killed your own sister?"

"You would have too if you knew what I knew, what I saw. She deserved to die, right alongside that despicable husband of hers."

"What are you talking about?" Liam asked, his disbelief turning to confusion.

June moved to the brick wall and ran her fingers in the mortared grooves. "My father helped lay these bricks," she said, her face slightly turned away. "This was his first job after my family moved here almost fifty years ago. They added this room as a coal-storage chamber when they switched the furnaces from wood to coal. He and my mother had no place to stay, and the owner of the foundry took pity on them."

"Jerry Shevlin's father," Liam said.

June nodded. "Yes. He was a good man." Her face hardened. "Nothing like his bastard son. He let my father build a small house not far from here, let him work off his rent." She turned to face them again. "In fact, you've seen it out in the woods, the day you trespassed here. My father and mother were happy to live away from people, as they'd been ostracized most of their lives."

"Why?" Liam asked, his eyes flicking toward the empty doorway.

June touched the protruding contours of her face. "My mother had a disease of the bones. Paget's disease, it's called. It was mostly confined to her shoulder and back, but she walked with a limp and had a hump that people found . . . unsightly. My father fell in love with her despite her disfigurement."

June looked away for a moment before continuing. "He was a special man in many ways. He protected us from the prying, judging eyes of the world. He asked Jerry Shevlin's father to keep our existence quiet, so rumors wouldn't start about the *freaks* living across the river. He even went so far as to have our groceries delivered to the docks on the opposite side, so no one would even see him in town." June's eyes became wistful in the low light. "I remember how he used to sing to Karen and me at night in that little house, his voice so soft and low. It was home, a good one filled with love. But my sister wanted more."

June spat on the ground, as if to curse the memory, then looked up at them in the low light, hatred etched into every line of her face. "Karen had no disfigurements, and I heard my mother and father speaking at night when they thought we were asleep. They said that she might not even have the disease at all. Karen was beautiful and she knew it. By the age of twelve she was flaunting it in my face whenever our parents weren't around. She loved the fact that I was like this and she wasn't—she reveled in it."

"How did she come to live across the river without the rest of you?" Liam asked.

June snorted. "She ran away when she was sixteen. It broke my parents' hearts. The things she said to them before she left, the horrible things she called our mother. Karen was disfigured in the soul rather than in the flesh.

"I started to follow her shortly after she left. She found a boarding house and charmed the owner's wife into letting her stay for free, claiming she'd been abandoned by her family. She was intelligent and charismatic. It wasn't long after that she met the only son of the richest family in town."

"Jerry Shevlin," Liam said, enthralled by the story despite himself.

"Yes. By the time they met, our mother had fallen ill, and my father worked himself ragged trying to care for her and hold down his job. Then the foundry shut down, and we had nothing. If my father had been a lesser man, he would've gone to the elder Shevlin and tried to gain favor with him since Karen was courting his son, but he had a stout honor that wouldn't let him. Secretly I think he hoped that Karen would come back to us." June closed her eyes and swayed like the candle flames that illuminated her. "My mother died soon after, and my father gave up. He fell into a deep depression, quit eating, quit moving, and slipped away. I was alone."

"How old were you?" Dani asked.

June shifted her gaze to Dani. "I was twenty. Karen was two years younger. She married Shevlin shortly after that, and I observed from the shadows, always there a few steps behind her, watching her perfect life unfold. I learned stealth from my father. Whether stalking a deer or watching people, I was always there but unseen. Truth be told, I was jealous. As much as I hated her, she had everything that I wanted: a rich and handsome husband, a big house, a new car. But I knew what would be coming down the line even before she did, although she figured it out soon enough. And that's when your brother entered the scene."

Liam let the gun sink to his side, though he kept a firm grip on it. "The blood tests."

June nodded. "Yes, there were many trips to your brother's clinic before they became pregnant. I knew what they were doing, making sure that they wouldn't have a deformed child—that would put a damper on their perfect life. I watched and waited, always just outside the line of sight. Although, when you travel in the circles that I do, most overlook you."

"What circle is that?" Liam said.

"The society of the homeless. People don't really see beggars and drunks, they see trash—if they notice at all." June smiled at him. "Even you don't recall the times we passed each other."

Liam blinked, his mind flitting over the past week. The memory of sitting in the hardware-store parking lot watching the pack of kids ambling across the street, along with a hooded woman. The homeless woman he'd almost run over with the truck, her face shrouded from view.

"Oh, I see you're remembering now. I kept a close watch on you from the moment you entered Tallston."

"Why?" he answered, feeling unhinged by the discovery of her surveillance in plain sight.

"To see if you were like your brother, meddling, without ethics."

"What does Allen have to do with all this? He ran tests for your sister, it was his job."

June's face hardened again, her malformed jaw sliding even more to one side. "They told him their fears, about the disease being passed down. He had no more than opened his clinic when they came to him carrying money that he needed to expand his business. I watched her belly grow, an untold sorrow and fear building within me." June fixed them both with a hard stare. "I knew what type of callous nature my sister had, but I didn't know just how far she would go."

"What do you mean?" Dani asked, and Liam felt unease rising like dirty floodwater inside him.

"I knew they were going to have the child at home—I'd heard them speak of it when they thought no one was listening. So I watched every night, and then one evening in the beginning of summer, the doctor came to visit. I could hear my sister's screams inside the house, and after hours of labor, another set of lungs joined her cries. But their fears were confirmed the moment they saw him. Peter was born with many deformities on his face and arms. The disease my mother carried left Karen untouched but set its claws into their little son."

A bang issued from somewhere in the darkness behind June, and Liam snapped the Sig up again, trying to see past her. June made no indication that she'd heard anything and continued speaking in a low tone.

"They came out of the house hours later, my sister and her husband, hand in hand, holding poor little Peter. I watched from the edge of the trees as they walked to the corner of their yard and Jerry began to dig a hole."

Liam heard Dani sob, and shuddered at the image the other woman conjured. "They didn't," he heard himself say.

"Oh yes, they did. Karen held Peter until Jerry had the grave dug. They even secretly had a little coffin already made up. They placed him inside it, then buried him alive."

June's words hung in the air, vile and undoubtedly true. The thought of burying a child alive was almost too much for Liam and he took a deep, steadying breath.

"But how?" Dani asked.

"You saved him," Liam answered, watching June's face. "You dug him up and saved him."

Slowly, June nodded. "I ran to his grave as soon as they went inside, and dug down with my bare hands. I flailed in the dirt until I found his casket and lifted him out. It was fate that he calmed as soon as I embraced him, otherwise his murderous parents may have come to investigate. I think he knew, even then, that I was sent to save him. Then I replaced everything back the way it was, and swam across the river with Peter. The whole while, my sister and her husband sat in their house with your brother, who was writing out Peter's death certificate at their kitchen table." June spit again on the floor. "Waiting for his check, I'm sure."

"Oh my God," Dani whispered. Liam reached down and placed a hand on her shoulder, not sure whether to steady her or him.

"God wasn't there to help him, dearie, I was. He would've died down there, alone in the dark, but I got him out. I nurtured him and clothed him, kept him warm and safe through the long winters and cool in the sweltering summers. I am his mother, not her, and God did nothing to help us."

"So you waited until now to exact your revenge," Liam said, stepping forward. "You poisoned his mind with your hatred until he became a monster."

"I told him the truth!" June shouted, her lips trembling with rage. "I told him his real parents abandoned him to death because of the way he looked! I showed him a world that had no place for people like us! I loved him and cared for him while everyone else turned their backs on him!"

"You made him into a murderer!" Liam roared back. "He tried to kill an innocent boy. He killed my sister-in-law, who had nothing to do with this." He felt his finger tightening on the trigger of the handgun and eased the pressure off, but didn't lower it.

"I let him fulfill his destiny," June whispered. "He righted wrongs set in motion long ago. He is righteous and powerful and true. He has a will of his own, and I don't think he meant to kill your brother's wife, but . . ." She swallowed. "He is my son."

Liam's chest heaved in and out, a river of emotion racing through him, clouding his thoughts. How could Allen have done it? How? He gritted his teeth and tried to clear his mind. "And what about the others? What about Haines and the mayor and Tracey? Why did they have to die?"

June stood straighter and raised her chin. "They were going to take our home from us. This place," she said, motioning to the walls, "is our sanctuary. We moved here when the house my father built began to fall in on us. We found shelter here and filled it with love, just as my parents did with their home." June's eyes hardened into glittering diamonds. "Jerry Shevlin and Donald Haines's company were going to rob us of that. They were going to shred the ground we hunted on, tear the walls of our home down around us, strip the land of everything that is good. The mayor was going along with it, as were most of the other people in Tallston, because they are filled with greed. Progress means money, and money equates to happiness. They would rape the earth of all it had to offer just for more wealth."

"And you would kill in cold blood to keep your home," Liam said, his hand that held the gun now shaking. A voice deep inside him screamed to pull the trigger, to right the wrongs that had been done to so many. He fought the urge and waited for her answer, all the while his eyes shifting toward the black doorway behind her.

"I would kill to survive, nothing else," she said.

Liam remembered the story Nut told him in the jail cell. The disappearance of the homeless man, the heavy tracks in the snow leading away across the river. He grimaced.

"You're going to come with us," Liam said, stepping backward until he stood beside Dani again. He bent over and was about to cut the ropes around her ankles when he heard June chuckling.

219

"We've survived this long against all odds, Liam, and you expect me to come quietly with you?" June shook her head in the wavering light. "No, I'll not be judged by people who would've shunned us if we would've asked for their help." Her face became poisonous. "You know nothing of living day in, day out with a hindrance such as this," she said, swiping at her face. "No one knows." She stepped to the side of the door and placed her hands into the pockets of her dirty sweatshirt. "I'm sorry, but this must be done."

Liam began to stand, but movement in the doorway caught his attention, a drifting of shadows that came nearer and then drew away before he could speak or even raise the gun. The cables he'd seen on the floor outside the room snapped tight, rising out of the filth until they hung taut in the air. The ground below their feet gave a sickening lurch, and he stumbled back, all at once realizing why the floor sounded so hollow before.

The grate they stood on slid from beneath them, empty darkness sucking them down, and he felt his hand clutching the Sig relax in an attempt to grab something to hold on to. The gun pirouetted away into the room as they slid out of sight, and June's disfigured face was the last thing he saw in the candlelight. Cold steel sung under their bodies as they slipped through the black. He reached out to where Dani's screams came from, but his hand met only empty air.

Then the chute was gone from around them, and they fell. The impact wasn't as hard as he expected but still forced the air from his lungs, leaving him paralyzed for a second, long enough for him to realize that Dani wasn't screaming anymore. He tried to move and found that all his limbs seemed to work and, other than the buffeting pain in his back from the fall, he felt okay. A dry clacking sound issued from the ground around him, and the smell of gasoline invaded his nostrils, almost overpowering with its cloying odor.

"Dani!" he yelled.

With a flick of his wrist, he folded the razor, which he somehow had maintained a grip on. Tucking it away in his pocket, he stood and attempted to walk, his feet sinking into the unstable floor. The darkness was liquid and complete around him, and as he moved, he held his hands out, blind to all else but touch. Liam reached down and felt the floor, his fingers coming back with a light, powdery chunk about the size of his fist. Coal.

"Dani," he said again, praying for a response. He dropped the coal and waded through its brethren, the sound of his movement like a thousand hissing snakes. His outstretched hand met a cold wall of rounded steel, and he followed it up as high as he could reach, his eyes gradually becoming accustomed to the darkness. Above him, he saw the rectangular opening that they'd fallen through. It was at least four feet over his head, and the sides of the container they were in were smooth and without any handholds he could see. He turned back toward the center and made out a darker form within the chunks of coal, and waded to it as he blinked against the gas fumes.

Dani lay on her stomach, her face pressed into the coal. Carefully, he turned her over, cradling her head in his lap. "Dani?" Nothing. He bent closer, felt the push of air from between her lips against his face.

A clumping sound filtered in through the opening above them and Liam looked up, listening, waiting. Soon the sounds became clear: footsteps, distant at first and then closer, and closer. He pivoted, trying to take in his surroundings again, and saw a flat wall of steel nearby that made up the end of the room. Several pipes and openings graced its surface, along with the heavy heads of bolts nearly two inches across. The footsteps approached, and he gauged they stopped only feet from the other side of the wall. A shrieking of rusted steel gouged at his eardrums, and he looked up in time to see a flap being pulled shut over the opening above them. The darkness became complete.

"Dani, wake up," Liam whispered, and tried to haul her to her feet.

She moaned in her throat, and with an immense effort, he picked her up and began to wade away from the end where the footsteps had stopped. He felt the scab on his back tear open and bit down on his lower lip as blood began to drool from the wound in streams that stopped at his belt line. A light scratching issued from behind them, and the sound registered somewhere inside him, drawing the already constricting band of fear in his chest even tighter.

It was a match being struck.

The smell of gas, the coal sliding around his feet, and the steel container all assembled into a horrifying surety within a breath.

They were inside a furnace.

Liam doubled his speed, and nearly cried out when they ran into the rear wall. He set Dani down and heard the match scrape against steel again, knowing they had only the space of seconds. Liam traced the steel, rust flaking off beneath his touch. He bent his knees, his fingers searching for a handle or seam. They found only the corroded heads of old rivets and the pocked surface of steel. He dove down deeper beneath the layer of coal, and at the bottom of the furnace, the rust became toothy and sharp. He felt the edges of it bite into his skin as his fingers poked through into open air, and he spun onto his back and kicked with both feet as hard as he could.

The sound of ancient rivets popping loose filled the air. Liam kicked out again and felt the steel, thinned by years of moisture and oxidation, break loose beneath his feet. The coal around him poured away, and he grabbed on to Dani's arm just as he felt heat bloom against the back of his neck.

Fire ripped toward them as he lunged through the gap in the steel, dragging Dani as he went. The flames kissed the back of his neck, releasing the sweet smell of burning hair, and he felt his skin blister and then pop, amazed at how fast the reaction happened.

Then they were on the floor, cool concrete rubbing against his forearms and a puddle of water soaking into his clothes. He pulled on Dani's arm again, yanking her legs free of the furnace just as flames shot out with reaching tongues nearly four feet long. Dani's pant legs caught fire, and she began to scream, her voice louder than anything he'd ever heard before. Scooping up handfuls of water, he doused her burning legs until all the flames were gone. Her scream reached a vocal-shredding crescendo, and then she fell silent and limp against him, the threshold of her pain tolerance exceeded and capped by unconsciousness.

Over the roar of the fire chewing the coal inside the immense furnace, Liam heard the sound of someone coming nearer. He stood and pulled Dani farther away from the glowing inferno, before spinning and drawing out the straight razor from his pocket.

Peter was there, his oblong skull half-lit by the fire, his eyes glinting with the reflection of flames. With an enraged bellow, he charged, bringing up the massive blade at his side. Liam waited, his hand twitching the razor open. His muscles flexed, even as the rest of his body cried out in pain. Peter swung the sword in a vicious downward arc, and Liam dove past him, drawing a line across the other man's dirty clothing with the razor.

Liam rolled to his feet and stood, the heat from the furnace making the burn on the back of his neck feel as if it were blistering all over again. Peter's weapon clanged off the concrete where Liam had been a moment before, sparks shining in a flutter of light. Peter turned and put a hand to his chest where a chunk of cloth hung like a limp sail and began to grow red.

"Come on!" Liam yelled, as Peter bared his teeth and glanced at Dani's prone form. "No, you want me! You leave her alone!"

Peter's gaze locked on him once again, and he lumbered forward, his rounded shoulders flexing as he re-gripped his weapon.

Liam backed up and looked over his shoulder, spotting the stairway that led up to the main level. A massive conveyer system sat to the right of the stairs and blocked the lower treads. Liam turned from Peter, stowing the razor away, and scrambled over the piled machinery until his feet were on the stairway. Peter climbed after him, the massive sword clanking against the steel components. Liam turned and sped up the stairs until he set foot on the main floor. Searching the area for weapons, he ran forward, his hip glancing off a solid worktable. He hissed with pain and spun, seeing the table roll a short distance before stopping. Liam grabbed the nearest edge of the table and pushed it toward the head of the stairs just as Peter emerged.

The table struck Peter in the chest, and his eyes flew open. He cried out as he tipped backward, Liam shoving with all his might on the other side. With a flailing motion, Peter swung the long sword down, and Liam felt it connect with his hand, the bones within vibrating like a struck bell, the flesh around them numb. The table continued down the stairway, jostling Peter in front of it. Finally, the other man fell beneath its stout form as it toppled end over end.

Liam glanced at his hand and saw the skin flayed open and the white glare of bone within the torn tissue. He groaned as he tucked it close to his body, and looked down the stairway. The table lay on its top, its legs in the air like a dead insect. For a moment everything was still. Then, the table flipped to its side and Peter crawled from beneath it, heaving his weapon up with him.

Liam staggered back from the stairway, looking for something else to throw at the juggernaut. A long steel rod leaned against the far wall, and he ran to it, tugging on it with his good hand to no avail. Looking up, he saw an iron strap holding it to the wall, and another anchoring it to the floor. He slid to the right, his hand seeking anything loose in the cobwebbed darkness. Behind him, he heard Peter step onto the main level and begin to stalk toward him, his breathing ragged and wheezing. Liam wondered if the other man had broken a rib or was bleeding internally. He hoped so.

With nothing at hand, he pulled the straight razor back out of his pocket and snapped the blade free of the handle. The puny length of knife looked so disproportionate when compared to Peter's sword,

Liam almost let out a bray of crazed laughter. Peter came closer and wound up, swinging the blade at Liam's midsection. Liam leapt back and felt the passage of air as the weapon sliced by him. Peter swung again, this time at his head, and he ducked, placing his clenched fist on the floor for support. A hard chunk of concrete nudged his knuckles, and when Liam looked down, he saw a pile of bricks lying beside him. Dropping the razor, he grasped a brick and stood just in time to dodge another wide swath of Peter's sword. Lunging forward, he drove the heavy brick into Peter's head.

The other man staggered from the blow, dropping his weapon, which clanged onto the floor. Liam drew the brick back and whipped it forward again. Peter turned just enough to deflect the attack with his shoulder, and Liam lost his grip, the brick spinning away into the darkness.

With a roar, Peter swung a fist at Liam's head and caught him with a grazing punch that sent stars flying across his vision. Liam fell back and was about to skirt a workbench to regroup when a thundering report filled his ears and blinding white pain lanced through his left shoulder.

He fell to one side, bracing himself with his right arm on the nearby table. June stood a dozen yards away holding his gun in both hands. He opened his mouth and gasped with the rolling pain that continued to shoot veins of fire down his arm.

"You're industrious, Liam, I'll give you that," June said, taking a step closer. "I don't know how you got out of that furnace, but it doesn't matter. I won't let you walk away from here. I won't let you destroy everything we've worked for." She turned to Peter. "Finish him, son."

Peter grunted and ambled forward. Liam tried to back away, but the other man caught hold of his bad arm and wrenched him close with a grip like a vise. Liam felt his feet leave the floor as Peter hugged him to his thick chest and wrapped both of his tree-trunk arms around his back, beginning to squeeze.

Liam's eyes bulged as all the air fled his lungs under the immense pressure. His spine popped as it adjusted and then bent as it flexed beyond its designed curve. He screamed and brought an elbow down on top of Peter's head, but the other man merely tightened the bear hug. Liam felt one of his ribs break. He slammed a fist against Peter's ear and tried to press a thumb into his eye, but the darkness around him was deepening. He felt light with agony, and in that moment he wished for it to end, as his intestines relocated to new territory. With his last stores of energy, he brought his head back and slammed it forward into Peter's temple. The grip around his back loosened for a split second, and he drew a breath in, knowing it was his last. Liam managed to lift his head again and saw Dani standing behind June, a length of pipe raised over her shoulder.

The gunshot was louder than the first, and before the ringing began in his ears, Liam felt a strange tug at his stomach. Looking down into Peter's face, he saw the other man's eyes open past the whites, dark blood coating his crooked teeth.

Peter's arms fell away, and Liam dropped to the floor, his legs holding him long enough to allow him to heave in a mouthful of air and then collapsing under his weight. He waited for Peter to step forward and end him where he sat, but instead, he fell too, like a tall tree cut at the base. Peter plummeted backward onto the floor. A gurgling cry came from the darkness, and Liam squinted, straining to see who made the sound.

"Momma."

The word was garbled and indistinct, but Liam heard it just the same. Blood bubbled at Peter's lips, and he coughed, a rope of crimson flying free onto his chest where a black stain was already spreading.

"Momma!"

Liam grasped the edge of the table and pulled himself up, still gulping down air like a starving man at a buffet. Then Dani was there, her shoulder beneath his armpit, her hand clutching at his stomach.

"Oh God, Liam, you're shot." She moaned.

"I know," he said, looking at the hole in his shoulder.

"No, your stomach."

He looked down and saw a dark patch on the front of his shirt near his navel.

"When I hit her with the pipe, she fired, and it went through him and into you."

"Noooo!"

The cry cut through their conversation, and Liam looked at where Peter lay. June crawled toward her son, her right arm hanging at a strange angle.

"Momma," Peter moaned, his voice half as strong as before.

June reached him and pressed a palm to his face, wiping away the blood from his cheek. "I'm here, baby. I'm right here."

"Momma," Peter gasped, and more blood boiled over his lips. His chest heaved and convulsed before he exhaled for the last time.

"Momma's right here, son. She won't leave you." June clutched Peter's head and sobbed, her wails becoming louder and louder.

"Liam!" Dani shouted.

The foundry toppled to one side, and his body met the cool floor. Darkness flooded his vision, and he felt as though he were floating away on the currents of the river outside.

# CHAPTER 26

Liam opened his eyes to sunshine.

The light streamed into the room through a high window, and he thought he was at the farmhouse. Then he felt the familiar pull of the blood-pressure cuff against his bicep and inhaled the smell of disinfectant. Not yet, but soon; today he could go home.

Liam sat up in bed, wincing at the snagging ache in his stomach. The wound itched. He supposed that was a good thing. His father always said that was the body's way of saying it was healing. Swinging his feet out of bed, he pushed himself free of the covers, with his bandaged left hand. His fingertips were still numb, but the doctor said that the feeling might come back, at least partially. With an agitated jerk, he pulled the Velcro cuff loose from his arm and flexed it. He stood and felt emboldened by the strength in his legs. Taking a few steps, he grabbed the thin, blue robe off the visitor's chair and managed to get it on before a plump nurse with frizzy black hair strode into his room with a clipboard.

"Mr. Dempsey, what in the hell do you think you're doing?"

He smiled. "Morning, Bernice."

"Don't you 'morning, Bernice' me! You're not supposed to get out of bed without help, you know that," she said, coming toward him, the prepared look of anger barely holding on her kind face.

"I'm going home today," Liam said, searching the floor for his slippers.

"Yeah, we'll see about that."

"Listen," Liam said, his eyes still on the floor. "I know you'd like to keep me here permanently, and your infatuation with me is flattering, but I really do have to leave sometime."

Bernice's dark eyebrows rose in unison, and then she let out a burst of warm laughter. "Your slippers are over there, sweetie. Let me get you your ride."

A few minutes later, after donning the slippers, which were no more than glorified socks with rubber patches on the bottom, he watched Bernice push a wheelchair into the room.

"You know, I'm perfectly capable of walking down there," he said, seating himself in the padded chair.

"Oh, I know you are, handsome, but my orders are to keep you in the chair until discharge," she said as she wheeled him around the end of his bed. "You aren't expecting any more company today, are you?"

Liam knew she was referring to Phelps and Richardson. The two agents had visited him almost every day since his admission at Fairview. At first Phelps's demeanor remained unchanged, his questions hostile and accusatory. But gradually over the two weeks that had passed, the agent became more docile and even respectful as the evidence mounted into a chain of facts that couldn't be ignored. Nut had been released, and June Harlow now sat in a cell in Hennepin County awaiting a trial and transfer date.

"No, I don't think they'll be coming back today," he finally said.

As he watched the corridor scroll by, Liam adjusted himself in the wheelchair, listening to the soft squeak of Bernice's shoes behind him. "You know, Bernice, I think I can make it from here. I've been down there a few times."

Bernice laughed again. "A few? Boy, I'm surprised you haven't driven that young girl mad with your constant pestering." He craned his neck around to shoot a look at the nurse. "Oh, I get it, you don't want your gal seeing you pushed in by an old lady."

"You're not old, Bernice, you're ancient."

Bernice cackled and gave him an extra shove, letting go of the chair as she did so. "You have a nice visit, and I'll find Dr. Mason, see if you really are going home today."

"Thanks, Bernice."

He spun the chair's wheels and glided to the end of the hall, smiling occasionally at nurses or candy stripers that he knew by sight. Turning left, he went through a set of double doors marked *Burn Unit* before coming to a stop in front of a wide desk manned by a severe-looking nurse with a long nose and tightly cropped blond hair.

"Good morning. Is Dani awake yet?"

The nurse glanced at him over the top of a folder before going back to reading. "Yes, go right in, Liam."

"Thank you," he said, and rolled across the room to a closed door in the far wall.

Opening it, he was glad to see Dani alone. The questioning hadn't been relegated solely to him, and the agents as well as the local law enforcement had questioned her rigorously about their version of events. He sat in the doorway for a few seconds, admiring how the sun shone off her hair draped across the pillow, and thought about what he wouldn't give to climb into bed with her at that moment, to hold her tight to him.

Turning her head, she finally noticed him sitting there. "Hi."

"Hi."

"You're up early. Did you sleep okay?"

He rolled across the room and stopped beside the bed. "Better than ever."

She smiled. "Good."

"How do you feel?"

"As well as can be expected. They said I'm healing nicely, but . . ." She threw a glance at her bandaged legs, covered with gauze from just above the knees down.

"But what?"

She just stared ahead at the wall for a long while, and he waited.

"Are you sure?" Her voice came out small and strained.

"About what?"

"About me and what we talked about? I wouldn't blame you if—"

Liam shook his head and slid his hand into hers. "I wouldn't care if you lost your legs completely, you're beautiful." He watched her, trying to judge her expression. "Unless you've changed *your* mind."

Her eyes darted to his. "No, I haven't, but it's just . . ." She blinked away the tears that threatened to spill down her cheeks. "I don't feel whole anymore, not just because of this," she said, motioning to her legs, "but everything. I dream about it, about what happened, and I just want to wake up from it and not have it be real."

He squeezed her hand. "I know, and the fear will get better. We can help each other, you'll see. I promise, it just takes time."

Dani sniffed, looking down at her lap. "And you don't mind Freddy Krueger legs?"

He laughed and stood from the wheelchair, bending over the rail of her bed to kiss her long and deep. "Like I said, you're beautiful."

She smiled and stroked his face. "You shouldn't be up out of that thing, didn't the doctor say that?"

"He says a lot of things."

"You're just lucky the bullet didn't go any deeper. You would've—"

"But I'm not," he said, cutting off her words. "I'm fine, and you saved me." She rubbed the back of his hand, her eyes shining. "Wanna go for a ride?"

They acquired a wheelchair for Dani and rolled along next to each other until they came to the elevator. They rode it up to the third floor and went to Eric's door, the uniformed cop long since departed, and knocked before hearing the boy answer.

Eric sat propped in the bed, an iPad on his lap. His face lit up with the sight of Dani alongside Liam, and he got out of the bed and raced to her to give her a hug.

"I was going to come see you again today!" Eric said, pulling back from her.

"You've come to see me every day," Dani said, laughing.

"I know, but I didn't think you'd be able to leave your room yet."

"I pulled some strings," Liam said.

Dani rolled her eyes as they followed Eric back to his bed. The stump of the boy's arm was bare now, and only an S-shaped row of stiches could be seen over the puckered red scar that lay beneath the thread. With an already practiced-looking heave from his remaining arm, Eric shrugged himself back into bed.

"How are you feeling?" Liam asked.

Eric tipped his head to one side. "Okay. It's weird how I can still feel my hand, you know? And . . ." His face darkened. "I miss Mom and Dad a lot. Champ too."

Liam didn't know what to say to that. He hoped to shield Eric from the facts surrounding his parents' death as long as possible, perhaps until he was old enough to understand them, if there was such an age.

"Some of my friends from school came by yesterday, and so did Mr. Swanson, my Little League coach."

"Really? That's great!" Liam said, grateful for the change of subject.

"Yeah, Mr. Swanson said I could still be on the team this fall if I wanted!"

The boy's rising mood was contagious, and Liam felt himself grinning. "I told you, you're going to be an MVP!"

Eric smiled and began to chatter about when the first practice was and how he'd let some of his friends touch the stump of his arm. A half hour later, after they'd shared cookies and a few juice boxes that a nurse brought in, Eric began to grow quieter and quieter, soon only nodding or shaking his head in response to their questions.

Liam rolled closer to the bed, setting down his half-eaten cookie on a tray nearby. "What's wrong, Eric?"

The boy glanced at him and then looked away. "You're both leaving soon, huh?"

Liam examined the boy's features; his hair poked past his ears. His father would've called it "the shags" from around his cigarette, and would've commenced to say that hair should go behind ears, not over them.

"Yes, we're being discharged today or tomorrow."

Eric nodded. "I have another week before I can . . . well, I guess I can't go home." The boy faced Liam, and he saw that he was trying not to cry, his lower lip trembling slightly. "A lady came and told me a few days ago that I'd be in a foster home for a while before they could find somewhere else for me to live."

Liam swallowed. "And how did you feel about that?"

Tears spilled over Eric's eyes, and he wiped them away with the back of his hand. "I'm scared. I don't want to live with people I don't know—I want my mom and dad."

Liam reached out and squeezed his arm, and Dani approached from the right to pat Eric's legs.

"I know you do, buddy. And I know they want you to be happy," Liam said.

Eric nodded, wiping another flood of tears from his face. Liam licked his lips, his heart beating harder than he'd expected it to.

"Eric, what if the foster home the lady talked about was my place?"

Eric swiped once more at his eyes before blinking, searching Liam's face for a long time. "You mean, I could come stay with you?"

Liam nodded. "Only if you want to."

The boy looked as though he might start crying again, and Liam mentally kicked himself. Why would Eric want to live with him? The boy didn't even know him other than the visits they'd shared over the last two weeks, although it had almost been a daily ritual. He was just about to tell Eric that it was okay if he didn't want to when the boy shifted his gaze to Dani.

"Will you be there too?"

Dani nodded, tears clouding her vision. "Yes, I think so," she said, reaching for and holding Liam's hand.

Eric began to grin, and bobbed his head. "I'd like that a lot."

The apprehension inside Liam's chest broke like a dam, and relief flooded through him. A smile pulled at his mouth, and although it still seemed alien, he liked the feeling of it there. He was pretty sure he could get used to it.

# ACKNOWLEDGMENTS

No book gets written alone. There is the author, that's for sure, but there's also a bunch of people behind the author, helping and guiding in small ways that most never see. *The River Is Dark* is no exception. Thank you to my sister, Ang, for once again answering my odd questions about cases and procedure; you're a big help whether you know it or not. Thanks to my cover artist, Kealan Patrick Burke, for coming up with my favorite cover so far; you sir, are not only an extremely gifted author, your skills as a designer are second to none. To my wife, as always, honey, you make everything happen; from concept to fruition, you're there, and without your help there would be no stories. And to you, reader, you're the reason my mind won't rest, and I thank you.

# ABOUT THE AUTHOR

Photo by Jade Hart, April 2014

Joe Hart was born and raised in northern Minnesota. He's been writing since he was nine years old in the horror and thriller genres. He is the author of five novels and numerous short stories. When he's not writing, Joe enjoys reading, working out, watching movies with his family, and spending time outdoors.

Learn more about Joe by following him on Twitter @AuthorJoeHart or connect with him on Facebook at www.facebook.com/pages/Joe-Hart/345933805484346.